# Praise for Stuart R. West's
## *Dread and Breakfast*!

"Like Stephen King and Joe Lansdale had a freaky,
hyperactive baby and it wrote this book!"
–Somer Canon, author of *Vicki Beautiful*

"A fast-paced, uncanny, and hugely entertaining
horror novel!"
–Vanessa Morgan, screenwriter and author of
*Drowned Sorrow*

"A suspenseful, twisty ride! Heart-pounding horror!"
–L.X. Cain, author of *Bloodwalker* and *Soul Cutter*

# DREAD AND BREAKFAST

# Stuart R. West

A
Grinning Skull Press
Publication

The Skull logo with stylized lettering was created for Grinning Skull Press by Dan Moran, http://dan-moran-art.com/.
Cover designed by Jeffrey Kosh, http://jeffreykosh.wix.com/jeffreykoshgraphics.

Published by Grinning Skull Press, P.O. Box 67, Bridgewater, MA 02324


ISBN: 0-9984055-1-5 (paperback)
ISBN-13: 978-0-9984055-1-3 (paperback)
ISBN: 978-0-9984055-2-0 (ebook)

# DEDICATION

As always, I'd like to dedicate this book to my lovely wife, Cydney, and my beautiful daughter, Sarah. They're my rock(s). Couldn't do it without them.

# Contents

# ACKNOWLEDGMENTS

A big shout-out to the wonderfully weird and twisted state of Kansas. Endlessly fascinating and creepy place to live, lots of fodder for creepy story-telling. Probably why I still live there.

# Chapter One

"*Why* are you *doing* this?" The chains binding her wrists drew taut as she lurched forward. Her chin cracked down onto cement, triggering her bladder. Urine warmed her legs. Dignity didn't matter, not anymore. Nothing made sense. As she dragged her locked hands toward her, she pushed up on her knees. Pleading, her last hope. "*Please* don't do this, oh God, please don't hurt me. Just ... tell me *why*."

Two figures stepped in front of the floodlight. Joined at the hip, hands entwined like lovers on a stroll.

A dry voice, crisper than crackers, said, "Why? Because it's date night."

The hatchet swung down, delivering date night's goodnight kiss.

❄ ❄ ❄

Snow swirled in the wind, dropping like feathers. Rebecca knew a storm had been forecast, hardly good driving weather. But she wasn't about to let up. Not 'til she put Hollington far behind her and then some. Dangerous? Absolutely. But navigating through a snowstorm sure as hell felt a lot safer than what she'd left behind.

The wipers beat the windshield, struggling to clear it. Snow piled on the hood. Rebecca brushed a hand through the condensation and hunkered down to peer out the narrow opening. She cursed herself for not getting the Chevy's defrost fixed; it never had worked worth a damn. Of course, she also didn't think she'd be fleeing for her life during what one weatherman had gleefully called "the Storm of the Century." Maybe she should've thought this out better. Should've, would've, could've; the old game she'd been playing a lot lately.

She glanced at Kyra, sound asleep. The seat-belt looked tight, confining her daughter's small frame. Kyra's stuffed dog rode with her, the safety belt covering its mouth, its eyes: say nothing, see nothing. The way Rebecca had lived the past ten years of her life.

But enough.

Rebecca had thought — if not accepted, exactly — she understood Brad's violent streak. It didn't happen often, but when he hit her, it hurt. Not so much physically; she'd developed a surprising tolerance to the pain. Emotionally, though, it pummeled her worse than fists. Yet she accepted it, justified it as the norm. After all, her daddy treated her mother the same way. And, as Brad often told her, his job weighed heavily on him, the stress too much. "Being a police detective is a load-and-a-half for any good man," he'd said before punctuating his insight with a blow to her cheek. Now Rebecca thought it nothing more than a load of shit.

Was Brad a good man? At one time she'd thought so. But when he hit their daughter last night, her perception, her entire world, changed.

*Enough.*

Kyra had sought safety in Rebecca's arms, crying, asking why Daddy hated her. The breaking point. And Rebecca hated herself for not having made the decision long ago. She knew then, absolutely knew, she and Kyra would leave in the morning. After Brad went to work.

Right now, he probably just arrived home and found her note. Then flew into a rage. Fine. Let him find a new punching bag.

As Rebecca tapped the brakes, the car swerved, the back tire edging toward the ditch. Finally, the car shuddered to a stop, Rebecca's heart threatening to stop as well. With white knuckles over the steering wheel, she blew out a deep breath, staring into the storm. Nothing but endless snow, drifting into dunes along the road. Fear fueled her; not just fear of the storm, but fear of the future, the unknown. Starting over at the age of 32, no college degree, no practical work experience. All very scary. But she still had her life. And Kyra's. This time she'd make it count.

Last night, after Brad had struck Kyra, things turned even worse. She knew Brad wouldn't let her leave, so she suffered in silence one last time. She'd consoled Kyra the best she could, even though she'd lied through her teeth. Hanging a pretty picture on abuse isn't easy. After Kyra had settled down, Rebecca dragged herself up to the bedroom, dreading what she knew awaited her. Five minutes later, Brad was pawing at her, acting like he hadn't hit their daughter. As if his abuse had turned him on. Business as usual, Rebecca a sex object purely for Brad's pleasure.

It felt like rape, torture of body and mind.

*Enough.*

Once the tears started, she couldn't stop them. Ten years' worth of bottled-up sorrow finally spilled. She covered her mouth with an arm, muffling her sobs. A small whimper birthed in her chest, a sad, little thing that matured into a growl.

*That bastard. That miserable bastard. And I took it.*

"Mommy?" Kyra yawned, staring at her. "Why're you crying?"

"Shh, honey, it's okay. Mommy's just tired, that's all. Everything's fine." Rebecca wiped away the tears and erased all thoughts of Brad. Time to pull it together. Kyra counted on her.

"Where are we?" Kyra leaned forward, wiping a viewing space through the windshield.

"I think … the sign said Hilston, Missouri." A place she'd never been, nor ever heard of before. Not that that was uncommon. Brad never took her out of Hollington, Kansas. Her entire life she'd been trapped in a lousy Kansas City suburb, her prison.

"Is this where we're going?"

"No, honey. We're going to stay with Aunt Jill and her family for a while. Like we discussed."

"And Daddy's not coming?"

"No, he's not."

Kyra said nothing, reacted indifferently. But a barely audible sigh escaped from her, one possibly of relief. Of course, Kyra loved her dad, warts and all. Yet she wasn't blind. She'd seen Brad at his worst. But he'd never hit Kyra before. It'd been foolish thinking he never would either. Brad was a ticking time bomb more often than not. Hell, she may as well have triggered the bomb herself. She should never have kept Kyra in that situation. Not for six years. *Shoulda', woulda', coulda'.*

"Mommy, I'm sorry I knocked over Daddy's beer. It was an accident. I'll never do it again." She blinked at Rebecca, sincerity sparkling in her eyes.

"I know, honey. Accidents happen." Slowly, Rebecca backed the car up and straightened it out; she noticed the snow was already covering her tracks. Nice and steady, twenty miles per hour. Maddening, like her life, steadily going nowhere. But not any longer.

"That's why Daddy hit me, isn't it?"

Again, Rebecca felt an emotional punch to the stomach. She couldn't have Kyra accepting Brad's abuse as just punishment. Not the way Rebecca had. "Kyra, Daddy's sick. He doesn't —"

"Is he dying?"

*I wish.* "No, honey, he's not sick like that. He ... he has something wrong in his head. Something that makes him do bad things. Like hitting you. He can't help it. It has nothing to do with his feelings for you. He loves you. But he should never have hit you. And I don't want you blaming yourself. You understand?" Rebecca watched Kyra carefully, ensuring the message took.

Kyra nodded. "Daddy's sick." A simple reiteration, but delivered with firm resolve. Relief coursed through Rebecca, a realization that Kyra would survive to live a healthy life. She marveled at her daughter's resilience, the kind children uncannily possess.

Rebecca reached over and dropped her hand over her daughters'. "Love you."

"Love you ... *Mommy, look out!*"

She had only taken her hand off the steering wheel for a few seconds. Not that it really mattered. The car took on a life of its own, angrily determined for the ditch. Rebecca tromped on the brakes. The car fishtailed, the back end sliding. In a panic, Rebecca cranked the steering wheel, forgetting to steer opposite in the snow. Kyra screamed. A complete 180 tossed Rebecca's stomach, then they twisted into a second loop. Closer, closer to the edge of the road. Snow sprayed from the drift they plowed through. The front of the Chevy lowered into the ditch, the back two tires banging down. Trees rushed up. Rebecca flung an arm over Kyra's chest, an impotent shield. Metal roared as they smashed into the tree. Rebecca flew against the steering wheel, sharp pain jagging into her chest. Glass tinkled, something hissed.

She held onto the wheel for another few seconds, uncertain their wild ride had ended. Smoke drifted up from beneath the sprung hood.

"Kyra, you okay?"

Kyra clutched her stuffed dog to her chest, eyes wide. She nodded, not reassuring enough for Rebecca.

"*Say* something, Kyra. You okay?"

"I think so. Gotta potty."

The damage to the Chevy appeared extensive. The front end resembled an accordion, a web-like vein crossed the windshield. A heavy tree limb lay over the hood. No signal on her cell phone. And the snow kept falling, God's frozen tears.

Rebecca wanted to cry. But she didn't. Instead, she laughed. Just a little at first, then it swelled, nearing hysteria. Nothing else seemed appropriate. Kyra joined her, a nervous titter.

*Welcome to the first day of my new life.*

Harold really shouldn't have done it, pretty much a no-brainer. Betraying the Kansas City mob is hardly the smartest career move. But money can be a strong motivator. Over the last several years, Harold had managed (or "mismanaged" might be more apt) Vincent Domenick's books and financial affairs, skimming a few tips off the top for his hard work. It's not like Domenick would miss a few bucks; the man had more money than several countries combined. Besides, the money had blood all over it, supposedly the net gains from Domenick's trucking company. But Harold knew better, knew where the cash really came from. Not exactly stealing from charity.

Things had heated up, though. Fast. Men wearing dull suits and flashing shiny badges had taken a sudden interest in Mr. Domenick's affairs, poring over his financial records and asking Harold uncomfortable questions. They had instructed Harold to keep Mr. Domenick blissfully unaware. No problem, he could live with that. But what really sealed Harold's bold career move was when one of the feds flat out stated that ignorance of Domenick's crimes wasn't a valid legal defense. He said it with a shit-eating smirk, as if he enjoyed watching Harold squirm. Harold received the message loud and clear: once Domenick goes down, Harold would be dragged to prison along with him. No thanks.

After Domenick's goon dropped off the monthly briefcase of cash that morning, it practically beckoned to Harold, screaming like a wild lover, "Take me, Harold, take me!" He would've been a fool to turn a deaf ear on such wanton lust. The time felt right to get out of town, his start-up funds handed to him in an easy-to-take briefcase, perfect for the man on the go. He'd always wanted to visit the Caribbean, never thought he'd live there. Life is sweet.

By now, Dominick had probably realized his money had vanished. Then again, maybe not. The man never did have an eye for numbers. Still, jumping on the first available plane seemed risky, too easily traced. And Harold swore he had spotted several suits following him over the last week. Pretty damn lousy at their jobs if an accountant could sniff out the feds. On the other hand, it could've been his imagination. Seven hundred thousand dollars' worth of hot can make a guy paranoid. But he hadn't seen anyone on his tail over the last couple of hours. Hell, in this weather, even the feds must've called in for a snow day.

He had a plan. As far as winging it goes, a pretty decent plan — catch a flight out from Los Angeles. Dominick's reach didn't extend to the west coast. But first Harold had to get there. And the damn snow didn't make it easy.

Married to his work, as they say, he had no real goodbyes to make. He could always call his ex-wife from the Caribbean, rub it in her nose a little. She'd always wanted to go there. A smile crossed his lips as he planned what he'd say to her: *Eat it, Barb.*

But now he needed sleep. Absconding with mob money wears a man out. He couldn't get very far in the storm anyway. The sign he'd just passed had read, "Welcome to Hilston, Missouri. A lovely place to antique."

Of course, the sentiment made him gag. Pretty twee using "antique" as a verb, not to mention bragging about it. And he really hated "antiquing." Barb had forced him to join her on some of her expeditions, wasting numerous hours in musty shops full of crap the owners tried to pass off as collectibles. But Hilston was the closest place to stop. Surely he could stomach it for one night.

He followed a sign pointing toward the downtown district. Downtown amounted to basically one block lined with antique shops. At a stoplight, he stepped out onto the empty street. Snow buried his shoes. Squinting from the blizzard, he looked beyond the one-storied shops, searching for a tall building along the skyline. Nothing. Crummy little town didn't even have a single hotel. But he knew there'd be a bed and breakfast, possibly several, a mainstay for those foolish people who just can't get enough "antiquing" done in one day.

Several blocks over, on a hilly street so narrow only one car could safely drive down it at a time, he spotted his destination. His tires lost traction, plunging him into sickening helplessness. At the bottom of the hill, the car slowed, then popped up on a curb, delivering him in front of the "Dandy Drop Inn." Even the name nearly made him wretch. Everything in this damned town wanted to be "cute." "Cute" was about as relevant to him as nipples on men. But the inn promised a bed, and what the hell, breakfast to boot.

\* \* \*

"Got his location, boss."

"You gonna give it to me or have I gotta guess?" Winston's patience had run thin. Not only did he despise driving in the snow, but talking on the phone while driving was something he rarely did. Just not safe; kinda stupid, really. But tonight it couldn't be helped. He wanted to get the job done, get out of the storm, get back to Julie and the kids. Tonight, multitasking trumped safety.

"Sorry. You're never gonna believe it ..." The kid paused, still forcing Winston to play "Twenty Questions." Yep, patience had about run its course. Still, in Winston's line of work, patience is a virtue.

"For Christ's sake, just tell me, Lenny."

"Yeah, uh, sorry, boss. The accountant's holed up at a bed and breakfast. In some shithole called ... let's see ... Hilston, Missouri. Want the address?"

"No, I'll just read your mind. Yes, *give* me the damn address." He really shouldn't snap at Lenny; the kid had proven himself time and again with his crazy computer and hacking skills. If he wanted to find anything or anybody, Lenny was his go-to guy. When you're in the "security consulting" business, assets like him are invaluable. Sometimes he wondered how people in his line of work made do before the advent of computers. Didn't matter. Lenny'd sussed out the missing accountant's location in no time at all. The accountant may be a whiz with numbers, but apparently didn't know jack about technology. The fool didn't realize his cell phone could be triangulated. Gotta love progress.

"Okay, got it." Winston pulled over, then entered the address into his G.P.S. Quickly, he switched the "creepy man's" voice his kids delighted in to a British woman's voice. On a night like this, Mr. Creepy made a lousy traveling companion. "Thanks, Lenny. We'll talk soon."

Hilston, Missouri. *Crap.* Another forty miles or so. Since he'd only been able to travel about fifteen miles over the past hour, he still had a good three-hour trip ahead of him. Long night. Better call home.

"Hey, Julie, it's me."

She laughed as she always did when he identified himself. Old habits and all. "I know, Win, we have Caller I.D."

"Yeah, yeah, right. Hey, the storm's not letting up, and I'm still trying to get home. I'd better find a spot to hole up for the night. It's coming down like ... I dunno, blankets. It's bad."

"Blankets, huh? Lame metaphor, hon."

"Hey, a poet, I ain't."

"Just be careful, 'kay? Promise?"

"Promise. Love you, honey. Kiss the kids good night for me."

"Will do. Love you back."

Spending nights away was a necessary evil in the security field. Lousy beds, paper-thin walls, diner food that could start a grease fire in your belly. But, mostly, Winston hated being away from his family. He lived for his wife and two daughters, pretty much the reason he extended his field of expertise in the security industry.

Of course, he'd been hesitant at first. Ever since childhood, he'd never had a stomach for violence, always preferring to talk his way out of a bad situation if possible. But Mr. Dominick had planted the idea in his head. Just a small seedling at first, but it blossomed, watered by Dominick's pushing. And, frankly, when Winston looked at the resources he had available — the entirety of his company, "Ashford Security Solutions" (unfortunate acronym and all) — pushing "Security Consultant" to the next level seemed like a natural step. Via Lenny, he could access anyone's personal accounts and files; false identities and papers were a snap to acquire; and, of course, his business led him to people who had no qualms about securing untraceable weapons for him. Sure, his company was profitable, but just not quite enough. When he considered his house mortgage and his daughters' costly private school tuition, well, pulling the first trigger wasn't so bad after all. Just as long as he never made it personal.

Family came first, though, one hundred percent. Several years ago, when he had first started taking on out-of-town assignments, Julie had grown aloof, her frustration evident in her uncommon silence. Once — and only once — she'd straight out asked him, "Are you having an affair?" Her lower lip had trembled, obviously dreading — yet antici-pating — his answer.

He swept her up in his arms with an amazed chuckle. "No, Julie, I swear to you I'm not. I never would and never will." Within his hug, he felt her physically lighten, her tense shoulders relaxing.

"I know, Winston. I'm just being silly. Forget I said anything."

And they both had. She never questioned him again. He told her about the more mundane details of his workload, the majority of it. But he never mentioned anything about his extra duties for Dom-enick. If she suspected, she never let on. Sure, guilt gnawed at him from time to time for withholding the complete truth, but he didn't outright lie. He reasoned it was for her benefit. What she didn't know wouldn't hurt her.

He glanced at the glove box where he stored his gun on road trips. The .22 LR handgun was small enough to conceal, yet packed a punch like a charging rhino. It hadn't let him down once.

Yet he dreaded using it. Sometimes completing duties for Dom-enick left a sour taste in his mouth. Especially when the assignments pleaded for their lives. Usually why he liked to take them out without any personal contact. Never put a story to the face. It helped him sleep at night.

How this job was shaping up worried him. He couldn't very well sleep in his car, not in this storm. And there didn't appear to be a motel in Hilston, not according to his phone. Against his better judge-ment, he'd probably have to stay at the bed and breakfast until the storm blew over. Then he'd make his move.

As his car crunched over the snow-packed highway, he flipped the visor down, kissed his fingers, and tapped the photo of his family. *This one's for you.* Then he drove on into Hilston.

❄ ❄ ❄

From an early age, Heather Peterson knew she was different. She just couldn't quite put a finger on how. Her schoolmates had shunned her, running in exclusive packs, which suited Heather just fine. She had other interests; not the typical sort either, the ones the silly girls thrived on. Growing up on a farm enabled her to pursue her new-found hobby. But she'd longed to share her passion with somebody, something that seemed out of the realm of possibility.

Until God, in His kind and gracious manner, led her to Tommy.

Or rather, led Tommy to her. Miracle of all miracles, Tommy had strolled up to her at her first Young Christians meeting, drawn to her inner light, and boldly stuck his hand out. Handsome, and with more confidence than a movie star, Tommy Goodenow regaled her with tales of his accomplishments. Heather had listened with rapt attention, drowning in his blue eyes, and swimming in his deep, soothing voice. Smitten like a silly schoolgirl — which, she supposed, she was — Heather knew Tommy was the man for her. Knew it as sure as she knew God had gifted Tommy to her. Once the meeting had ended, Tommy asked her out. Her hopes soared, then crashed back down to earth. What if he found her strange like the other students did? What if he found her impossible to love, the way her parents had?

But she should have had faith in God. Things worked out better than she dared hope.

Holding her ring up next to the car window, a street lamp caught a glint of diamond. Her smile stretched, grew even wider when she looked at her new husband behind the steering wheel.

*Mrs. Tommy Goodenow. Heather Goodenow.* She couldn't believe she was now a married woman. Something she had only dreamed of before.

Tommy must've sensed her thoughts, the way he innately knew so many things about her. He swept his brown hair out of his eyes and flashed his killer smile, incredibly toothy and white. "Penny for your thoughts, Missus Goodenow?"

"Why, Mister Goodenow, a girl has to keep some secrets." Truly a miracle how he brought out her playfulness, a daring flirtiness. Still, she didn't want to tell him what really bothered her, something that caused butterflies to swarm in her stomach. While her newlywed status thrilled her, to be frank, the inevitable consummation terrified her. Momma'd never been much help in such matters, never taking the time to explain things. Heather'd pieced things together as well as she could from stories overheard in the high school locker room. She thought she knew what to expect. But did she truly? Was it possible to be petrified and exhilarated at the same time? Something burned in her lower regions, a warmth that spread throughout her body and spiked in her brain. Her mind toyed with her, teetering on the verge of unlocking the secrets of the human body. All led there by God, of course. She turned toward the window, hiding, but not out of shame, never shame. Rather, she didn't want Tommy to see her surely pale complexion. Fear of consummating their love. *Sex.* There she said it;

well, not out loud, but she put a label to the act. And it didn't sound dirty at all, not really.

Tommy's hand crawled on top of hers. "We'll be there soon, babe." Always so darn self-assured, Tommy had enough confidence for both of them, and then some.

"Both hands back on the wheel," she chided. "With this crazy storm, you'll need all your attention on the road." She swept back a lock of her blond hair and tucked it behind an ear. "You'll have all the time in the world later to attend to me." Had she just said that? She couldn't believe her audacity. Tommy had that effect on her.

She'd told Tommy she was a "V." Honestly, she'd never even had a boyfriend until him. Sure, she kissed a few frogs, stupid boys hopping around on the playground. But never one like Tommy. And he'd handled the news of her virginity like a true Christian gentleman. He didn't laugh, as she suspected he might. He didn't ridicule. Instead, he'd seized her hand within his, held it to his heart, and said, "Then we're meant to be together. I've been saving myself for marriage."

Which totally blew Heather away. How in Heaven could a boy this gorgeous have gone untouched? She pretty much assumed Tommy had indulged in "lighter" petting, making out, who knew what. Part of being a boy. But she never asked, he never volunteered. Some things are better left unknown.

God had smiled down upon them both that fateful day. And they had agreed to help others see the light as well. Spreading the wealth of God.

As they approached a traffic light, Tommy tapped the brakes. The car slid a few feet into the intersection before crunching to a halt.

"My goodness." Heather fanned herself with a hand. Mostly to calm herself from the slight scare, maybe to cool herself down for more intimate reasons. "Be careful, babe." Funny how comfortable she'd become calling her new husband "babe." Before, she would've thought it juvenile, vulgar even. Now it sounded daring, liberating.

"Always with you, babe. I'd never put you at risk." Again he patted her hand. This time she allowed it since they were stopped. "We're almost there." Another knowing grin. "G.P.S. says just a few more blocks."

Anticipation crawled inside her, an uncomfortable scratching at her private parts. Only several blocks separated them from their marital bed. How far they'd come along God's path, all building to this moment. "Can't wait," she said quietly.

After months of chaste dating, she had expressed her innermost feelings to Tommy, told him of her unusual passion. Bravely, she'd demonstrated her hobby, leaving any judgment in God's hands. At first, he'd watched slack-jawed, an uncommon look for him. Nothing ever seemed to faze him. When she finished, she stood up, looking at him in silence. Waiting. Finally, his grin fell back into place. He strutted forward, the cock in the henhouse, and kissed her. Then, dropping to his knees, he picked up where she left off. Finished the job and followed it with another kiss, full-on, sensual, exciting. *Forbidden.*

She closed her eyes, basking in the blissful memory, and silently prayed: *Thank you, God, for leading us to one another.*

Tommy jarred her out of her reverie, concern tightening his handsome features. "Okay, babe?"

She nodded. "Never been better. Just ... praying. I'm thankful for us and wanted to let God know."

"Amen," he said.

The wedding had been a small, slap-dash affair. With no friends to speak of, Heather's side of the church had been fairly barren, occupied by a few relatives she didn't really know. Tommy, on the other hand, had invited a raucous group of male friends who laughed and hooted throughout the ceremony. Since Tommy had graduated a year before her, she didn't really know them either. To be honest, based on their childish actions, she didn't think she wanted to get to know them. The louder they carried on, the redder Reverend Paxton burned. Not nearly as bad as her father, though. He sat in the front row, red as dawn, ears on fire from a head full of hate. He had been dead set against the wedding, actually believing it to have been a "shot gun" affair. *Hardly.*

After the glorious event, they stopped by home to say goodbye to her parents. Her father had grown even more sullen, falling into a whiskey fit. And he hadn't even blessed them with a wedding gift.

But that was okay, though; turn the other cheek as the Good Book says. Heather and Tommy had left her parents with the ultimate gift, the true Christian thing to do.

Heather smiled at the memory, warm in the afterglow.

Close-set, quaint houses and trees lined the street. Heather's heart knocked, practically jumping up the hill ahead of them. Ready for the final mystery to be unwrapped. She swallowed, an audible dry click.

The car hurtled down the hill, Tommy grinning behind the wheel, letting gravity take over. At the bottom of the hill, he pumped the brakes, *thunk, thunk, thunk, hiss.* The car slalomed to a stop, deep tire grooves in the snow-laid street behind them. Wind rattled the chains on a sign reading, "Dandy Drop Inn."

"We're here, babe." Tommy leaned over and kissed Heather. His tongue darted into her mouth, a hand gently caressing her breast. His reward for having conquered the snow storm.

"Tommy!" Heather pushed him back, not too much. She couldn't resist a smile, giving away her true desire. "Not in public!"

Tommy looked around, seriously puzzled and nearly comical. "This ain't exactly public. No one out on a night like this but us."

"I'm no slut, Tommy Goodenow, to be pawed on the street. You just wait."

"Reckon I can, at that. Reckon I will. Lookin' forward to it."

"Me, too." She tossed her arms around his neck and gave him a quick peck. Just a tease, enough to titillate, not enough to ignite his male hormones again.

"Okay. Ready?"

*Not really.* "I suppose. As long as you're gentle," she whispered.

"Always, babe. Always."

They stepped out into the snow. Heather cinched her coat beneath her chin against a sudden, brutal gust. Snow blew into her face, biting cold. "*Oh.* Don't forget the knives."

"Right, babe." Tommy pulled open the car door, reaching into the back seat. He gripped the knife sleeve, waving it as validation. "Can't forget God's work."

The wind seized and conquered his words, everything except for "God." But she intuited what he'd said. With her gloved hand coiled around the crook of Tommy's arm, he escorted her down the side-walk to their honeymoon abode.

# Chapter Two

Hunkered down in the back seat, Rebecca hugged her daughter tight beneath the blanket. The grease-stained blanket smelled of gasoline. She hadn't remembered why it was in the trunk, but was certainly grateful for the discovery.

Even though she'd known better, several times she'd stepped outside, holding her phone in the air like a torch and seeking different angles for a signal. Pointless, really, but at least it made her feel proactive. Anything beat passively freezing by the roadside.

Trying to keep things upbeat, she led Kyra through songs, their breath expelling condensation with each note.

Kyra dropped the current song in mid-verse. "Mommy, what're we gonna do?"

"We're going to wait for help. Or until I get a phone signal."

"When's that gonna be?" Kyra looked up, her head and shoulders shivering.

"Soon, honey." She hoped. Rebecca launched into another song, one Kyra listened to constantly on her iPod. She stopped when something rumbled outside.

"Mommy, what —"

"Shh, honey." Rebecca cracked the back window, tilting her head to listen. From a distance, snow crunched, steady and growing louder. A motor's struggling hum. Headlights swooped past them, a disheartening sight. Then the car stopped and backed up. Rotating lights blinked over the top of the ditch, bathing Rebecca's car in artificial reds and blues.

With her hand shielding her eyes, Rebecca jumped out of the car. "Stay here, honey!"

"But, Mommy, I —"

Kyra's words cut off as Rebecca shut the door behind her. A man's silhouette appeared in front of the headlights, a flashlight held at his center. "You folks all right down there?" The flashlight beam fell on her, then swept toward the damaged car.

"Thank God! My daughter and I ... we slid into the tree." Rebecca waved her hand over her eyes, hoping the man would get a clue about his flashlight. Although, honestly, she welcomed the light after the last hour of darkness.

The man stumbled down the ditch, wading through the snow. She noticed the badge pinned to his chest, not a welcome sight these days. Her husband had demolished her trust in law enforcement. Still, she'd only sampled one bad apple. Now she'd accept aid from any orchard.

"Are you okay? Any injuries?"

When the cop gripped her shoulders, she flinched. An instinctual reaction, one that couldn't be helped. "We're fine. But ... *freezing*. Could you call a tow truck? Or —"

"Ma'am, on a night like this, ain't nobody out but you, me ... maybe abominable snowmen." He grinned, a good look for him, but she had no tolerance for jokes now. Or flirting. Apparently, he noticed her edginess and adapted a serious cop face. "Okay, tell you what ..." He swept the flashlight over the back windshield. Kyra looked out, hands splayed on the window, helpless as a dog locked in a car. "... step into my office for a spell. We'll work something out. Heater's working jus' fine."

The first thing that sounded good to Rebecca all night. With a nod, she turned, the policeman on her heels. Kyra bolted out of the car, practically falling into her arms.

"You okay, sweetheart?" The cop ran the beam up and down her shaking body.

Rebecca struggled to lift Kyra, her arms frozen and numb, ice needles prickling her.

The policeman said, "Let me help." He swooped up Kyra, a more-than-willing passenger. Her daughter flung shaking arms around the cop's neck, no jaded fear of law enforcement in her small world. While Rebecca put on a smile, or at least tried to, her nerves jangled, echoes from her past.

Snow lit in the cop's wavy brown hair, a premature graying illusion. His hair hung over his ears, almost reaching his eyes, definitely not standard length, at least according to her husband's anal-retentive buzz-cut standards. Apparently impervious to the cold, the cop's muscles rippled beneath his short-sleeved uniform. As he dashed by Rebecca, he shot her a self-impressed, admittedly attractive smile. But she'd had more than her fair share of cops with charming, dashing exteriors. Hardly the time to indulge a little rebound fantasy.

Snow enveloped his legs as he trudged up the ditch. Rebecca retrieved her suitcase and followed in his path toward the running cruiser. As she crawled in next to Kyra, the heat embraced Rebecca like a long-lost friend.

Their savior hopped into the car, out of breath, and draped an arm over the bench seat. "I'm Deputy Randy Gurley." He stuck his hand out. Reluctantly, Rebecca accepted it, the least she could do after his efforts. His hand froze in hers, in more ways than one, lingering a little too long. "Okay, let's get it out of the way. I'm Gurley. Go ahead, get it out of your system." Smiling, he waited. Rebecca refused to laugh, or rather, couldn't dredge up the energy. Kyra, on the other hand, giggled, a nice reaffirmation of youth. "The other fellas sure let me have it about my name. Anyway ... you are?"

"I'm sorry. I'm Rebecca, and this is my daughter, Kyra."

"Nice to meet you gals. Wish it was under better circumstances. So, what happened? And why're you driving through Hilston in this storm? Didn't recognize your plates."

Rebecca'd never noticed him checking out her plates, unsure of when he could've managed it. And she didn't like all of his questions. A cop's training, she supposed. But Brad always bragged how cops were one big brotherhood (don't worry about the poor suffering sisterhood at home, thank you very much). "The information highway in blue," Brad'd called it. Rebecca worried that "highway" might travel through Hilston. Even though Deputy Gurley seemed like one of the good guys, she thought it best to play it close to the vest. Cop's wives have instincts, too. "We're going to see my sister. In St. Louis. Road trip from Kansas City." She looked at Kyra, waiting for her to object or add anything. But she remained quiet, awestruck by the rifle in the front seat.

"Helluva ... ah, excuse me, heckuva night for a road trip, Rebecca."

"I hadn't listened to the forecast. Dumb mistake, I know."

"As a teacher of mine used to say, 'There's no such thing as a dumb mistake'."

*Well, yes there is,* Rebecca thought. And even though she knew he'd misquoted, she let it ride. The sentiment counted. "Thanks. But it was a dumb mistake. We should've waited another day."

"Don't think the snow's gonna blow over anytime soon. Is your car drivable?"

"There's still life in the engine, but it won't catch. Are you sure you can't get a tow truck out here tonight?"

"Ma'am, I got the unfortunate call to patrol tonight, and believe me, there ain't no one out. We can try in the morning."

With a sigh, Rebecca fell back against the seat. Until they reached St. Louis, every setback amped up her anxiety. "Fine. Whatever. Can you drop us at a hotel?"

"No hotels in Hilston. Sorry. Just a couple bed and breakfasts. I can recommend the Dandy Drop Inn. If for nothing else, you gotta try Dolores's chocolate pecan pie. I can't get enough, myself." He patted a flat stomach, a solid thump. It bothered Rebecca — not necessarily in a bad way — how there didn't appear to be any fat on his frame. Wicked flames licked at her libido as she wondered how those solid abs might look beneath the shirt. Then she doused the flames quickly. *Ridiculous.*

"Okay, then. The Dandy Drop Inn it is."

He smiled, nodding, his eyes flitting away as if lost in a chocolate pecan pie daydream. "Good. Tell you what. Let me phone this in, take care of a lil business. Then we'll be on our way."

Gurley's radio crackled, the sudden static making Rebecca jump. A woman's voice, mechanical and bored sounding, blurted out some numbers, no doubt codes. Quietly, Randy spoke into the mouthpiece, his lips practically kissing the device.

Kyra tugged on Rebecca's coat sleeve. "Mommy," she whispered, "can we get some pie? I'm hungry." Chocolate, Kyra's kryptonite. Rebecca's, too, actually. Her stomach gurgled, reminding her she hadn't eaten since morning.

"Sure, honey. Let's just get there first, 'kay?"

Deputy Gurley ended his hushed conversation with an assertive

"Roger that," then snapped off the radio. With a skillful touch — a man unafraid to drive in snow — he straightened the police car and headed down the highway.

Rebecca leaned forward, gripping the seat. "How far is it, Randy? Kyra's hungry."

"Not far, not far at all." He caught Kyra's gaze in the rearview mirror, his brown eyes solemn even in the darkness. "You hang in there, honey. I'll get you there in no time." He stole a glance at Rebecca's left hand. "Oh. Married, huh?"

Reflexively, Rebecca drew her hand back, running her fingers over the small stone. She'd meant to take off her ring, one last physical embodiment of her pain. But in the midst of their panicked flight, she'd forgotten. She slipped it off, dropped it into her purse, noting a pawn shop would be her first stop once she arrived in St. Louis. "No. Not anymore." Out of the corner of her eye, she saw Kyra staring at her, obviously confused, probably disappointed. But now wasn't the time for a long discussion. She kept her gaze locked ahead and a hand on Kyra's knee for quiet support. "What about you, Randy? Married?"

"Nope. Guess I just haven't found the right woman. So … you're divorced?"

A moment's hesitation. Then she looked at her daughter. Kyra's eyes had moistened, priming tears. Rebecca squeezed her daughter's knee harder, both for Kyra's benefit and to boost her own courage. "Yes. Divorced." Kyra's knee flinched, just slight enough to notice. Of course, Rebecca wasn't divorced, not legally. In her mind, though, the papers had been signed, dotted, and filed. Saying it added a touch of finality, the last nail in her terrible marriage's coffin.

But, strangely, she kept dwelling on how she'd heard the defeat in Randy's voice when he'd asked about her marital status. More astonishing, she'd asked him right back. For the first time in a while, she felt like a woman, not a punching bag. Desirable, even. She knew this silly, fleeting infatuation with Deputy Gurley would lead nowhere; an unrealistic whimsy kick-started by her awful past. But it gave her hope for the future, for a possible true relationship down the line, one based on love.

A grin tugged her cheekbones high. And, damn, if goose bumps didn't ride across her arms.

"Well, while I'm sorry to hear that, Rebecca, one man's loss is another lucky man's gain. Good-lookin' woman like you won't be single for long."

"Why, Deputy Gurley, that's the nicest thing anyone's said to me in a while. Thank you." Kyra rolled her eyes and plopped back. Actually a preferable reaction over her earlier sadness. Typical for a young girl who thought her mother's flirting was too much to stomach.

Throwing all caution to the wind, Rebecca added, "You're not so bad yourself, Deputy."

Kyra had grown bored with the chatter, idly staring out the window and sulking a little bit. Rebecca patted her daughter's knee. And she immensely enjoyed the rest of the ride to the Dandy Drop Inn.

\* \* \*

"Yes?" As usual, Rebecca's sister sounded cold, a human refrigerator. Didn't surprise Brad a bit.

*Thanks for the warm welcome. Bitch.*

"Put Rebecca on the *phone*, Jill." Two can play at that game. Brad looked at the damage to his home, taking inventory, the way detectives do. Broken mirror, a chair thrown through a window, upended sofa, all of Rebecca's figurines beheaded and smashed into shrapnel. And at his feet, Rebecca's hateful letter, shredded into confetti.

"She's *not* here, Brad."

"Bull*shit*. Put her on the *goddamn* phone. *Now*." A rustling hiss — probably a hand held over the mouthpiece — then some marble-mouthed mumbling.

Phil — spineless, weak Phil — took over the phone. "Rebecca's not here, Brad. *Don't* call again." More forceful than Brad had ever heard Phil, but still about as effective as an ant defying a stomping boot.

"God*dammit*, Phil, you pussy! Put my damn wife on the *phone*. And don't give me any more of your *bullshit*. I *know* she's there. Bitch doesn't *have* any friends."

"And I *said* she's not here. I mean it, don't call again. Even if she was here, she wouldn't want to talk to you." Tough talk from a little man, especially from a safe distance. But Phil's fear played out as gulps issued between his words. *Pathetic*.

Brad lifted a foot, kicked the wall until his heel broke through the drywall. Their wedding photo dropped off the wall, the glass cracking on the floor. He finished the job, rubbing his heel over Rebecca's smiling face. Her phony smile, the one she faked all those years. "She's my *fucking* wife, Phil! You can't —"

"If you call again, I'll call the police."

Rage ripped through him. Yellow spirals obscured his vision. Lightheadedness threatened to drop him, but anger propped him up. "You *stupid* son of a bitch. I *am* the *police*. You're *not* going to keep me from seeing my wife! I *paid* for her goddamn life, *asshole*. I'll *get* her! I'll get *you* and your *goddamn* family, too! Asshole!" Of course, he knew Phil had hung up. But things needed to be said, things that had been building.

Clapping the phone shut, he hurled it across the room. Not nearly as satisfying as slamming down a land-line phone or ripping it out of the wall. Sometimes a man has to act out his aggression, the way men are wired to do. Why couldn't she *see* that?

Pacing the hallway did nothing to alleviate his anger. With each footstep, he recalled things Rebecca had done in the past, things he'd turned a blind eye to. And, as always, he'd forgiven her. Every *goddamn* time. Unlike her. One slip-up and she bolts.

*Bitch.*

He wasn't sad she left, not at all. Giving her the heave-ho had been in his plans for some time, but he wanted it to be on his terms. She didn't get to choose. He ran the house, paid for everything, gave her a good life. Did she appreciate it? *No.* Their wedding vows obviously meant nothing to her.

*Bitch. Goddamn, ungrateful bitch.*

All he asked from her — all he had *ever* asked — was for her to cook, keep the house clean, and don't nag him when he came home. She failed on all three counts, three little things that were as natural as breathing. The rare times she managed to serve him a warm meal, it tasted like shit. The house was a pit, Kyra's toys scattered everywhere like debris from a highway accident. And her bitching, constant and irritating. "Brad, let's go out" and "Brad, how about we take a vacation," and worst of all, "*Brad*, can't you *ever* come home in a good mood?"

*Jesus Christ.* A housewife's work *isn't* hard; it's not even work. Not like his job. The things he saw, the people he had to deal with on a daily basis. She never worked an honest day in her worthless life.

He gave her a daughter, thought that'd make her happy, shut her up. A little living doll she could dress and show off. But nothing satisfied her. *Nothing.*

*Bitch.*

His hands slapped at the front door, grabbed hold of it, grasping an anchor to keep his ship from capsizing. He rested his forehead against the door, unsuccessfully trying to stave off his mounting headache. Standing push-ups followed, pointless and futile. His head banged against the door until a Botoxed numbness spread. As a final touch, he heaved his fist through the small window. Sharp, surprising pain triggered more fury, more memories. Blood dripped down onto his lips, salty, bittersweet. Like his joke of a marriage.

"God *damn bitch!*" Dropping to his knees in the foyer, he bellowed. No words, just raw screams. Dizziness swam up again, a vertiginous tsunami. He collapsed, exhausted, curling up. *Humiliated.*

No one does this to Brad Stanchfield. *No one.* Bitch doesn't know who she's messing with. Take the kid, he didn't care. Go live in a trailer park, suit her right. But she needed to pay for his pain. He needed to make her understand, teach her one final lesson.

Across the room, the *Hawaii Five-O* theme song belted out from his phone. Work calling. Maybe they had news. Earlier, the first thing he'd done was call his partner. Actually, it was the second thing. After a little impromptu home renovation. But he'd told his partner Rebecca had vanished, told him to spread the word. Gave him license plate, make of car, the whole nine yards including a description of her scrawny, worthless ass.

"Stanchfield."

"Hey, Brad, listen, I think I might have something ..."

"I'm listening."

"Now, don't lose your shit or anything ... It might mean nothing. Rebecca might just —"

"For *fuck's* sake, Steve, just *tell* me. You *don't* need to hold my hand." For a moment, Brad thought something might've happened to Rebecca. He didn't know how he felt about that. Obviously, she deserved punishment. But he damn well better be the one to administer it.

"Okay ..." Steve cleared his throat, taking his sweet time. He never did have the balls for this part of the job. "... I just saw something come up over the wire. Rebecca's car was found banged up pretty good in Hilston, Missouri." He paused, waiting for the news to sink in, a trick usually reserved for civilians. "But there was no sign of injury, no blood. Just an empty car. Looks like they slipped off the road and hit a tree. I'm following up —"

"Got it. Keep me posted." While Steve continued to blather on, Brad cut him off. He had everything he needed. He'd driven through Hilston before, knew its location.

But, to add insult to injury, his ingrate of a wife banged up her car, sure to be hell on his insurance rates.

Time to hit the road. And Rebecca. No way she'd made it out of Hilston yet, not without a ride and not in this storm. With his four-wheel drive truck, he could easily make it to Hilston in three hours, even in the snow.

*You're about to get a heaping pile of payback, bitch.*

The snow chilled Harold's ears to the burning point. Having forgotten his gloves, he wished he could dig his hands deep into his pockets. But there was no way he'd chance tucking the briefcase of cash beneath his arm, much too flimsy of a hold. He retracted deep into his overcoat, collar up, and quickly released one hand from the briefcase to knock on the door. The overhead light flicked on, a yellow oval spotlighting the drifts at his feet.

The man towered over Harold, large and oval shaped, his girth tucked into a burgundy vest that threatened to snap apart at the buttons. As he nudged his wire-rimmed glasses up on his nose, his red cheeks pulled up into a smile. Son of Santa Claus. "Good evening, sir. Come on in out of the cold." With a little bow, he ushered Harold in. Even though Harold saw nothing remotely amusing about his situation, the big man chuckled nonetheless.

"Thanks." In the foyer, Harold unwrapped his scarf. He stomped snow off his feet. The other man grimaced like he'd just discovered a painful tooth. But he quickly recovered with another belly-based chortle.

"I'm Christian, host of the Dandy Drop Inn." Bending down to fit his image inside a hanging mirror, Christian studied himself, no angle left unchecked. Quickly, he dabbed a small tuft of blond hair to the left, apparently didn't care for the results and readjusted it to the right. He straightened, his hands reverentially clasped in front of him. "How may I help you, sir?"

"Well, I was hoping for a room. Kinda got stuck in the storm." Harold hitched a thumb behind him. "You full?"

"Why, no, we're not. Not on a night like this. And what kind of reputation would the Dandy Drop Inn have if we didn't show hospitality during a storm? It's what we're about after all." Again with the annoying laugh. The guy probably laughs at funerals. "We only have one other couple tonight. Here ... let me take your coat and scarf." He held his hands out like an infant stumbling toward his mother.

Carefully, Harold set the briefcase between his feet, locking it into place with his knees. The coat slid off, shedding more snow onto the floor. Based on the way Christian pursed his lips, it was something he didn't care for.

Christian held the coat at arm's length like he couldn't stand the stink of it and draped the scarf around his wrist. "And may I help you with your briefcase?"

"No!" Harold swept it up, clutching it against his chest. Until he deposited the money, he wasn't letting go. Might even sleep with it under his pillow. "Ah, no, I can manage. Thanks."

Another half-bow from Christian, complete with closed eyes, ever the obedient genie. "Ah, fine, sir. Any other luggage in the car?"

"This is it. I travel light." Harold hadn't really had time to pack a suitcase. His life meant more to him than his drab, moth-eaten suits. Soon, he'd be decked out in a new wardrobe, something appealing to the ladies. "You take cash?"

His lips moving side-to-side, Christian furrowed his brow and gazed up at the ceiling. Apparently a tough question. "Of course we'll honor cash. It's just ... we don't handle many transactions like that these days." He leaned in as if ready to share a dirty joke. "If you know what I mean." Harold didn't, not really, but Christian certainly ladled a hearty spoonful of laughter over his perceived wit. Just as suddenly, he stopped. His cheeks dragged down in a frown. Guy can turn on a dime. "We do, however, require a deposit. Credit cards are the preferred method of payment." He stared unblinkingly at Harold as if he knew his secret, sweating him like a cop.

"Hm? Oh, yeah, sure, whatever." Harold didn't think anyone scoffed at cash, especially in a rinky-dink town like Hilston. But, if the crush-ass insisted on a credit card, what the hell, he could swing it. It's not like Domenick and his thugs even know what a B&B is. He smiled at the image of Domenick, napkin tucked beneath his chin, asking politely, pinky finger extended, for another crumpet. Whatever the hell a crumpet is.

"Fine. Fine. Step this way." This time when Christian bowed, Harold swore he heard the backs of his heels click. Magician-style, the host floated his hand toward a tall counter at the back of what Harold presumed to be a rec room of sorts. A large fireplace centered the room, the stone walls impeccably clean. Incredibly deep-looking sofas and loveseats were strategically placed about the room like giant game pieces facing off against one another. Hardwood floors — the visible parts that weren't devoured by Persian rugs — glimmered like a lake beneath an armada of floor and table lamps. Overhead lights appeared to be extinct at the Dandy Drop Inn. Harold thought it a miracle they even had electricity, buncha backwoods hillbillies. He looked around for a TV, disappointed he couldn't spot one.

"Are you coming, Mister ... ah, I'm sorry, sir, I didn't get your name. How impolite of me." For a big man, Christian moved fast and had already reached the back counter.

"Carsten. Harry Carsten."

Christian pushed through a swinging door set into the counter and assumed his position. Like a welcoming bartender, he stretched his arms over the wood. Light caught on his cufflinks, twinkling stars, an accessory Harold hadn't seen in years. Behind the counter, Christian stood tall and commanding, Harold reduced to an accused man waiting for final sentencing before a judge. "Very nice to meet you, Mister Carsten. The deposit is $250.00. We accept MasterCard —"

"Yeah, yeah, yeah. Here ya go." Harold tossed his battle-worn credit card on the counter. The last time he intended on using it.

"Very good. This should only take a few minutes." Painstakingly, Christian tapped numbers onto a hand-held device. Without glancing up, he asked, "What brings you to these parts, Mister Carsten? Visiting family?"

"No. No family."

"I see. Are you married?" Christian glimpsed up, not so covertly checking out Harold's hands, searching for wedding rings, no doubt. Christ, that's all Harold needed, some love-struck gay guy hitting on him. Time to set him straight. In a manner of speaking.

"No, I'm not married. Got an ex-wife, though." He dropped his voice an octave to emphasize his heterosexuality.

"I'm sorry to hear that. Ah, I mean about your divorce. What line of business are you in?"

*What the hell is this?* Harold's goodwill had about come to a crashing halt. "I'm in business. I travel." He didn't want to appear too evasive, but no sense in giving out too much info either. "Look, I'm tired. I just want to go to bed."

"Oh, my apologies, Mister Carsten, if I'm being too intrusive. That's not my intent." Chuckles let it rip again. "It's our policy here at the Dandy Drop Inn to make everyone's stay a very memorable — *comfortable* — event. 'Hospitality is dandy' is our motto. You'll just love the innkeepers. The Dandys own the house, been in their family for years. They renovated it and opened up their home and hearts to the public. Just wait until you try Dolores's muffins. She's the finest cook in Hilston, Missouri." His mouth hung open, his tongue bobbing, practically salivating.

"Sounds good. But I'm tired. Maybe breakfast."

"Breakfast will be between 6:00 a.m. and 9:00 a.m. Tell me, Mister Carsten, do you perchance enjoy antiquing?"

He had to go there. Yanking Harold's trigger. "No, I don't like damned, stupid *antiques*! I need *sleep*. What *room* am I in?"

The color fled the host's face. Red, puckered lips offset his chalky pallor. His gaze lowered as if ashamed. In a quiet voice, a chastened child, he said, "I see. You'll be in ..." He ran a finger down an open ledger. "... room three on the second floor." He swiveled and tapped a cabinet. The door sprung open, exposing hanging keys. He pressed a key into Harold's hand, his fingers cold, grotesquely damp. "I'll see you to your room, Mister Carsten."

"I can find it myself."

The big man seemed to deflate even more. Actually, Harold enjoyed the moment immensely. It'd been some time — well, never — since he'd intimidated anyone. Hardly an imposing figure, Harold stood as short and thin as his hair. Except for the slight middle-aged potbelly created by too much fast food. But big money begets big confidence. He'd learned quite a few things already during his new beginning.

"Fine, fine. It's up the stairwell; take a right, second door on the left."

"Got it." Harold tossed the key up for show, actually managing to catch it when it dropped. Didn't even have to look at its trajectory, either. Instead, he kept his eyes glued on Christian, challenging him the way bullies do. Finally, Harold let the host off the hook and turned away.

Before Harold reached the staircase, though, Christian called out to him. The man never knew when to quit.

"*What?*"

"If you get a chance, would you mind signing the guest register? By the stairwell? It's another Dandy Drop Inn tradition."

*Jesus Christ!* "Fine, fine, whatever." An open book sat on a standing podium. Harold grabbed the pen, scratching harshly through his name. The pen tip ripped a hole in the page. On the side sat a comments column. With a much lighter touch, he wrote, *Antiques can kiss my ass!*

Grinning, he hopped up the stairs two at a time, feeling ten years younger.

✳ ✳ ✳

His nerves fried, Winston let out a breath of relief once he parked down the street from the Dandy Drop Inn. Quite a walk to the inn, especially in the snow, but keeping his car a comfortable distance away always worked out for the best. Of course, he had phony tags, but one can never be too cautious.

He scratched at his new beard, something he always grew for jobs. Once, with a put-upon grimace, Julie had asked him why he let his facial hair run wild whenever he left town. She likened it to kissing an ape. He explained, "When I'm living the life of a hobo, sleeping in holes in the wall, I might as well look the part." That seemed to satisfy her, although he'd never grown accustomed to beards, itchy and troublesome as all get out.

Again, he checked his cell phone. Still no bars. Earlier, as soon as he'd crossed the Hilston city limit, the signal had dropped. Which concerned him. He'd been instructed (well, ordered) to call Domenick every hour until the job was completed and he had the money in hand. But several hours had passed since their last contact. He imagined Domenick, the world's most impatient mob boss, climbing the walls like a snake in a pit. In the past, Winston had witnessed some of Domenick's snap decisions, and the results frightened him. Definitely not a man to cross. Winston almost pitied his mark. Then again, the foolish accountant made his own decision, time to face the consequences.

Surely the inn would have a phone. Hopefully without curious ears listening in. Shouldn't be a problem in this weather, he imagined. Only fools and murderers out on a night like this. He grimaced at his little joke. He didn't consider himself a murderer, not really. Just a businessman trying to keep his family afloat by whatever means necessary.

*Yeah, keep telling yourself that, Winston. Maybe someday you might actually believe it.*

In his wallet, he thumbed through several phony driver's licenses, wondering which of his stock repertory players to put on stage. Dave Harton, insurance salesman operating out of Omaha ("The best steaks on God's green earth. Come on down; you'll taste what I'm talking about."). A bland backstory, a bland job, even blander name. Perfect.

Sort of like Winston's appearance. By no means ugly (at least according to Julie), not quite handsome (as he judged himself), he looked remarkably average (gauged by most everyone's non-reaction). Finally, he'd found an advantage to his dull outer skin. Before he met Julie, he hadn't had much luck with women. He attributed it to his plain looks. But now he'd have it no other way. His wife loved him for who he was. And, should he ever be so unlucky, no one would ever be able to pick him out of a police line-up. He favored suits slightly too large for him — always dull, muted shades — to cover up his muscular physique. Everyone remembers a sharp-dressed man; no one recalls a schlub. He wore current, trendy glasses, the ones with the huge, dark frames that people used to associate with high school outcasts. Not because they were trendy; rather, they covered up a good portion of his face, a huge dark frame obfuscating his features. Between that and the beard, he looked quite different. And still incredibly average.

But the thought of spending the night in the same quarters as his target filled him with apprehension. He'd never taken such a risk before. Actually, calling it risky seemed like a massive understatement.

Headlights brightened his rearview mirror. He dropped down in the car seat, eyes barely above the dash, and killed the engine. *Shit.* A cop car. *Keep on going, keep on going, keep on …*

The police car rolled down the road, the tires snapping over the snow with a popcorn crunch. It passed within inches of Winston's car, so close Winston could practically smell the cop's authority. Then the car kept on at an even, steady pace. Finally, it pulled into the

Dandy Drop Inn's driveway.

*Dammit.*

Snow blanketed Winston's windshield. He flipped the key to auxiliary, ran the wipers once. He watched a cop exit the patrol car and escort an attractive woman and a young girl through the knee-deep snow down an invisible sidewalk. Now Winston had an even bigger problem. The girl appeared just slightly younger than Ellie, his youngest daughter. No way would he take Carsten out in the B&B. Absolutely not. The thought of the girl possibly discovering Carsten's body sickened him.

Time for Plan B, probably a better plan anyway. He'd wait for the storm to pass, then leave the inn directly after Carsten. Make his grab for him outside. Or better yet, follow him out of town and flag him down. Not ideal, but improvisation had worked out so far.

Now he just hoped the cop would leave soon and damn near prayed he wasn't there to spend the night with his wife and daughter. Surely he wouldn't take his cruiser to a B&B.

Once the trio entered the inn, Winston turned the car on and cranked the heat. Holding his hands over the heater didn't help; nothing but cold air coughed out. He rubbed his hands together, blew into them. Wished he and his family lived in Arizona, somewhere warm.

Dammit. He'd have to spend the night at the Inn. He had to.

Just as soon as the cop left.

❆ ❆ ❆

Heather lay in bed, her head on her husband's chest. She wouldn't exactly categorize herself as relaxing in the afterglow of their marital consummation, not the way she'd heard the other girls talk about it. Rather, she considered — from a fairly clinical viewpoint — what she had just experienced.

Prior to their love making, she had spent a good half hour in the bathroom. "Preparing," she had hollered to Tommy through the closed door. More like procrastinating. She'd looked at her cotton pajamas lying on the sink, then studied the flimsy nightie in her hand. What in the world had possessed her to buy that at the mall anyway? It even had an opening for her private parts, leaving nothing to the imagination. What had she been thinking?

She could hear Tommy growing restless in the bed. Sheets rustled, his weight shifted. A loud sigh, followed by his singing her voice out like a seductive bird call. Marriage was always what she'd wanted; she just wasn't so sure about the sex part. Her folks had always implied sex was a dirty act; a necessary evil for procreation, nothing to be talked about. Which just made her more curious. But now it seemed so terrifying. Yet Tommy didn't frighten her; her prince, patiently waiting for her. They had shared true passion; they had experienced something much more intimate than sex. After the wedding, at her parents' house. Sex probably wouldn't even compare. So, why worry? Taking a chance, she wiggled into the nightie. She smiled at her reflection in the mirror. Her long hair draped over her bare shoulders, straight and wispy blond. She thought her body looked a little too thin, but maybe not when compared to the bony look models favored today. And her breasts stood small and firm, her nipples erect and visible through the flimsy material. Her "naughty bosom" as Momma used to call it. But she felt empowered, for the first time comfortable in her body. Severing ties with her dominating parents had been all it took.

And severing their heads.

As she left the bathroom, Tommy's expression pleased her. Literally, his mouth hung open. His eyes widened, lechery the culprit. Aimed at her, of all people! When he sat up in bed, the sheet fell to reveal his naked chest, so muscular, so tight. She couldn't help but notice the tent pitched over his groin.

And it hurt, Lord, did it hurt. She didn't know sex would be so painful. Sadly, she hadn't experienced an orgasm; at least she thought not since she had nothing to compare it to. Years ago, she had ruptured her hymen while horseback riding, a pleasant, warm sensation preceding it. At first, the blood had horrified her. When she studied up about women's parts the following day, she felt relief, understanding her body a little better. Then shame took her. She hadn't wanted her first orgasm to be that way. She kept her dirty, dark secret to herself all those years. Until Tommy.

Of course before the wedding, Heather had read about sex, at least as much as the local library had on hand. Someone — she couldn't remember who — had defined the orgasm as "a small death." Now this part of sex truly interested her. Once she'd discovered her hobby years ago, the part she enjoyed most had been the moment of death. She saw the animals' souls leave their carcasses. Nothing flashy, not very noticeable, just a shimmer in the air, a feeling that also reverberated through her body.

That glorious afternoon, the one she'd shared with Tommy, when she'd taken the rock to the stray cat, she'd explained the phenomenon to him. Excited, he jumped in, delivering the death blow — or as she liked to call it, "the soul-saving blow." Curious, Heather asked Tommy if he saw the cat's soul leave its body. With glazed eyes, he smiled and said, "Yeah."

She didn't know whether to believe Tommy or not. He'd never lied to her before. Maybe he could see the souls leave, maybe not. It didn't matter.

While she hadn't achieved an orgasm, her husband certainly had. Of course, he'd been gentle with her, she expected nothing less of him. Several times he'd paused to ask her if she was okay. She'd simply nodded.

But during their love making, she kept her gaze glued on her husband's face, curious if she could see a small part of his soul leave his body at the point of climax. "A little death." Tommy had kept his eyes closed, sweating over her, his face contorting into what looked like discomfort, his brow crinkled and angry looking. How could something that's supposed to feel wonderful look so agonizing? Finally, he shuddered, gasping as if dying. Disappointed, she saw nothing.

And now Tommy slept. If it wasn't for his chest lifting her head up with each slight breath, he appeared dead. His heart thrummed through his chest, beating into her ear, her lifeline to happiness. With a sudden *snurk*, Tommy's eyelids lifted.

"Hey, babe," he said. "That was great."

*Yes and no.* "It was."

A lascivious grin teased at his lips. "Wanna go again?"

"No, not now." She couldn't imagine it. Not so soon. She felt sore, dry. With his every thrust, she'd experienced pain, a raw, flesh-tearing pain. "Babe, I'm still sore from earlier. Too much man for me."

His grin bloomed into a broad smile. One thing she'd learned from the locker room girls: boys love to brag about their size. "Aw, sorry, babe. I'd never intentionally hurt ya'."

"I know. You won't next time. Just need to get used to it."

They lay in silence. Heather looked at the room, more like a large apartment. Tommy had splurged for the separate loft above the garage, a beautiful place, nicer than anything she'd ever seen. He'd said, "Nothing's too good for you, babe." A fireplace sat at the foot of the bed, warmth trickling out from the logs' orange glow. Thick, ornately designed burgundy drapes covered the window behind them and the door leading to the lower level. Posts on the bed had rattled during their love making. *Posts!* Talk about classy. It even had its very own small kitchen, complete with dining table. And the *bathroom.* The bathtub was big enough for the two of them, something she wasn't quite sure about. Cleanliness seemed like an act of privacy, next only to Godliness.

Tommy hitched up on an elbow. "The Dandys sure seem like a nice, ol' couple."

"That they do."

She could tell something bothered him. He blinked repeatedly, frowning slightly. "They kinda remind me of my folks. Babe?"

"Hmm?"

"Are you sure we have to ... you know, send them to their maker like we did your folks?"

When Heather shot up, she made sure to bring the sheet with her, covering herself. Intimacy seemed far from her mind now. "Tommy Goodenow! We talked about this. I thought you understood we're doin' the good Lord's work."

"Yeah, but —"

"No 'buts'!" She struck an iron finger in front of him. "You know darn-tootin' well what we're doin' is for their own benefit. We're helpin' to hasten their departure from this sinful world, sendin' them onto their immortal afterlives. Doin' God's work."

"I know that, babe. It's just ... the Dandys seem so nice and —"

"Exactly. And nice folks get their just rewards. I thought you understood all this."

Heather watched realization crack like an egg over Tommy's face. With a smile, the one she liked so much, he gripped her shoulders and playfully brought her back down to bed. "You're right, babe. 'Course you're right. They'll thank us when we get to Heaven. You think ... your folks went to Heaven? I mean, after everything you tol' me about 'em?"

"I been kinda thinkin' about that myself, babe. All I know is it's God's plan for us to carry out His work. If we hasten some sinners on their path? It's what God wants. That's why I see souls fly away."

"Yeah. *Sinners.*" Tommy drew a hand down his square jaw. She noticed he didn't mention his ability to see souls. "Kinda like that Christian fella."

"Whaddaya mean?"

"Well ... seems kinda obvious to me, Christian, the host ... he's one of those ... homosexuals." Tommy lowered his voice as if not to offend God.

Heather hadn't really thought about it, having never met a homosexual. At least not that she knew. "You don't think —"

"I do, babe. He's ... funny. Speakin' of funny, it's funny he, of all people, has a name like 'Christian'."

Shock nearly bowled Heather over. First sex, now a homosexual. Two things she thought she'd never experience. The world, indeed a wicked place, seemed to be changing all around her. It strengthened her conviction, her mission more urgent than ever. "Well, then, maybe he should be next. After the Dandys."

"I think I'd like that, babe."

"Me, too." She burrowed down on his chest again, breathing in his manly aroma of sweat and heavy cologne. "It sure was nice of him to light the fireplace for us, though."

"Even sinners do nice things on occasion."

"Love you, Mister Goodenow."

"Love you back, Missus Goodenow."

The tingling sensation in her body, the one she'd experienced in the car, returned. She unclenched her legs, discovering a natural lubricant had soothed her privates. Reaching over, she turned off the lamp, and this time made sweet love, definitely not sex, to her husband.

# Chapter Three

For a moment, as Rebecca walked up the steps of the mammoth southern-looking abode, she felt swept into the past. Only the snow diluted the fantasy. Impeccably kept and restored with an artist's eye, the inn — a quaint gothic-styled, three-story domicile — stood tall and solid, a sentinel against the storm. A sprawling porch, supported by pillars, wrapped around the house, an architectural napkin. Green shutters, fresh and newly painted, flattened against the walls. Through thin curtains, light filtered out of the windows on the lower two floors, a nice welcome on a wintry night. Only the top floor's two windows lay shrouded in darkness. Each story grew progressively smaller as they climbed, reminding Rebecca of something Kyra might build with her blocks. Barren bushes surrounded the porch, branches poking out of the snow like skeletal fingers. Rebecca imagined the inn would be even lovelier in the Spring or Fall. Perhaps she'd visit again. And maybe look up Deputy Randy Gurley when she did.

"Deputy Gurley, nice to see you again," said the large, blond man at the front door. Immediately, he ushered them inside. "And you've brought company." He bent over, hands on knees, to reach Kyra's level. His voice raised an embarrassing notch. "And what's your name?"

Kyra gripped her mother's arm tight, small fingers digging in. She kept quiet.

Randy rushed to the rescue. "Christian, this is Rebecca and her daughter, Kyra. Little bit of car trouble put 'em in a fix. I was hopin' you had an open room for the night."

He straightened with a little chin curtsy. "We certainly do. Quite honestly, I'm surprised at the number of visitors we have tonight. There's a lovely newlywed couple in the loft. And another gentleman has joined us for the evening as well."

Rebecca stuck her hand out. "It's fine, no judgment here. A pleasure to meet you, Christian. And thank you for helping out two ladies in distress."

"Trust me when I say the pleasure's all mine." He grabbed her fingertips and shook them with a delicate touch. "Any luggage you need help with?"

Holding up her suitcase, Rebecca demonstrated its light weight with an easy shake. "What you see is what you get."

"Very good. I imagine you're very tired after your, ah, travails. But, alas, we have some minor formalities to take care of first."

"Of course." Once Rebecca shed her coat, a shudder followed like an after draft.

"I'm sorry, are you cold? I can turn up the heat if you wish. And I'll see to it you get the first room floor with the fireplace."

"That'd be great." Rebecca hadn't even thought to inquire about the costs. It hardly seemed important now. Nothing mattered more than a nice warm bed, a temporary place to sleep her troubles away. During their trip, she'd been adamant about not using her credit card again; Brad's money, after all, at least that's how he saw it. But she reconsidered once she thought of it as severance pay, one last go-round. With a small grin, she hoped the pricing would be exorbitant.

"Say, Christian, Dolores got any of that chocolate pecan pie tonight?" Randy tossed a thumb over his shoulder, presumably toward the kitchen.

"You're in luck, Deputy. Fresh out of the oven."

Kyra tugged on Rebecca's sleeve again. "Mommy? Can I?" Rebecca saw hunger in Kyra's eyes. She'd felt bad about not stopping for food along the way, but she'd been hell bent to get away, food a forgotten notion. Of course, she also never thought a tree would've stopped them before they had a chance to refuel their bodies.

"It's okay, Rebecca," said Randy. "I'll take her." He offered a hand toward Kyra.

Rebecca's first instinct had been to snatch Kyra to her side, fold her in, not let go.

Apparently, Randy noticed her hesitation. Gently, he placed a hand on Rebecca's arm, and said, "It's fine. I'll watch her. Nothing's gonna happen to her." This time Rebecca didn't flinch from his touch. His trustworthy touch.

"Okay, fine. Go get pie." Kyra raced in front of Randy, snatching his hand as she went. She practically dragged him behind her in her quest for pie. "One piece only, Kyra! You hear me?"

"Yes, Mommy!" She had turned and was running backward, with Randy stumbling after her. Then they vanished around the large stairwell.

Christian waited for her behind a beautiful oak counter, pen in hand. A closed door stood behind him.

"Your home is gorgeous."

He tossed a manic laugh toward the ceiling like a coyote baying at the moon. "No, no, I'm afraid you're mistaken. I'm merely the host, not the owner. That would be the Dandys, Jim and Dolores. I'm sure you'll meet them." He gave her a wink as if defining their "character" status.

"Hope so."

A little bit of paperwork, a whole lot of deposit, and an avalanche of personal questions consumed the next fifteen minutes. Rebecca kept looking over her shoulder, waiting for Kyra to return. Then she realized how silly she'd been acting. No more paranoia. Not everyone's evil. She left evil behind in Hollington. Kyra's fine, in the hands of a nice deputy. Not to mention handsome. Why not enjoy her little vacation?

"All right, Missus Stanchfield —"

"Miz," she corrected.

"Excuse me?" His eyebrows rose like twin arches.

"It's Miz. I'm divorced." It rolled out of her mouth with ease this time. Funny how she felt another brick load of angst shoveled away.

"I'm very sorry to hear that, Miz Stanchfield."

"Don't be." She felt the corners of her mouth prick up, a grin, ten percent bitter and ninety percent victorious.

On the other hand, she'd obviously tossed Christian out of his comfort zone. His cheeks flushed red, his eyes flitting everywhere but on her. Judging her. Maybe everyone in Hilston considered divorce a sin. "Anyhoo, anyhow ..." He busied himself with more paperwork, humming a nonsensical melody that surely he just made up.

Rebecca looked around. Wooden framework, the kind you're more likely to see in a log cabin, braced the tall ceiling. Table lamps lit up the large room, a dazzling display of electric warmth. A log snapped in the fireplace, the smell of burning wood taking Rebecca back to her childhood. The happier days. It'd been some time since she'd had the pleasure of warming herself in front of a fireplace.

Christian hovered over his ledger, practically oblivious to Rebecca's presence.

Behind him, the door now sat open a crack. Just enough to allow a sliver of orange light to bleed through. And within that light, an eye appeared. Staring at her. Bloodshot, narrowed. *Unblinking.*

A chill raced down her back. Goosebumps rippled across her arms, this time not the pleasant sort. Over her shoulder, she called out, "Kyra?" When she looked back, the door behind Christian had closed. Then she wondered if she ever saw anything in the first place. Lord knows she was exhausted enough to imagine things, her eyes dry and blurry. Still, she wanted her daughter at her side. *Now.*

"I'm sure your daughter's fine, Miz —"

"*Kyra!*" Rebecca raced away, her boots slapping against the hardwood floor. "I'll be right back, Christian." He said something, but Rebecca couldn't hear him. She had a bad feeling, a sudden feeling Kyra was in danger. A mother's sixth sense.

She picked up her pace, swiveled around the stairwell. Breaking into a sprint, she shoved through a swinging door. The door smacked back against the wall with a resounding bang that echoed through the large kitchen like a firecracker. Her nerves buzzed like live wires, her pulse a rattling jackhammer.

Kyra and an elderly woman sat at a large oak table, room enough to accommodate a dozen people. With the kitchen counter at his back, Randy stood stuffing his face, his fork frozen in midair. Hunched over her daughter, the woman gently stroked Kyra's chin. She looked up at Rebecca, her eyes nearly forced closed from a beatific smile. Rebecca rushed to her daughter, marking her territory by grabbing Kyra's shoulders.

"Ah, hello, I'm Rebecca. This is *my* daughter." She punched "my," a sign of ownership. And, really, it made her feel strange, considering her daughter as property, but she felt a driving need to protect Kyra, now more than ever. Irrational, sure, and just maybe she needed to help atone for Brad's sins as well. Still, she hardly felt like "Mother of the Year."

"Hello there. I'm Dolores. Dolores Dandy." The elderly woman held her hand out. Rebecca tread lightly, afraid to squeeze her offered hand too hard. But Mrs. Dandy gripped as hard as many of Brad's cop buddies. "Kyra was just telling me about school. And I'm very sorry to hear about her father."

Rebecca shot Kyra a look. Not only did she prefer to keep her personal life — such as it was — her own business, the fewer people who knew about her dangerous husband, the better off they'd be. Kyra sunk her head, probably working up alligator tears. A survival technique she learned early.

"Nice to meet you, too, Dolores. I'm sorry Kyra's —"

Dolores stood and shooed away Rebecca's words with a flurried wave of her hand. But the raspberry sound the old woman made really surprised Rebecca. "Pshaw, child. No need to apologize for what happened to your family." She approached Rebecca, arms out. "Should be me apologizin'. You need a nice hug after the passing of your husband."

Rebecca stepped back as Dolores embraced her. Like an old friend, she dropped her head onto Rebecca's shoulder, her hands massaging a circular pattern onto her back. A smirk tightened Kyra's face, the look kids get when they try to rein in complicit laughter. She'd get hers later. But as far as lies go, it might work nicely given the circumstances. If Rebecca weren't so on edge, she'd be proud of Kyra. Just a little. Reluctantly, Rebecca patted Dolores's back, then gently edged away.

Still propping up the counter, Randy grinned around the pie wedged into his cheek. Apparently, he'd let Kyra's lie fly. More cop instincts, no doubt. When Rebecca glared at him, he straightened, polishing off his mouthful like a hyped-up cow.

Rebecca turned her attention back to Dolores. "Thank you, that's very kind. But I'd just as soon not talk about it."

"I understand, I understand. I've lost someone I loved ..." Her voice floated away as she lowered back into her chair. Her blue eyes misted, one hand rubbing a cheek. But her mourning didn't last long. Her hands flew beside her, wringing away her melancholy. "What do I know? I'm just a silly ol' woman, don't mind me."

Finally, Randy surfaced, his food submerged. "How 'bout a piece of pie?" He offered his empty plate toward Rebecca for all the good that'd do her.

Food sounded like a good idea. Not the taste. Rebecca had no yearning for anything, almost as if her taste buds had retired. But she knew she needed the protein. And maybe a sugar rush could clear her head a little, if only temporarily.

"Don't mind if I do." She crossed the room toward Randy.

The swinging door flew open. A deep voice bellowed, "*Hold* on there, young lady. Jim Dandy to the rescue." The tall man swept across the room, his stride nearly twice as long as Rebecca's. With a chef's polish, he slid a utensil into the pie plate and slapped a healthy-sized wedge onto a plate. Then he set it down, wiped his hands on his flannel shirt, and stuck his arms out.

*Good grief.* Rebecca'd stumbled across the world's most hug-gingest people. Still, she gave in, accepting the kindness. Warmth she hadn't felt at home. After a respectable length of time, Jim disengaged. "Here at the Dandy Drop Inn, everyone's family." With his solid baritone voice and full head of silver hair, Rebecca thought he could've once been a movie star. Every move he made leaned toward theatrical sweeping gestures; everything he said sounded like a radio announcement.

The Dandys made an interesting — albeit, delightful — looking couple. As short and lovably compact as Dolores stood, Jim had everyone in the kitchen beat by at least a head's height, maybe more. "And as everyone knows, family's everything," he said.

He stared at Rebecca as if waiting for affirmation. "It is. Thank you both for having us tonight. For welcoming us."

"Ain't nothin' we wouldn't do for anyone, child," said Dolores.

Jim leaned down behind his wife, his back cracking, and laid a tender kiss on the crown of her head.

A small part of Rebecca died; she wondered if she'd ever experience love and companionship into her senior years. This couple had managed to keep it together for a lifetime, their love so thick you could slice it like Dolores's pie. Rebecca couldn't even sustain a ten-year tenure. Of course, that tour of duty had been fought under battle-field conditions. But enough feeling sorry for herself

"Land of Goshen, Mother, we surely do have a full house tonight. Who woulda thought it during this storm."

"That's precisely why all these young folks have stopped in, Poppa. To get out of the snow."

"Ceptin', of course, for the nice, young newlywed couple." He winked at Randy, his eyes sly. "And we all know what they're up to."

Dolores shoved an elbow back at him. "You just hush now, none of that kinda talk." Yet a case of the giggles weakened her protests. He dropped down, their cheeks next to one another. A painting, a Norman Rockwell portrait of America, captured in a B&B kitchen. With a stubby finger, Dolores scratched beneath his chin. "Forgot to shave again, didn't you?"

Good-naturedly, he grumbled something — part of their ritual, Rebecca imagined — then looked at Kyra. "And who do we have here? My goodness, you're a pretty lil gal. You driving yet, sweetheart?"

As wary of strangers as Kyra can be, she immediately warmed to Jim. Other than food, the trip to her heart rode the funny bone. "I don't drive, silly. I'm six!" She giggled, her feet kicking madly beneath the table, a sugar surge of delight. "I'm Kyra."

"Sure had me fooled. Thought you was at least sixteen. I'm Jim, Jim Dandy. Ain't that name a hoot-and-a-half?" He squatted behind her, his arms folded over the back of her chair.

Kyra appeared ready to burst out a comment, but still uncertain in the land of the adults. Rebecca knew what she wanted to say. With a smile, she nodded her approval.

"'Ain't' isn't proper. But your name's funny."

The Dandys' laughter mushroomed through the kitchen, loud and resonant. A nice sound. "Why, Kyra, you've properly schooled me. I stand corrected."

Obviously, Kyra didn't understand everything Jim said. She switched her head back and forth between the laughing adults, her blond hair whipping her shoulders. Rebecca couldn't control her own giggle, a wonderfully cathartic feeling.

When Randy clapped his hands sharply, it sounded like a gunshot's report bouncing off the vaulted ceiling. The handcuffs attached to his belt loop jangled, a coda. "Welp. Gotta get back to patrol now that everyone's all nice and snug for the evening. Thanks for the pie, Dolores." He dropped low, giving her a quick hug. Rebecca wondered if Hilston's favorite pastime leaned toward hugging. Although Randy favored Jim with a mere rigid handshake.

"You're certainly welcome, Deputy. Do drop in any ol' time."

Randy hesitated at the kitchen doorway. "Rebecca, Kyra ... nice to meet you both." The door swung after he dodged out.

Rebecca hadn't properly thanked Randy for his help. She darted after him, not quite wanting to say goodbye yet.

"Randy?"

"Oh." With one foot out the door, snowflakes breezed in, alighting in his hair. As she approached, he closed the door and opened a smile; a big, handsome, cocky smile. One she couldn't get enough of. "I forget something?"

"No, but I did." She stepped closer, smelling mint on his breath, a clean odor. "Thanks. You know, for everything you did." For one crazy, uninhibited second, she wanted to toss her arms around his neck and kiss him. Common sense won out. Instead, she wrung her hands like a dishwater housewife.

"Hey, my pleasure. Not often I get to help out a beautiful woman."

Blood rushed into her cheeks. A care-free light-headedness made her loopy. "Well, thanks again." She meant to lean in, give him a quick peck on the cheek. He'd earned that, at least. Even if it was brash and extremely out of character for her. But at the last moment, he turned, meeting her lips with his.

Shock coursed through her. Reality yanked her back down to earth. She pushed him away. Her heart pounded as she tried to cover her shortness of breath. And parts of her absolutely sizzled, catching fire after lying dormant for so long. But it felt wrong. "Holster it, cowboy. I'm flattered. I really am. But I'm just not ready for … anything like this. Sorry."

"Hey, don't apologize, Rebecca. It's all good." He gave a nonchalant shrug.

Rebecca laughed, feeling a little duped. She knew his type, a cad, a player. Still, the attention was a welcome diversion. For the most part. "Fine, I accept your apology."

"I didn't apolo —"

"Then maybe you should." Rebecca's smile hinted at more than a desired apology. She had lit the match, now playing with fire. But it was time to douse it. "Okay, okay. Enough." She swept her hair back with both hands, hoping to sweep the rush of arousal away with it. "Anyway, I'll be out of here tomorrow. It'd be —"

"I wouldn't be so sure about that. I mean, the storm's supposed to last 'til Friday." He tossed another shrug, no skin off his back.

"We'll see. But now? I'm exhausted. Good night, Randy." His

foot stopped the door before she could close it.

Playfulness slipped into impatience. "*What?* Look, I'm sure your boyish charm and good looks get —"

"No, no, nothing like that." Concern added five years to his face. Crow's feet that hadn't been there before creased with worry. He handed her a business card. "If you need anything ... anything at all ... give me a call. No matter the time."

She accepted the card, playing a finger along the edge. His Jekyll-and-Hyde switcharoo threw her for a loop. "I'll do that. But ... why would I need to call you?" Paranoia, her old friend, just tapped her on the back. "Something you're not telling me?"

"No, I didn't mean it like that." Faster than she could keep up with, he slipped back into his "aw, shucks" routine, all grins and charm signifying nothing. "Guess I just wanted you to call me." He locked his supersized smile back into place. "Hey, you think I have boyish charm and good looks?"

"Good night, Deputy." As he rambled through a list of his good points, she closed the door. So damned annoying. Yet kinda cute. And he knew it. Didn't matter, though. She twirled a lock of hair around a finger, another smile dawning. A rare experience these days. Then she realized she had an audience.

At the bottom of the stairwell, Dolores and Jim stood with their arms around one another, grinning like proud parents on prom night. No taller than Jim's kneecaps, Kyra, so tiny and fragile, yawned. Rebecca wondered how much they'd seen, hoping not too much. Based on Kyra's dog-tired indifference, probably not a lot. Still the Dandys' twin grins held a knowing look, the kind that said, "We know your secret."

"Just seeing Deputy Gurley out," she mumbled as she scurried toward them, head down.

"That's nice," said Dolores as if having witnessed anything but "nice." "We're just showing Kyra to your room. You'll be staying in room number one, the best in the house. Has a personal fireplace and bathroom, too."

"Sounds wonderful." Aggravated with herself, Rebecca slapped her hands down against her jeans. She hadn't been as gracious to the kind couple as she should've been. They'd been knocking themselves out to accommodate her, while she'd been oscillating between a harried drama queen to a stupidly smitten schoolgirl. Time to pull up her big girl panties. "You both have been so nice to us. I truly appreciate it."

"Not a problem, child." At first, when Dolores raised her hand, Rebecca thought it the precursor to another hug. Frankly, she felt flat hugged out at this point. But Dolores chopped the air with finality. "We'd do it for anyone. Besides, we have a gentleman on the second floor. Wouldn't be proper to have two young ladies sharing a bathroom with him."

"No, sir. Mother's right, jes' wouldn't be proper. Now if you'll follow us, your room awaits. I 'spect you're plumb tuckered."

"Plumb tuckered," parroted Kyra, rubbing her eyes.

Behind the stairwell lay a hallway Rebecca hadn't seen earlier. Electronic sconces lit portions of the walls, yellow circles dissipating into darkness. Paintings lined the hardwood walls, most of them pastoral vistas. At the end of the hall, a painting of a grim man glowered at them. His suit looked too tight, his hair sticking out like a mad clown's. Kyra shrunk into Rebecca's arm, the painting too much for her. Rebecca couldn't say she blamed her.

Jim rattled a key in the lock and pushed the door open. As if Kyra'd just received her second wind, she rocketed toward the king-sized bed. She hopped onto it, bouncing animatedly, the effects of late-night sugar.

"I'm sorry there's only one bed in the room, but we thought you wouldn't mind," said Dolores. "'Specially with what y'all have been through tonight."

*Preach it, sister.* Honestly, Rebecca didn't want Kyra out of her sight. She just hoped it wouldn't be a long-lasting issue, transforming her into one of those overprotective parents who just can't let go. But tonight? She'd fall asleep, arms wrapped around her daughter.

"It's perfect, Dolores."

"Bathroom's over yonder." Jim jabbed his finger around the room like a man on a hunting expedition. "Pitcher of water on the bed stand. If y'all need anything else, ring the bell." As if prompted, Kyra clutched the bell, pulling it back for a good thrash.

"Kyra, *no*. Put it down."

Kyra looked disappointed, pouting, but complied nonetheless. Of course, the Dandys found her behavior the most precious thing in the world and showed their appreciation with a round of chuckles. Rewarding discourteous behavior. But it was late, too late to run parental damage control. Besides, Rebecca didn't want to hurt the Dandys' feelings. Like most grandparents, they meant well.

"Christian will come a-runnin' at the sound of the bell. Boy has ears like a rabbit. Anyhow, anyhoo, reckon we'll say good night."

"Night. Thank you, again. I mean it."

"Ain't no thing." When he left, Jim left the door slightly ajar. Although the light was weak, Rebecca thought she saw a shadow, a black smudge, shift beneath the door. Someone standing just outside the room. Quietly, Rebecca padded toward the door. Bending down, she peeked through the keyhole and saw nothing but blackness. Suddenly the darkness lifted. Muted orange light replaced it. Startled, she fell back. She pushed the door closed until she heard a reassuring click. Footsteps receded down the carpeted hallway.

Another chill scurried through her, causing her hands to tremor. There wasn't an internal lock on the door plate.

She knew the Dandys meant no harm to her or Kyra. Knew it in her heart. But her heart had failed her in the past. Lifting a chair away from the desk, she wedged it beneath the doorknob. It didn't seem too steady, yet it always worked in the movies.

Perched on the bed, Kyra watched her, obviously loaded with questions. But before her daughter could begin her interrogation, Rebecca fell into bed, fully clothed, out faster than a weak-jawed boxer.

❋ ❋ ❋

The harder Brad pushed through the snow, the more his head pounded. An equation of sorts, the kind any good detective looks for. He'd damn near demolished the bottle of baby aspirin riding shotgun next to his pistol. *Baby aspirin!* How many times had he asked Rebecca to buy adult aspirin? Like Kyra was the only one in the house susceptible to headaches.

That was the deal. He didn't know when it happened. Seemed like overnight. But he'd been pushed out. Once the brat came along, he'd been bounced to the curb. Kyra, Kyra, everything Kyra. Maybe his daughter deserved punishment for his misery as well. Sure, she's just a kid, probably not entirely her fault, but she needed to be reprimanded. For once. His damn wife always let her get away with murder, making excuses for her unacceptable behavior.

He ratcheted against the steering wheel until his arms hurt. His hand deadened when he smacked the windshield, but not his internal pain. Why didn't that bitch, Rebecca, appreciate his hard efforts? His sacrifices? All she cared about was her daughter.

Tapping the bottle into his mouth, he chewed the last four aspirin. They left a bitter, metallic taste in his mouth, a taste similar to his blood he'd tasted earlier.

"Goddamn *bitch*!"

He hadn't turned on the radio. Definitely kept the police radio off. He didn't need other voices rattling around in his head. Plenty crowded in there already with Rebecca's whining and Kyra's crying playing on an endless loop. They were even pushing him out of his own head. Couldn't get peace of mind anywhere.

He swigged his fourth Red Bull and crushed the can before tossing it to the floorboard. Red Bull and baby aspirin, about the only damn thing to consume in his house. How hard is it to keep food in the refrigerator?

The snow pummeled down, taunting him with its relentlessness. He'd severely underestimated the storm, believing the trip would be over by now. Instead, he'd been on the road for over three hours, slow going and getting nowhere. Damn road crews too lazy to get off their asses and do their jobs. Whatever happened to a good work ethic?

Not that Rebecca'd ever given two shits about work.

Three hours behind him and only halfway to Hilston. *Shit*. At this rate, he wouldn't make it 'til dawn. Several times he considered pulling over, catching an hour of shut-eye. But he wouldn't let nature beat him down. Hell, he was a force of nature, one to be reckoned with. He could conquer this goddamn storm. Yes, sir, Hurricane Brad's coming to Hilston, Missouri. God help anyone who gets in his path.

Her note had stabbed like a knife in his gut and dragged up to his heart.

*Brad, we're gone. You know why. I don't want anything from you, I don't expect anything from you. Just leave us alone. Rebecca*

Or some such shit. He couldn't remember it all. Just the letter's extreme hatefulness. It didn't make sense either. He tried to put the pieces together, struggled to understand it. Too much work, too much self-torture.

*You know why.*

What the hell did that mean? Was she referring to the tap he gave Kyra? Crybaby. It didn't hurt her. Hell, he'd been holding back.

Mustn't harm the precious little princess. Besides, she deserved worse. Running around the house, screaming for attention. *Daddy, Daddy, watch this! Daddy, look at me!* Just like her mother, needier than the homeless. Then she spilled his beer, icing on the cake. All he'd wanted was to be left alone for the night. Why couldn't they get that?

He'd make Rebecca understand. His daughter, too. No matter what.

As he cracked open his last Red Bull, Brad howled, releasing his rage to the world, but mostly to his "loving" wife.

❄ ❄ ❄

Well, obviously there was a party raging downstairs. At first, Harold could only hear mumbled voices. Until the old woman launched into the first of many high-pitched screaming jags, the only way she apparently knew how to communicate. Worse than an adolescent yodeler, she reminded him of his ex-wife when she'd hoot at the TV.

Dealing with the host, Christian, had been bad enough. He hoped not to see anyone else for his safety. Honestly, he'd never had much use for other people. Living life like a hermit had its rewards, fully preparing him for a life on the run. It's just his bladder disagreed with this arrangement.

It throbbed, full and angry.

An hour ago, he'd been ready to trip down to the john, but he heard footsteps coming up the stairwell. Two men chatting. He recognized Christian's effete voice. The other man kept his voice low, how most people should speak. When they walked by his room, his heart sped up. The way Christian had been all over him earlier, he thought he might invite him for a game of pinochle or something ludicrous. But they passed his room. A door across the hall opened with a mousey squeak, then closed. Other than the slight sound of bedsprings settling, he hadn't heard a peep since. Probably asleep, a respectful neighbor.

He listened. After a loud rallying at the bottom of the stairwell, the voices finally died down. Nice and quiet, conditions that appealed to his bladder. He scuttled off the bed. With his hand on the doorknob, he remembered his traveling companion. Couldn't believe he nearly forgot it. Snatching the briefcase from beneath the pillow, he raced toward the door.

*Hold on S.S. Bladder, you're about to come into dry dock.*

He opened the door a crack, peered out. No one in sight. The lamps on the wall had been muted, nothing more than a firefly's weak glow. Even though he took extra care to tread lightly, he may as well have been stomping. Every time he lifted a foot up, the floorboards beneath him groaned. Not even the hall-length runner softened the sound. *Damn old houses.*

To his right, a door clicked open. A vertical line of light dropped over the paisley patterned carpet, expanding across the floor and the wall. Harold's throat dried up, his bladder clenching like a fist. Backlight splashed off a man's silhouette.

He stared at the figure, silent, frozen. Finally, the man stepped out into the hallway, his hand reaching for Harold. "Oh, sorry, guy. Didn't mean to startle you. Name's Harton. Dave Harton."

Harold fumbled the briefcase into his left hand and offered his neighbor a clammy-handed shake. "I'm Harry. Hope I didn't wake you. Just, ah, going to the john."

"Oh, right. Won't hold you up then." He looked at Harold, stone-faced, waiting, damn near challenging him to say something else. Social amenities and all.

For an instant, Harold forgot his mission. Until his bladder urged him on. He clenched his groin muscles, gritted his teeth. Yet he noticed Harton staring at his briefcase. Feeling it necessary to offer up an explanation — not everyone takes their briefcase to the bathroom — Harold offered, "Um, brought my own toiletries." An inspired lie.

Harton nodded, an "aha" look on his face. "Well … 'night." His door closed, light peeping out beneath it. Then a shadow darkened the middle section.

*Jesus.* Harold stood still for another moment, his heart tripping, looking at the door at the end of the hall, his endgame. So close, yet so far. Forgoing stealth, he lifted his feet, running, the briefcase bouncing against his leg. He slammed the door open, flailing around for a light switch. His thigh muscles squeezed involuntarily just as the light blinked on. No time to undo his belt, just unzip the fly. Then his bladder locked up again, a petulant baby throwing a fit.

*Jumping Jesus!*

He supposed he should've expected it. His bladder had always been shy and the hallway encounter sent it fleeing for cover. With his johnson in hand, he leaned over the toilet, resting his head against the cool wall. *Come on, come on …*

Something about the guy bugged him. First, what was he doing at a bed and breakfast? By himself? Harold hadn't heard any other voices, hadn't seen anyone behind him in his room. A romantic night for one can easily happen at home; God only knew Harold had plenty of practice. Then again, maybe the storm forced Harton to suck it up, seek shelter, just like it had Harold.

The guy looked strange, though. A wanna-be hipster, one of those too-cool-for-school guys who hang out at coffee shops and unemployment lines. A beard fringed his face, his designer glasses screaming pretentiousness. He was only missing a stocking cap and a guitar strapped to his back. Yet he seemed too old for that look, his suit at odds with his appearance. Maybe it's a Missouri thing.

Twisting the knob in the sink to full blast, Harold waited for the washing sound to influence his bladder. A false start, a single drop plopping into the bowl, made him groan.

And had Harton taken a particular interest in his briefcase? The man gaped at it like it was Harold's third leg. Which reminded Harold to give his "third leg" another couple of shakes.

On the other hand, Harold might find it odd if he saw someone lugging a briefcase to the toilet, too. Dammit. Seeing ghosts where there weren't any hauntings, something his mother used to say. Still, it pays to be aware, on guard at all times. Pays a helluva lot, actually. The proof lay at his feet. Might be best to keep an eye on Dave Harton.

But for now? Nothing mattered but sweet, sweet relief. Time for another tactic, one that rarely failed him. He dropped trou, lowered the lid and sat, tucking his penis into the opening. When he grabbed the briefcase, he clutched it to his chest. A relaxing, calm swept through him, coddling his bladder, telling it to "Release. Just ... let it go." In a woman's sexy, alluring voice, natch.

The gates opened, the torrent flowed. When he thought he'd finished, round two fired up. A sense of serenity relaxed Harold, the first time since he'd left Kansas City. He patted his briefcase, a fine anti-anxiety medication.

❋ ❋ ❋

Hardly the luck of the Irish. Not only did Winston now reside across the hall from his mark, but they shared the same bathroom. Not an ideal situation. Roommates in a dormitory of death, a crappy horror movie title if he'd ever heard one. To top it off, the host had told him the inn's phone was out. "Not uncommon during a storm like this," he'd said with a laugh. Winston met his merriment with a stone face. Pissing off Domenick hardly seemed like a laughing matter.

Running into Carsten had shaken him up. He thought he'd bounced back gracefully enough during their encounter, but it felt like bumping into an old girlfriend, a relationship where things had ended poorly. Their conversation hadn't amounted to much of anything. Yet it filled him with guilt, possibly even a little melancholy. "Melancholy" didn't quite seem like the right word, though; as he'd told his wife earlier, "a poet I ain't." But instead of considering Harold Carsten a cipher to dispose of, Winston now knew enough about the accountant to see him as a person, flaws and all.

On-the-job training had honed Winston's analytical skills. Based on their brief meeting, he pegged Carsten as neurotic, fastidious, lacking in social graces, possibly anal-retentive. And worried for his life. Not exactly someone he'd go out of his way to have a beer with. But someone recognizable, all too human.

Which made his impending job tough. A cannonball of trepidation loaded into his gut. And he'd have to fire it even if the enemy waved a white flag.

Giving himself a mental slap, he reminded himself Carsten was a crook. Something that made his work a little more tolerable.

The grumbling in his stomach required immediate attention, though; actually a nice respite from his mental gymnastics. The host, Christian, had told him the innkeepers always kept a selection of cookies and muffins available. Not the healthiest of food choices, but he hadn't eaten since this morning. Besides, his stomach wouldn't know the difference.

He waited until Carsten finished in the bathroom; then he gave it an extra half-hour. At 2:00 a.m., quiet had settled, the inn having tucked everyone in for the night. Safe for him to make a covert grab and gobble.

Still wearing his suit, minus the jacket, he left the room. He'd abandoned his traditional work shoes — the leather ones — at home in lieu of loafers. Much quieter, but shit in a snow storm as he'd found out the hard way. In his room, he had laid them over the vent, trying to dry them. Now they felt stiff, unyielding. But nice and toasty.

With his hand riding the stairwell railing, he took the steps at a fast clip, descending quietly. Already, he'd logged a mental blueprint of the inn's layout — at least the parts he'd seen — usually the first thing he did in an unfamiliar environment, so the darkness didn't bother him. Counting down the steps, he reached the first floor. A single sconce, lonely in the night, illuminated a partial path to the kitchen.

Beyond the swinging door, a lamp burned dully above the kitchen sink. Not until he'd tread halfway through the kitchen did he notice he had company. He stopped, staring at the girl sitting at the table. The same girl he'd seen outside the inn earlier. Chocolate blemished her cheeks, the tip of her nose. She lapped at an empty plate, scrounging for leftovers.

Winston swallowed the lump in his throat. While her eyes never left him, her priority clearly remained the plate. She watched him like a wary dog hovering over food.

Too late to back out now. If the girl was wired anything like his daughters, her intuition could prove problematic, bringing more attention his way. Casual small talk and non-threatening body language, the best way to diffuse the situation.

"Hi there. You're up late."

She nodded, finally dropping her relentless gaze. She lowered the plate, wiping her index finger around the rim. Sticking the chocolate-tipped digit into her mouth, she pulled it out with a pop.

"What's good to eat around here?"

"Pie."

"Save a piece for me?"

She grinned, perched somewhere between mischief and sincerity. Chocolate darkened parts of her teeth. "Two pieces left."

"Sounds great. How 'bout if I have one … and if you don't tell your mother, I'll give you the other?" He made his way to the counter, his heart settling to a normal beat.

Her smile widened. "'Kay." Carrying her plate, she skittered his way. "But remember, don't tell my mommy."

With a finger pressed to his lips, Winston made a shushing sound. "Our secret."

She bounced up and down on bare feet, plate outstretched. He didn't keep her waiting. One bite in and Winston thought he might end up licking the plate as well. Still warm — a culinary mystery given the late hour — the pie slid down fast and tasted nearly as fulfilling as Julie's pumpkin pie. The girl watched him carefully as if wanting to hear his food review.

"Wish there was more," he said, coming up for air.

"Me, too."

"What's your name?"

"Kyra. What's yours?"

"Dave. Just Dave to you since we're secret, late-night kitchen pals."

She giggled, sing-songy and worry-free, the way his youngest daughter carried on. He marveled at children's abilities to find joy in the smallest things. Before the world clubbed them with a good dose of adult anxiety.

"Anyway, does your mom know you're down here?"

"Uh-uh. She's asleep."

"We wouldn't want to wake her, would we?"

She shook her head and opened her eyes wide, crazy wide for two in the morning.

"Part of our secret." Holding out a fist, Winston waited for her to bump it. "Don't leave me hangin', Kyra."

Winston nearly laughed at the way she scrutinized him. But he remained solemnly quiet. To gain a child's trust, you take everything seriously. One of her eyebrows lifted, the other eye narrowed. Her lips tightened with doubt. Apparently, she'd learned to be suspicious of adults at an early age. Smart girl.

Finally, she popped his fist with hers, both of them shedding imaginary shrapnel with wiggling fingers. "Why're you and your mother here?"

"We're going to see Aunt Jilly." Her chin dropped to her chest, her eyes searching the floor. She had a secret. Seemed everyone had a secret at the Dandy Drop Inn tonight. She looked up and added, "Stupid storm."

"Stupid storm is right. That's why I'm here, too. No one should be out driving in this mess."

A roll of her eyes spoke volumes; a master of sarcasm at an early age. "Tell me about it. Mommy wrecked."

"Aw, that's too bad. You guys okay?"

"Uh-huh. The car's broke."

With a shrug, Winston said, "That stuff happens. I'm sure your mom's a careful driver."

"I guess."

Hitching up his trousers a bit, Winston knelt. Speak to children on their level, figuratively and literally. "We both should get back to our rooms now. It was really nice talking with you, Kyra. And becoming secret buddies."

She giggled as she shook his proffered hand. He imagined no one treated her in such a mature fashion. Her chin bobbed along with her "one-two-three-and-out" shake. "Nice to meet you."

Winston blinked, rubbing his beard as if deep in thought. "Say, Kyra, if we're secret buddies, I'm not supposed to tell anyone you were down here. Especially eating two pieces of pie, right?" Again with big eyes and a bigger nod. "Well ... then you probably better not tell anyone you ran into me. Right? 'Cause then they might wonder where we'd met. Am I right?"

"Mm-hmm." She held her finger to her lips and shushed, mimicking Winston's earlier move. "Secret buddies."

"Okay, good girl." As he straightened, he forced a smile. Not because Kyra didn't charm him; she did, right down to his core. But he'd used her, making her complicit in keeping his presence on the down-low all for a slice of pie. Heavenly pie, though, so maybe that counted for something in the afterlife. "'Night."

He watched her scamper off, her feet smacking the tiled floor. The door nearly caught her blond hair before she sailed through it.

What was he thinking? Flitting around like a social butterfly with his target, then a young girl. Stupid, but both incidences couldn't be avoided. Unless Karma chose tonight for some payback.

Winston's night couldn't possibly get any worse. He told himself this a lot during jobs, superstitiously so. Whenever he thought this, as if by magic, somehow his nights never did get any worse. A stupid fallacy, no doubt, but why tempt fate?

Doubling down, he knocked on the wood cabinet three times before going to bed.

✳ ✳ ✳

This time Heather experienced what she'd hoped for. *The tiny death.* Her heart had raced. Her body tightened to unfathomable heights, shaking uncontrollably. And her private parts absolutely quivered, impossibly so, building to a crescendo, climbing, climbing. The intensity frightened her. She didn't know what to expect, how it would end. But it ended. Just as she thought it couldn't get any better, any more extreme. And she swore — bona fide knew — a little part of her soul fluttered away. The proof hovered above Tommy's sweating back. Shimmering and dancing. Then she reclaimed it.

Just a smidgeon of how death must feel. She ballooned with pride when she thought of how God had singled her out to bring this beautiful gift to people.

Tommy rolled over, one arm splayed over his head, huffing out deep breaths in his sleep. Exhausted. Yet she wouldn't let sleep claim her, not tonight. She had a message to spread, one she couldn't wait to continue. After years of searching, she'd finally found her lot in life. More exciting than waiting for Santa Claus.

They'd agreed to start with the lovely older couple, the Dandys. So sweet, so ready for Heaven's touch. Heather couldn't wait. Tomorrow night, though. Their reservations ran through the following morning, after all.

She smiled at her husband, gently wiping a matted brown lock of hair away from his forehead.

Aside from seeing a part of her soul earlier, she'd also learned something else. Knew it as Gospel as sure as the sun would rise in the morning. Her very own secret. One she looked forward to sharing with Tommy. He'd impregnated her tonight. She felt it, witnessed it. Just as God had gifted her with the ability to see life depart, He must've likewise blessed her with the power to see a life created. When Tommy had finished, she saw a small light sparkle next to her. Unlike a passing soul — sort of sad in a fading, falling-apart-at-the-seams way — the light had danced, entering her, nesting in her womb.

Rubbing her hands over her belly, she closed her eyes and prayed. The luckiest girl in the world. Miracles followed her, surrounded her. She couldn't, wouldn't deny them.

*Thank you, God. We'll continue your work tomorrow night.*

# Chapter Four

When Calvin sneezed, spittle flung onto the windshield.

"Jesus *Christ!* Cover your mouth!" Domenick grabbed the can of disinfectant from the glove compartment and gave his idiot nephew a spray. For good measure, he hit him with it again.

Calvin swatted around his head as if fending off a wasp attack. "Uncle Dom, what're you —"

"How many times I tell you not to call me 'Uncle' when we're workin'? It's unprofessional. How many?"

Slumping back in the driver's seat, Calvin sighed. "I dunno. Lots?"

*Dumb ass.* Domenick should never have hired the boy, always best to keep family separate from business. But his sister just wouldn't let up. "Yeah. 'Lots'. You got a real good head for math, Calvin."

Calvin brightened, obviously eating up Domenick's derision as a compliment. "Thanks, Unc ... Mister Domenick."

"Better not be catching a cold, that's all I'm sayin'. Keep your germs to yourself." Fast as a whip, Domenick shed his leather gloves, then stripped off the underlying skin-tight rubber ones. Using his glove to grip the glove compartment lever, he popped it open and snatched a bottle of sanitizer. Like a prepping surgeon, he slathered it on his upraised hands thoroughly, then shook them until they dried. He unrolled a new pair of rubber gloves over his hands, then followed those with his leather set. A tedious process, but in today's disease-ridden world, why take chances?

"Don't have a cold," mumbled his nephew.

The Humvee rolled over something in the road, pitching them up and dropping them back into the snow. Domenick's hat crunched on the ceiling. "Dammit, watch out."

"Sorry, Mister Domenick, can't see much of anything."

At least the moron got that part right. The snow hammered down with no relief in sight. Last night, Domenick thought the storm would've moved on by now. Kansas City storms rarely stuck around for longer than twelve hours. But this doozy just wouldn't leave, kind of like a woman who wants to cuddle after sex. He knew he should've set off last night, should've listened to his gut. But, no, his wife scolded him, telling him, "Your business can wait." She might've had a different opinion if she knew three-quarters of a million bucks of his — well, "their" — earnings were at stake.

Domenick pulled out a stack of paper surgeon's masks and tossed one to Calvin. "Put that on."

Calvin grumbled like a surly schoolboy, then complied. Looked ridiculous as hell, too. But good hygiene was important.

"It itches."

"Man up, Calvin. And shut up."

"You really think Winston's joined up with the accountant? He seems like a pretty stand-up guy. I don't think —"

"No, you don't! I don't pay you to think, so stop thinking." As far as what Domenick thought? Hell, yes, Winston had gone rogue with the accountant. Sure, maybe it didn't start that way, but that's a lot of dough, enough to turn any man's head. He probably offed the accountant, then fled with the cash. How the hell else do you explain his not contacting him?

He hadn't heard from Winston since yesterday. When he'd called with Harold's location. Or general location. Hilston, Godforsaken Missouri. What the hell would all that money buy there? Goddammit. Winston's probably halfway across the world by now.

Whatever happened to honesty making the man? Loyalty? Hired help's not what it used to be. Probably have better luck advertising on the damn internet for a trustworthy killer.

It wasn't like he hadn't given both men a shot, offering them more money than they'd ever see in a lifetime. And this is how they paid him back? By ripping him off?

Sons of bitches. Wait and see what kind of "shot" he had in

mind for them now.

The snow caked the windshield like icing. Calvin — slow on the uptake, as usual — took forever to kick the wipers into fast speed.

His anger simmering, Domenick wanted to smack the dash. Repeatedly. Throw a tantrum. But then he might rip his gloves. Count to ten, find his center, all that yoga crap his wife ranted on about. Yeah, well, yoga wouldn't return his hard-earned cash, now, would it?

So, since Winston and Carsten had disrespected him, he'd play the game their way. Show them payback. True payback. They'd set the rules, he'd win the game, always did. As soon as they reached Hilston.

From behind the mask, Calvin loosened a sneeze, wet and disgusting sounding.

With a sigh, Domenick cracked his window, his lips sucking in the cold, fresh, germ-free air.

❄ ❄ ❄

Rebecca woke tired. She'd slept through the night — what little there'd been left — a rare event. Mercifully, she'd had no dreams, the usual ones of Brad on a violent tear. Scratch that; not dreams, all-too-real nightmares.

She stretched across the bed until her muscles drew taut. Her ankles cracked. Sludge muddied her head, similar to a hangover. Darkness outside the west-facing window disoriented her.

Kyra lay next to her, curled up. By morbid instinct, Rebecca held her hand in front of her daughter's nose. Reassuring breath warmed her fingers. But something dark clung to her daughter's cheek. Blood? Rebecca leaned closer, studied it. Chocolate? Another splotch on her pajama top betrayed Kyra's late-night dessert jaunt. Even though Rebecca didn't approve — for many reasons — she couldn't help but admire her daughter's incorrigible spirit. Not that she'd ever let Kyra know that, of course. But she'd go easy on her.

As Rebecca rolled out of bed, she braced herself against the morning cold. Outside the window, endless white blanketed the countryside. Cars lay buried, large whiteheads on the face of the street. Same old, same old, nothing but endless snow. The sky captured an almost nausea-inducing gray uneasiness. In many ways, much worse than the previous night's crushing darkness. Just as Randy had told her, they weren't getting out of here anytime soon. Defeated, she trudged back to bed. She bounced onto the bed, hard, sighing loud enough to wake the dead.

Her tactic worked. Kyra stirred, stepping through her usual wake-up routine: an eye rub, a jaw-dropping yawn, arms stretching. "Morning, Mommy."

"Morning yourself, sleepyhead. 'Bout time you got up." She wiggled her fingers the way Brad used to do on his rare good days. "Tickle alert!"

Kyra rolled over, clutching her belly, giggling. "No, Mommy! Don't! Gotta potty!"

Rebecca surrendered. "Okay, no tickling." She swabbed at Kyra's cheek as if just discovering the chocolate. "Hmm, what's this? Kyra? Did you go back to the kitchen for more pie last night?"

Kyra's grin drifted away. "Uh-huh." With her knees drawn up, she anchored her chin between them, looking properly chastised.

"You know you shouldn't have done that, right?" A small nod. "It's not our house. Also, I don't want you wandering in a stranger's house."

"But, Mommy, they're not strangers."

A tough argument, the way Kyra always challenged her. "Technically, no, I suppose they're not. But it's a strange house. Just don't do it again, alright?" Another bob of the head. "If you're truly hungry, let me know."

"But you were asleep. I didn't wanna wake you."

"Doesn't matter. I won't get angry if you wake me." She jumped out of bed, mustering false energy. As if sleepwalking, her body was present, but her brain had a hard time tracking. "Let's go. Time's a-wastin'. You want some breakfast? If you're not too sick from chocolate?"

"Yeah." Kyra scurried to the bathroom, fire on her tail. Even though she'd had even less sleep than Rebecca, nothing slowed her down.

Rebecca grabbed her phone from the nightstand. 6:44, a lot earlier than she'd initially believed. Her heart bottomed out a little more at the sight of no service bars. She'd use the inn's phone, find out the status of her car, then let her sister know why they were late.

But breakfast sounded good, her taste buds practically begging. Baby steps, an encouraging thought. First her appetite, then maybe she could reclaim her self-worth in time.

She gave her sweater a quick sniff, pulled it on, then stepped into a clean pair of jeans. Her undergarments could wait until later, squeezing in a nice hot shower to boot. Maybe she'd even indulge herself with a bath. Why not? Like it or not, they were on a forced vacation.

Looking at herself in the mirror, she grimaced. Dark crescents hung beneath her eyes, making her appear older than thirty-two. A quick touch of make-up, a brush-through of her hair, and she felt reasonably presentable to rejoin the human race.

The chair beneath the doorknob hadn't moved, both a reassuring sight and one that seemed somewhat silly now. Of course, she had nothing to fear from the Dandys. Thoughts of Brad had her jumping at her own shadows.

Rebecca wrenched at the chair, but it stuck, wedged in tight. With another mighty tug, the chair loosened and flew back. How in the world could Kyra have jammed that in so tight? Her upper body strength hadn't yet developed fully. And as a general rule, Kyra stank at trying to cover up her misdeeds, lacking a seasoned criminal's eye for detail.

"Kyra? Kyra, honey?"

Kyra rushed out of the bathroom wearing a t-shirt, jeans, and an ear-to-ear smile. Ready to take on the world, just not dressed for it. But her daughter's youthful optimism warmed Rebecca. Having forgotten about the chair already, she folded Kyra into her arms. "Love you so much."

"Me too, Mommy. Let's eat!"

Voices rose from behind the kitchen door, the Dandys' laughter unmistakable.

"Why good morning, Rebecca, Kyra," said Dolores. She turned back to the stove, flipped something with a spatula. The pan hissed. Smoke curled up, twisting to the ceiling. The smell of bacon filled Rebecca's nose, hunger pangs on high alert. "How'd you sleep?" Dolores held the spatula high like a baton.

"Fine, thanks."

Jim tossed a wave and an eager "howdy-do," while the young couple seated across from him stared at her, emotionless. Rebecca filtered it all through a sleepy haze, half lucid and definitely not up for socializing.

The handsome young man jumped to his feet and swiped a hand

alongside his jeans. As he stuck his hand out, his t-shirt tightened across his muscular arm, so tight it looked like it could cut off his circulation. Rebecca wondered why cold weather never seemed to affect youth.

"Tommy Goodenow, ma'am." His intense handshake pumped some vicarious life into Rebecca. "This here's my wife, Heather." Pretty in a quiet, non-flashy way, the blond girl pressed her lips into a bare smile as if it hurt. Her hair hung down, long and straight, no doubt the results of a flat-iron marathon. Her gaze shifted to Kyra.

"Oh, look at you. Aren't you beautiful?" The girl held her hands out to Kyra. With a little nudge, Rebecca steered Kyra toward the girl. Hesitantly, Kyra tucked her hand into the blonde's. "One of God's precious gifts. I'm sure he broke the mold when he made you."

Kyra's brow wrinkled. Her hand still trapped, she shot Rebecca a helpless "save me" look.

"She's shy," said Rebecca. "Pleasure to meet you. I'm Rebecca, this is Kyra."

Still standing, Tommy thrust his chest out a little bit more. "We're newlyweds." He said it loud and proud, the kind of arrogance youth monopolized.

Rebecca thought, *Just wait until the honeymoon's over.* Instead, she said, "Congratulations. That's wonderful."

"It is," said Heather. "And we owe it all to God."

The girl — no, the woman; something about her eyes looked older than her age — unsettled Rebecca. Obviously a bible-thumper, she shared that same glazed-over, vacant look Rebecca had seen all too often in Kansas. Kyra must've felt it, too. Suddenly, she wrenched her hand away as if from a snapping dog. The blonde's smile faded, her eyes no longer blank, but smoldering with hostility.

Undeterred, Tommy favored them with another grin. Rebecca knew his type well; she'd had first-hand experience. Big promises and flashy charm didn't last, not in her charade of a marriage. And she suspected Tommy didn't have too much knocking around in his attic. Then again, she was making snap judgments. Everyone deserved a chance. "I'm happy for you guys, really."

Heather's hand felt clammy and cool in Rebecca's, a dead fish, perfectly complementing her demeanor. Then Rebecca chided herself for jumping right back into cattiness.

Christian swooped in, defusing the situation. With a dancer's grace, he dropped two plates onto the table. Obviously a man who enjoyed his work, he spun and bowed, waltzing in the spotlight. Finished, he patted his apron. "Fresh off Dolores's griddle, cakes and bacon. Have a seat, ladies. Your food's coming next."

As far away from the young couple as she could get, Kyra climbed into a chair at the table, her fork poised and ready.

Christian slipped a champagne goblet in front of Rebecca, bubbles rising in the golden liquid. "A mimosa to start your day off right?" Christian phrased it as a question, but his confident smile told Rebecca no one ever refused it.

Rebecca shouldn't, she really shouldn't. At 7:00 a.m., it was too early for alcohol. And she may have to drive later. Then again, one look out the window changed her mind. The snow beat down with a vengeance, a good three-quarters of a foot added overnight. What the hell? Why not enjoy herself, take advantage of the situation? Honestly, it'd been the most fun she'd had in some time. Her mind made up, she said, "Sure, you talked me into it. When in Hilston, do as the Hilstons do."

The host tossed back his shoulders, laughing heartily. "Indeed. I like the way you think."

The bubbles tickled Rebecca's nose, the alcohol warm in her chest, the taste delicious. "Wow. What kind of mimosa is this?"

"Dolores's special pineapple mimosa," Jim piped in. "Ain't it a beaut?" Catching his mistake, he slipped Kyra an apologetic look. "Sorry, sorry, young gal. I know 'ain't' ain't a word."

"*Mommy*." Although Kyra protested, she smiled, this time joining in the adults' laughter.

"Sleep well?" With an elbow hitched up over the chair, Jim turned his attention toward Rebecca.

"Mm-hm. Like a log."

The newlyweds ate in silence, yet their eyes never strayed far from Rebecca. Unnerved, Rebecca fortified herself by downing the mimosa in three gulps. Before she swallowed the last bit, Christian set a new mimosa before her. Rebecca rapped her fingers beside the glass, considering, then surrendered. She noticed the Goodenows hadn't touched their drinks, having set them far away, as if the mere presence of alcohol offended. Already feeling lightheaded, Rebecca forced herself to slow down. No sense in upsetting the newlyweds by getting sloshed. Particularly in front of Kyra.

"How're you likin' the Dandy Drop Inn?" asked Jim.

"It's gorgeous. How in the world did you find such a beautiful home?"

"Feh. Fact is, me and Dolores's families purt near founded this town. Dolores's family grew up in the ol' homestead, passed it down through the generations. By the time we got hitched, the place was fairly run down, but we decided to patch it up. Good investment. It's paid for itself several times over." A pocket knife appeared in his hand. He flipped a blade out from the ivory handle and dug the tip under a fingernail. The blonde gave a small, humorless grin. Probably offended, thought Rebecca, her normal reaction. "Heck, I was mayor of Hilston for a while, dang near runnin' the town. Brought in a lotta business, too, yessireebob."

From the stove, Dolores hollered out, "Poppa, don't clean your nails at the kitchen table. I swan, how many times I gotta tell you?"

With a chuckle, Jim folded the knife and pocketed it. "Sorry, Mother. Ol' habits die hard."

Unusual for Kyra, she sat at rapt attention, eyes alert. Generally, adult conversation bored her.

"Anyway, the house was too dang beautiful not to share it. So ... we opened it up to anyone who cared to drop in."

Rebecca sipped at the mimosa, grinning around the rim. Through the bottom of the glass, she glanced at the Goodenows, distorted and blurry, watching her. It gave her some comfort Kyra chose the far end of the table.

"Um, Jim, if it's no trouble, may I use your phone? I need to call about my car and make a long distance call. I'll be glad to pay for the charges."

Jim looked at his wife and dropped his ever-present grin. "Oh, I'm sorry, young lady. Didn't Christian tell you?" She shook her head. Dread built in her stomach. Sounded like bad news. "The phone's been out since last night. Ever' time we get a storm in these here parts, you can count on it like death and taxes."

*Dammit.* Rebecca wondered if they'd ever get out of here. And she imagined her sister was frantic by now, having expected them yesterday.

Finally, Christian lowered a plate in front of Kyra, then Rebecca. Still hot, smoke rose from the bacon. The pancakes appeared moist and fluffy. "Apple cakes and hickory bacon." He turned to Kyra and said, "I imagine the young lady will want seconds." Her fork already dug in, Kyra nodded. "Don't forget the homemade pecan maple syrup."

So hungry, Rebecca tossed manners to the wayside and devoured her breakfast. A race between her and Kyra, Kyra pulled ahead by a small margin. And Rebecca realized it wasn't such a bad place to get stranded after all. Around a cheek full of food, she mumbled, "This is delicious."

"Mommy, don't talk with your mouth full!"

Dolores hooted. She untied her apron and clapped it between her hands. "This darling lil girl's been brought up right."

Embarrassed, Rebecca felt her cheeks flush while Kyra beamed. But it didn't matter. The food tasted glorious, felt even better in her empty stomach. Then a tired sensation crept up on her, the food leaden in her belly, her head dizzy from the alcohol. At the end of the table, she heard muttering, a hair above a whisper.

Kyra scooted out of her chair and ran to her mother's side. Pinching Rebecca's elbow, Kyra whispered, "Mommy, what're they doing?"

With their eyes closed, the Goodenows clasped their hands in front of them, their elbows on the table. *Praying.* Although given their feverish intensity, it struck Rebecca as more like chanting, almost speaking in tongues. Words ran together, one train of a sentence chugging along at high speed.

Rebecca shook her head at her daughter and mouthed, "*Be quiet.*" To make sure Kyra received the message loud and clear, she embellished it with a finger to her lips. During Kyra's early years, Rebecca had tried to indoctrinate religious fundamentals into her, including prayers before meals. Due to Brad's constant chiding, though, it sort of drifted away. Obviously, the prayer after the meal confused Kyra. And it seemed sort of strange to Rebecca as well.

First Tommy, then Heather opened their eyes with a resounding "Amen." Slowly, Heather leaned across the table, her head and limbs low, like a lizard's. Her eyes — so wide, so unyielding — trapped Kyra in a hypnotic snake's gaze. The accompanying smile freaked Rebecca out the most, though; superficially sweet, yet Rebecca could imagine fangs beneath those tight, chapped lips. "Have you accepted the Lord, Jesus Christ, as your Savior, little girl? If not, you'd better do it. *Soon.*"

"Mommy?" Even though whispered, Rebecca detected fear in her daughter's tone. Kyra clutched onto Rebecca's sweater, wringing her arm. Yet she held Heather in a corner-of-the-eye stare, as if afraid to let the strange woman out of her sight.

Bolstered by the alcohol, Rebecca stood. "I'm sorry, but our religious beliefs are our own concern." She turned to Dolores. "Thank you for a delicious breakfast."

"You're welcome, child." The Dandys seemed to be taking in the unsettling encounter with mild amusement, their reaction to everything. Christian had vanished, his breakfast services apparently no longer needed.

"We need to get cleaned up," said Rebecca, excusing herself. And she hated that she felt the need to make an excuse to the Goodenows. Their behavior had been out of line, not hers. Brad had wrought not only physical damage, but he'd left mental scars on her psyche as well. It seemed she'd spent ten years apologizing, accepting the fallout of Brad's vile behavior as her own.

Kyra clung to her. With a protective arm around her daughter's shoulders, she scuttled Kyra toward the door, wanting to get the hell out of there.

"Accept Jesus Christ now." Heather's voice carried an edge with it, sharp as a razor blade.

Rebecca whirled, seeking courage to put this woman in her place. But the blonde's unwavering cold eyes chilled her into silence.

Then the door swung open at Rebecca's back.

❄ ❄ ❄

*Well, hail, hell, the gang's all here.*

Harold stood in the kitchen doorway, retracting like a turtle into its shell.

First thing this morning, he figured he'd grab some grub, early enough to avoid the other lodgers. After all, who didn't sleep in at a B&B, especially with a winter storm raising hell outside? The left side of his brain kicked in — years of accounting experience — tallying five adults and a kid in the room. More people than he'd been around in a while. And six too many to keep a low profile.

He swallowed the huge lump in his throat and managed to say to no one in particular, "Ah, hi. I'm Harold." His voice quavered. Blood rushed to his face, settling on his cheeks, his forehead. The moment seemed stuck in time, a stalled nightmare. Just like the general trajectory of his life.

A wiry, tall old fart jumped up from the table and rushed him, hand extended. "Good morn! A real pleasure to have you with us, Harold. Pull up a seat, take a load off. Eat some vittles. Good for the belly, great for the soul."

He pumped Harold's hand like he couldn't get enough. Reluctantly, Harold hurried toward the empty end of the table, his head down. Although mortified, he couldn't help but notice the good-looking woman who he'd brushed by on the way in. The kind of woman who'd usually never give him a second look. But that was then, this is now. He bet — damn near'd put money on it if he wasn't so frugal — if she saw what he carried in the briefcase, she'd do more than just look at him. Maybe he'd put some of his new-found confidence to work. The woman looked a little ragged around the edges, hardly fresh. But she'd clean up well. Strong features, starlet hair, great figure. Too bad about the rugrat in tow.

"Food'll be up in a minute. Welcome to the Dandy Drop Inn," called out the squat woman at the stove. With her back toward him and her head hunkered down so far it'd surely cause future back issues, she looked like Quasimodo. "I'm Dolores."

"Um, thanks. And hello."

The young couple opposite him stared at the briefcase clutched to his chest. Quickly, he put it between his legs, locking it with his knees, hooking it with his heels. The couple resembled some of his ex-wife's figurines; all doe eyed and cloyingly cute. He nodded at them and turned his chair away, hoping they'd take the clue and leave him in peace.

By the door, the attractive brunette cleared her throat and said, "Hi, I'm Rebecca. This is my daughter, Kyra." She knocked out a gratuitous smile, the bland, half-assed smile most women afforded him. When they bothered.

Emboldened, the world literally at his feet, he framed a seductive smile. Confident men made it look so easy. "Hi there, Rebecca. Real nice to meet you." He glanced out the window, made a cursory examination of the weather, pondering his next move. Then he came roaring back with a seriously strong gaze. Keeping things cool. "Looks like we're gonna be stuck here a while. Hope to see more of you." His words tumbled out easily, no tongue-tied gymnastics. *Is this what it feels like*, he thought. Big-shot status; a guy men want to be, a guy women want to be with. It felt good; he imagined it looked even better.

"Yes, well ..." The woman blinked, her smile fading. "We have to be going." Quickly, she glanced around the room, a visual adios, noticeably avoiding the young couple. But she had included him, not a bad start, not by a long shot.

"Hey, maybe we can —" The door swung shut, cutting off his seduction. Self-consciousness clubbed him in the head again. He stared at the empty place setting before him. Like a distaff Dorothy in Oz, he clicked the briefcase with his heels three times, waiting for the magic to happen. Wishing to be whisked away.

"Hey there, Harold, I'm Tommy Goodenow, and this is my wife, Heather. We ..."

The blowhard kid rambled on, standing in front of him, hand stuck out. But all Harold heard was "me this ...," "we that ...," "I'm great ..." Typical braggart crap. He zoned him out, the guy's wife as well. No need for them, not any of them. But a mate, even a sexual encounter — one he didn't have to pay for — *that* he could use.

✳ ✳ ✳

As dawn lightened Hilston, Brad reached the reported site of Rebecca's wreck. The gray skies, the relentless snow, the frigid temperature compounded his headache. And all the caffeine he'd practically injected into his veins just gave him a wide-awake migraine.

Slowly, he crawled down the road, the way he'd driven all night. He studied the woods next to him, looking for signs of a wreck. Nothing. Not within a mile radius of the location. Of course, here in Hicksville, they didn't have addresses, not even street signs. Buncha redneck inbreds.

The snow made it damn near impossible to see anything. Snow climbed up tree trunks, devouring them. Tree limbs draped ice like wedding dresses off arms. Which reminded Brad of the expensive dress he'd bought for the bitch. Ended up in a closet, a colossal waste of cash.

A drift next to the road rose solid and unbroken, a wall nearly three feet tall. As he turned his car around, a new white layer of snow had already covered his tire tracks. Every so often, he'd check his phone, hoping for a call from his partner. But the damn phone had no signal. Seemed like Hilston sucked it out the second he reached the city line.

Then he spotted something that didn't quite fit. He punched the brakes, the car continuing to skate down the road. Once he finally stopped, he backed up. To his right, the drift was smaller, definitely lower, almost mound shaped in the middle. Something a car could've carved out.

He shifted the gear into park and left the car running in the middle of the road. No need to worry about other traffic. Smoke coughed from the tailpipe as he passed it. With his coat collar clutched to his neck, he stepped over the wall. The snow rode up to his thighs, more resistant than walking through water. After brushing wind-blown snow away from a tree trunk, he examined it. Raw bark. Next to it, a large fallen limb poked tendrils through the drifts. He dug his gloved hand down, feeling nothing. Peeling back the fingertips, he stuck his hand in again. Something sharp pricked a finger. Glass. He licked the fingertip, savoring the taste of blood.

*But where the hell was her car? And where was the bitch, the back-stabbing bitch?*

He stumbled up the hill and collapsed into his warm, waiting steed of steel. But he couldn't relax, not now. It would all end soon, he could feel it. Definitely not the time for a nap or anything pussy like that.

This time the snow didn't slow him. Nothing could deter him. Right was on his side, after all. He sped down the road the way he came, his mind racing ahead of him.

What if she got a ride into the next town? By a truck driver or someone else? Some guy she'd let into her pants? Laughing at Brad while screwing him?

*Goddammit.*

The car couldn't go fast enough. Steering wheel in one hand, he held his phone just over the dash, checking it every few feet.

The trees along the road thinned, sparsely spaced and scrawny looking. Soon, he crossed the Hilston line into God knew where. Another half mile down the road, three bars on his phone bounced to life.

"*Yes*, goddammit, 'bout *time*."

The car fishtailed, slaloming across the road. He went with it, correcting the wheel, spinning it in the opposite direction. Adrenaline spiked. The way he always felt when closing in on a perp, closing in like a hunter.

After locating a number for the Hilston Sheriff's office, he dialed it. Five rings, six rings, seven ... His pulse raced, his breath fogging up the windows.

"Sheriff's department."

"I need some information on a Chevy reported in an accident last night —"

"Uh-huh." The cop sounded cocky, a little fish in a big ocean. "And who might I be talkin' to?"

Brad gave his stats, badge number, and detective status. Just enough to make the little minnow nibble at his toes.

"Got it, Detective Stanchfield. Let's see what I can pull up on the magic box ..." With a clunk, the cop dropped the phone. A *tap-tap-tapping* of computer keys accompanied the cop's inane humming. Like this wasn't more fucking important than anything else he had going on.

"Detective?"

"Still here."

"Sorry, can't find anything. No Chevy, no mention of a ..." Paper rustled. "... Rebecca Stanchfield, nothing of the sort. Sorry."

*Goddamn incompetents.* "Bullshit! I know *damn* well —"

"Hey, hey, easy there. We're all on the same team, dedicated law enforce —"

"I don't wanna hear your redneck, Mayberry feel-good shit! Why don't you get your head out of your ass and —"

"No need to be that way, Detective. I told you what I know. Listen, I was on duty last night. I would've either seen something come up on the wire or at least heard about it."

It made no sense. His partner didn't lie, wouldn't lie. Unless ... the bitch ran off with him. *No.* She was capable of doing it, but Steve would never betray him, not his partner. Maybe Rebecca somehow staged the accident to throw him off the trail. Blew town with a lover. Sure as hell would explain a lot. But that didn't track either. Idiot wife wasn't that smart, and she didn't have the connections to pull a disappearing act. More than likely, Hilston's finest screwed up. *Incompetent idiots.*

"Listen, dumb ass, after I find the car, after I find her, I'm gonna —"

"Sounds like a threat to me. We don't cotton very kindly to threats in these parts."

*Cotton? What the hell's that even mean?* "What's your name? 'Shit for brains?' I'm gonna report you to your sheriff and anyone else who'll listen in this Podunk town!"

The cop laughed, lazy and smarmy, completely condescending. "Go right ahead. But you won't be able to reach him. Off on a hunting trip. But, sure, you can have my name, no problem. Gurley. Deputy Randy Gurley. And I'm anything but. Girly, that is. Be glad to prove it to ya, if you're man enough to meet me."

✳ ✳ ✳

"Kyra, honey, there's no reason to be scared."

Yet, truthfully, Rebecca thought Kyra's fear might be merited. Something seemed off about the Goodenows. She'd met plenty of religious people in the past, some of them her neighbors. But not to this frightening extreme. The Goodenow girl's words had been strong, but her demeanor — her unwavering conviction — seemed to imply a threat more than any soul-saving venture. But no sense in sharing these thoughts with her daughter. "Sometimes very religious people want to share their opinions with others, that's all. Don't pay Missus Goodenow any mind."

Kyra looked up at Rebecca, her cheeks damp from tears. "Mommy, are we religious? Do you believe in God?"

Rebecca contemplated her answer, formulating something a good mother might say. "Yes. I think there's a God. Don't you?" Kyra's head bobbed up and down. "Then you just keep on believing. And keep on your nightly prayers. Then God will look out for us."

"I always do." Reinforcement of a benevolent God perked Kyra up. Instantly, she transformed from a frightened child to a care-free innocent, the way kids should be entitled to live. Damn Brad for stealing away much of Kyra's childhood.

Rebecca laid a lingering kiss on her daughter's cheek. Kyra scrabbled to escape Rebecca's bear hug, exaggeratedly fussing. Even though Kyra's nose wrinkled, her giggling indicated she didn't object too much, just part of the game. "Stop it, Mommy!"

"Never!" Rebecca finished with a raspberry blown onto her daughter's cheek.

"*Gross.*" On the bed, Kyra kicked her feet into the air. Rebecca joined her, still hosting the effects of the mimosas. She thought they must've looked quite the sight, mother and daughter laughing, bicycling their legs into the air. And Rebecca thought she'd remember this moment forever, her first worthwhile snapshot of their new life.

Once their giddiness settled, Kyra asked, "Mommy, can I go play in the snow?"

"Kyra, I don't —"

"*Please*, Mommy? There's nothing else to do."

Rebecca knew she was right, absolutely so. Kids need exercise, fresh air. She had niggling doubts, but she also realized they had to quit living cooped up, captives beneath Brad's lingering specter. A nap had sounded like a wonderful idea, but she wouldn't be able to batten down Kyra's hatches long enough, not now. Maybe later.

"All right. Just for a little bit. But only under two conditions." She held up two fingers; Kyra's eyes were glued to them, awaiting instruction. "One, you bundle up properly. I mean it. Zipped-up coat, boots, hat, gloves." Kyra looked like she debated the idea for a bit, then gave a thoughtful nod. "Two, you stay in my sight at all times." Which meant she'd have to go downstairs and keep watch from the front window, something that hadn't been in her itinerary. But parents sacrifice.

Already off the bed before Rebecca finished issuing her second demand, Kyra bolted for the suitcase and wriggled into her boots. "Okay, Mommy."

Six years old, the girl should be out playing in the snow. So why did Rebecca feel so hesitant to let her daughter go? Kyra had several storms of experience under her belt, suffering no mishaps, a perfect record. In fact, her first injury had been at Brad's hand the other night. And they'd left Brad behind in a cloud of dust. Well, *snow*.

So why did her protective instincts clang like a fire alarm?

Because of the people, not the storm. Sure, the Dandys were wonderful, and Christian couldn't help but charm. But she couldn't shake the newlywed couple. The woman looked fragile enough to blow away in a wind gust, though; hardly the type to venture out into the snow. And the new man ... Henry, Harley, something ... the way he'd looked at her, he may as well've been sizing her up for dinner. *My, what big teeth you have, Harley.* And he loved exposing those teeth when he grinned. Yellow corn kernels, the incisors pointed like a vampire's.

Rebecca sighed and shook her head. Whatever. A meek vampire. She'd be seeing ghosts next. Time for a reality check. She rolled out of bed, hating to leave its comforting warmth, and slipped into her shoes. Then she and Kyra raced toward the door; to the victor, the spoils.

❋ ❋ ❋

So cold his teeth felt numb, Winston bunched up his shoulders, dropped his chin to his chest. The smoke weighed heavy, yet calming in his lungs. As he expelled a long drag, it kept on going and going, the smoke indistinguishable from his frozen breath. The nicotine buzz started small, then grew, a tingling sensation creeping down from his brain. A welcome sensation. Propped up against a gazebo post, he thought he better sit before dizziness dropped him.

Actually, he'd kicked the cigarette habit after he'd graduated college. It hadn't been that hard, not really. Of course, he put on thirty pounds, but he shed that soon enough. Not until he took on his extracurricular work did he pick up the habit again. And only when he was actually on the job. He looked at it as a reward, plus it helped settle his nerves. Or so he told himself. A psychiatrist, on the other hand, probably would've had a completely different take on the scenario. Maybe they'd look at it as punishment — killing himself slowly — for killing people.

Regardless, the nicotine tasted fine, the deadly smoke in his lungs fulfilling. Hardly a good substitute for a meal, though; particularly one of Julie's wonderful suppers. He'd been existing on a nonstop diet of protein bars, which he'd been sensible enough to pack as soon as he'd heard about the impending storm. Still, the smell of food had wound its way upstairs earlier, practically seeking out his olfactory senses like a missile. More than once, he nearly caved, ready to burst into the kitchen, making like Oliver Twist pleading for porridge. But common sense held him captive. Once he heard the accountant going downstairs, presumably toward the kitchen, he snuck outside. Not only for a smoke, but to escape the tempting odors.

And he was still without a phone. Just like the inn. He hoped Lenny, his right-hand man, would call Domenick, explain Winston's situation. But that seemed unlikely. Brilliant guy, but Lenny lacked the motivation to take on anything less than a direct order. Perhaps Winston had been stupid not taking his laptop with him on assignments, but these days he could acquire all of his needs easily enough on his phone. A condensed computer, pocket-sized and tailor made for hired killers. Until they didn't work.

He looked at the back of the house, the southern side, the only side missing the wrap-around porch. He spotted a cellar entrance, the two closed doors set into the ground presumably leading underground. Strangely devoid of snow coverage. Maybe it's where Christian kept the firewood, nice and dry. Even stranger, though, was the lack of a back door. Nothing but a massive white-paneled wall with very few windows, all of them tightly shuttered.

As he inhaled slowly, a sudden chuff sounded overhead. Snow sprinkled into the gazebo. A silenced gun, his first instinct. He dove to the snow-dusted cement, the cigarette still between his lips. The butt snuffed out. He thrust a hand behind him, patting down the small of his back. No gun, still in the car.

Then, like a twittering bird, shrill laughter echoed across the snow. A white projectile whizzed through the gazebo above him.

"Are you scared of snow?" Kyra yelled while packing another snowball between her gloves.

Once his heart settled, he stood and brushed himself off. Bundled up, the little girl pushed stiffly through the snow toward him. Quickly, he tossed the broken cigarette out into the snow. Kind of silly, he thought, but he didn't want her seeing him smoke. Nasty habit and all.

"Guess I am. You almost got me."

"I play softball," she said, as if that explained everything. With the snow nearly to her waist, her coat ballooned out, and with her stocking cap pitching a point, she resembled a garden gnome. She hitched a leg up, took a giant leap, repeating her slow process one step at a time.

"Keep at it then, Kyra. Your mother know you're out here? Wouldn't want you getting buried in an avalanche or anything."

She looked around. "No mountains."

"Yep, you're about the biggest mountain around these parts." She giggled, and Winston couldn't get enough. Thoughts of home, his daughters, tugged at him. "Again, is your mother in the know?"

"Uh-huh." Finally, she reached the gazebo and climbed the steps like a swimmer exiting a pool. When Winston sat on the bench, she plopped down next to him. Her feet kicked, one after the other. An icy cloud of breath expelled from her scarf-covered mouth.

"Well, good. So we don't have to play secret buddies anymore." Which meant, sooner or later, Kyra's mother would find out about him. Of course she probably already knew about his presence — the host was certainly chatty enough about the other lodgers — but she hadn't seen him yet. He hoped to keep it that way.

And whenever he started thinking nothing else could happen, it usually did. Funny how he never used to be superstitious. Not before the jobs started.

"Secret buddies about what?" Kyra's mother stood behind them, wrapped in only a sweater, her arms folded, shivering like a detoxing junkie.

\* \* \*

Naked and kneeling, Heather and Tommy prayed before their makeshift altar. They'd pinned a sheet up to the wall. A crucifix hung over the sheet, Jesus staring at them in beautifully excruciating agony. Heather hoped the tacks wouldn't scar the room's walls too much. It'd be a real shame.

"And thank you, God, for bringing new life into my womb." Heather stopped, a couldn't-be-helped grin breaking over her lips. With one eye open, she peeked at her husband. She'd thought about the proper way to break the news to him. It seemed only fitting God should be their witness.

"Babe ... is it true?" Heather thought a cat could've crawled into his gaping mouth.

"Mm-hm." She wanted to elaborate, but, honestly, no words could properly convey her joy.

"I can't believe it! I'm ... we're gonna be parents!" As he hugged her, cheek to cheek, he suddenly tensed. Bracing her by the shoulders, he pushed back to look into her eyes. "But ... how is this possible? I mean ... we ... did you miss your, um, time of the month or whatever?"

She giggled at his naivety. Not too long ago she thought no one knew less about the female body than she did. And unlike Tommy, she wore one. "Babe, it don't work like that."

"Then how do you know?"

"The Lord showed me through a sighting. I saw our baby's soul enter my womb."

"That's *fantastic*, babe." He smashed his lips onto hers, the way old 50s matinee idols used to do to in the movies. Heather always thought it looked painful. But she now knew pain and pleasures commingle, can't have one without the other.

"I know, right?" They fell down onto the plastic tarp they had spread before the altar. The material crinkled, pinching up beneath their entwined bodies. "And I can't think of a better way to give our thanks than to begin our work tonight."

"I'm with ya, babe."

"The Dandys are set to come over at eight o'clock, just after supper."

"Mm-hm. To play Spinner Dominoes."

Heather sat up, clawing fingers through her hair like a comb. "Babe, what if they want to gamble? On the game?"

"I won't let 'em, babe." He pulled her back down. She fell onto his chest, her arms a barrier between them.

"I know you won't. It's just …"

"What's on your mind, babe?"

"I can't wait to usher on that Godless woman and her unholy offspring."

"Me, too. Lookin' forward to it."

"The way she looked at us this morn, like we was crazy or somethin'. Telling us her beliefs are none of our business. Won't she be surprised to find out we're working for God, with God. Ain't got a clue. I'm especially gonna enjoy sending her on to her immortal fate. And I think we both know where *that's* gonna be."

"Sure do." His male part grew, reaching out toward Heather. She squeezed it, no longer afraid of his naughty parts. In fact, nothing frightened her anymore.

# Chapter Five

They'd been in the Humvee for nearly eleven hours. Calvin drove worse than a little old lady with cataracts, stopping only once to let Domenick piss on the side of the road. Unsanitary, sure, but Domenick preferred it over using a public john. The germs that lurked in public facilities terrified him, a fate worse than death. His hands stung after he swiped them in the snow. The sanitizer burned even more. But the resulting redness at least looked clean, a newborn's skin.

Every time Calvin mounted a sneeze, Domenick cringed. His nephew's incessant snuffling grated like fingernails on a chalkboard. Even Domenick's favorite big band music couldn't soothe his anxiety.

It took forever and a day, but he'd finally tracked down Winston Ashford's assistant, some slacker kid named Lenny. Getting him on the phone shouldn't have been that difficult. After all, the kid was on his payroll.

"Mister Domenick, I'm sure Winston didn't take your money. He's not like that." The kid kept whining, saying the same thing over and over, trying to build a case for Ashford's innocence. Instead, it shoved Domenick the other way. No doubt the kid was on the take as well.

"Goddammit, you're not *listenin'* to me! I know for a *fact* he's got my money! Haven't heard from him in almost twenty-four hours. He's supposed to call every hour."

"I don't think he has a signal. Or his battery died."

"Excuses, excuses. That's all I'm hearin'. Wi-Fi's everywhere. You in on it, too?"

After a satisfying moment of silence, the kid said, "I swear I'm *not*, Mister Domenick. Neither is Winston. Let's just be calm and reason through this. *Please.*"

Lately, Domenick's wife had been shoveling all kinds of New Age crap on him. She told him he needed to be an open book, expose his emotions for people to read. Use the important "I" statements — "I think," "I feel," blah, blah, blah. He knew it was stupid, but he thought he'd give it a spin. "Listen, Lenny, I feel ... you should *shut* the *fuck* up."

As he hung up on the kid, Domenick felt marginally better. Maybe his wife's sensitivity classes had paid off after all.

His nephew looked at him, his blue surgeon's mask sucking in with every breath. No doubt waiting to hear what the kid had said, but too afraid to ask. Cowards everywhere.

"Kid's in on it, too," said Domenick with a sigh. "Covering for Ashford. He'll be our first stop when we get back to K.C."

Calvin nodded. One of his eyes twitched, clearly nervous about the job ahead of him. But at least he quit trying to defend Ashford. No denying proof.

"But we got a location on the accountant. The kid better not be lyin', that's all I'll say. Or our 'meeting's' gonna be extra painful." Again, Calvin gave a weak nod. Followed by a sneeze.

"Dammit, Calvin! Swear to *God*, if I get sick, *you're* goin' on my list."

"Sorry, Mister Dom. Think it's just allergies. I don't think allergies are contagious. That's all I'll say."

Domenick groaned. He hated when his nephew copied his catch phrase, never an original thought in his empty head. Idiots. Surrounded by backstabbers and fools.

Not trusting his nephew to do the job right, Domenick checked out the bed and breakfast on his phone. "Got the address. Some shithole called 'The Dandy Drop Inn'."

"We're only 'bout thirty miles from Hilston now."

"Good. Can't wait to get some payback."

"Me, too, Mister Dom ... *ah-choo.*"

*Jesus Christ.*

\* \* \*

"Mommy, what're *you* doing out here?" Kyra rocked, swinging her arms, her tell that she'd broken the rules.

"Freezing. You left from where I could see you." Rebecca's teeth chattered. A wind gust blasted her, needles shooting into her bones. She hadn't grabbed her coat, no time. One minute Kyra had been there, the next, gone. Every mother's nightmare. "I want to know about this 'secret buddy club'. I'm Rebecca. I see you've met Kyra. And you are ...?"

The man stood, extending a gloved hand. "Sorry, sorry. Ah ... Dave Harton, insurance salesman."

The handshake was short lived as Rebecca's hands folded back into her sleeves for cover. Warily, she stepped up onto the gazebo, sizing up the stranger. The stranger who'd been talking to her daughter without her knowledge. Kyra appeared fine, nothing out of the ordinary.

"Guess I need to explain why Kyra and I are secret pals." He rubbed the back of his neck, gave a sheepish smile, a shamefaced, "Aw, shucks" look. Rebecca didn't buy it, not for a minute. Strangers with secrets are *not* a good thing. "Well, I have to confess ... Kyra and I shared some pie late last night. I reckon after you went to sleep. I promised your daughter I'd keep her secret."

Kyra hung her head, her guilt-induced reaction saying more than words.

"Kyra, is this true?" Although Rebecca'd already covered Kyra's sneaking off to the kitchen, it concerned her Kyra hadn't mentioned the man. It made her wonder what else she might be withholding.

Harton said, "Sorry. Blame me. I just thought it might be fun for Kyra. You know, 'secret pal' and all."

A forest of beard obscured a bit of his smile, but he seemed genuine. Rebecca relaxed her guard. But not by much. "Okay, fine, whatever. So you're the other guest on the second floor?"

"That's me. Driving across the midwest on business. Got stuck here. But it seems like a nice place."

"Mm-hm. We're stuck as well. Any idea when the storm's gonna end?"

"No clue. But I'm anxious to get home."

"You have family waiting?"

Harton's face wrinkled. He said nothing, appearing pensive. Rebecca suspected a fellow "divorce" survivor. "Nothing but a cat and a coupla goldfish. But I'd better get home before they officially meet."

Rebecca said, "Sounds like you better hurry."

Kyra had been watching their exchange, remaining wisely silent. Probably relieved the attention had shifted from her.

"Yep, the sooner, the better. How about you? Family?"

Rebecca tilted her head toward Kyra and lifted a conspiratorial eyebrow. "Not really. We're going to see my sister. I think we'll stay with her a while."

"Gotcha. Well, you'll be there soon, I'm sure of it. Weather can't stay this way forever. Isn't that right, Kyra?" She smiled, her trust in the man uncomfortably apparent. "Hey, you look like you're freezing, Rebecca. Take my coat while we head back inside." Before she could object, he shrugged off his overcoat and draped it over her shoulders. While she considered throwing it right back at him, she had to admit it felt damned toasty.

"Going inside sounds like a great idea."

Kyra ran ahead of them, trailblazing a path through the snow. Harton strolled alongside Rebecca, apparently oblivious to the cold.

"So, what do you do, Rebecca? Besides raising a great kid, that is."

"Not sure yet. Starting over, I guess."

Harton — *Dave* — smiled at her, nodding like he'd mastered the secrets of the universe. "That's fantastic. I think ... everyone needs a second chance sometimes."

Dave hadn't yet won her trust, not completely. But he was growing on her.

※ ※ ※

As he sat on his bed, Harold watched the wall clock tick away, every click like a torturous drop of water falling into a steel sink. Time had slowed. And anxiety gnawed at him like a rat through rope. He felt hopelessly trapped, caught between a stupid, inconsequential town and his future. Unable to do anything about it. For all he knew, Domenick could be tracking him while he was forced to look at doilies and other cutesy crap.

And the pendulum swung, taunting, then teasing, choking out every agonizing second. At 4:00, he decided to kill time, rather than let time kill him.

In front of the dresser mirror, he combed through the remainder of his hair, spreading the strands across his dome, patting them into place. He still had hair, didn't look bad. Besides, he'd read women like prematurely balding men, found it sexy.

After he threaded the tie through his collar, he studied it. Incredibly wide and vibrantly yellow; a "power tie" the smarmy clerk had proclaimed it. Outrageously overpriced, Harold jumped on it anyway. Power didn't come easy in his world and, at the time, it seemed worth every buck. Of course, the tie hadn't brought him any power, too good to be true. Only money bought true power. Sort of a Mobius loop, wrapping around itself. Money buys money. But even millionaires have to start somewhere.

He slipped into his jacket. One last time, he admired his reflected appearance. Not too shabby at all. Running through his repertoire of smiles, he settled on one: seductive, confident, handsome. Just had to remember how to pull it off when he visited the woman in Room Number One. Since breakfast, he'd been thinking about her. Those ski-slope curves, her chocolate-rich brown eyes, perfect white teeth. Almost a fantasy woman. With briefcase in hand and a kick to his step, he hurried down the stairs.

For minutes, he stood in the hallway before her room, scrounging up the courage. He tossed his shoulders back, sucked in his pot belly, and threw caution to the wind. Confidently (but not too powerfully — he didn't want to frighten the woman), he hammered at the door. Even his knock sounded self-assured, he thought, proud and impossible to ignore. After no one answered, he knocked again. Where was she? It's not like she'd be "antiquing" on a day like this. God, he hoped she didn't "antique."

In fact, the entire inn seemed quiet, a heavy hush smothering the place. Nothing but settling floorboards or various clocks still counting down his wasted seconds. He knew the young, ridiculous couple was probably rutting away over in the carriage house. But the old owners, the host, the guy on his floor, even the brat — and surely he'd hear her even if he couldn't see her — were nowhere to be found.

He thought he may as well take advantage of the quiet time. It'd been some time since he'd eaten. The old woman said he could come down any time for a snack. Accommodating in the worst kind of way, just like his mother, pampering via a still-attached umbilical cord. Memories of his mother turned his stomach. Still, breakfast had been good, much better than the crap he'd been shoveling down his throat lately.

Outside the kitchen door, he heard voices. Hushed whispers. Obviously someone with secrets. Maybe they were talking about him, the sexy mystery man with the briefcase. Or maybe Rebecca was inquiring about him. Sweat greased his palm, the briefcase handle uncomfortably loose in his grasp. He had to hear the conversation, though, just had to. Whispers didn't exactly build a man's confidence.

He opened the door a crack, leaning in. And he listened.

The voices sounded a little louder now, more defined. He couldn't see the speakers, couldn't pinpoint their identity due to the anonymous nature of whispering. But he thought he distinguished a male and female voice.

"... *what do you think?*"

"*Not sure.*"

"*How 'bout we try them first ...*" Something shuffled, a chair leg, possibly. Then a rattling sound, metal clunking down onto wood. Harold barely contained a startled yelp. "... *move on to the others.*"

"*Sounds nice.*"

"*I think it's gonna be our best date night ever.*"

More scraping across the kitchen floor. Footsteps coming his way. On tiptoes, he scurried across the floor, picking up speed as he went. Once on the stairwell, he hit the steps hard. He didn't stop running until he slammed the door to his room.

Out of breath, he sat down in the depression the bedding had shaped around his ass earlier.

*What the hell was that about?*

Something sounded wrong, unnatural. *Date night.* Planned around the other guests. Good God, he'd stumbled upon swingers. Then he thought, maybe that wouldn't be so bad after all. Maybe it's why Rebecca was here. She did have a kinda wild energy about her, her sexuality barely contained. Hell, he'd even settle for the skinny, little, blond hippy chick. Just as long as the men left him alone.

Harold didn't swing that way, 100% man.

❊ ❊ ❊

Not an ideal situation, certainly not the disaster it could've been. Now Winston had met four people at the Dandy Drop Inn. But he'd learned, once you're on the radar, stay on it, just blandly so. Going into hiding after a social encounter raises people's suspicions like a polka-dotted flag rippling in the wind.

Rebecca had caught him, outed him. He hoped his "secret buddy" pact with Kyra didn't raise any warning signs. Suspicion mounts, creeping around inside like cancer, until it's diagnosed. And any parent's gonna eventually diagnose "secret pal" as malignant.

Actually, he liked Kyra and her mom. Reminded him of home. But thinking like that did nothing but carve another notch out of his soul.

After escorting Rebecca and Kyra inside, he'd chat a little longer, then make a gracious getaway. "Exhausted" always works wonders as an excuse, something no one questions, something everyone experiences. But he had to strive to be more boring than white bread. He grinned, thinking his wife wouldn't find that too much of a stretch.

Kyra led the way through the snow, no doubt enjoying every minute of helping the adults in her wake. Once they reached the porch, Winston told them he'd follow in a minute.

Something caught his eye, something out of place, like one of those puzzles in his children's books. Down the street, a steady cloud of smoke rose, too low, too small to originate from a chimney. Exhaust from an idling car. Winston's eyesight not being what it used to be — Jules had been on him for a year to get contacts — he squinted, making out what looked like a truck. Dark, either blue or black. Surprisingly clean and snow free given the storm, possibly a local. Not someone who might've traveled from Kansas City. Like Domenick. Or one of his men. He didn't recognize the vehicle, but that meant nothing. No one could connect him to his current car, either. But he saw a figure behind the wheel, little more than a shadow. Unmoving, or so he thought. Watching?

Again he patted down his back, force of habit, knowing full well his gun remained in the car. Something he needed to correct. Even though he didn't plan on using the gun until after he left, he would feel safer carrying it. Experience taught him Domenick didn't listen to reason. Only bullets spoke to him. And it scared the hell outta Winston where that trail might lead, and the possible fallout for his family.

Maybe when he'd pick up his gun, he'd take a closer look at the truck's inhabitant. Assuming he was still there. He knocked on a wooden post three times, then entered the house.

After tromping the snow off his feet, Christian magically appeared to take his scarf and hat. "Thanks, Christian."

"My pleasure, Mister Harton. I didn't know you'd left the premises." Christian nearly looked hurt that Winston hadn't informed him of his smoke break. And it concerned Winston the host seemed to know all, see all, hear all.

"Just for a bit. Smoker's habit." He feigned a cigarette between his fingers. But Winston had no doubt Christian smelled the smoke on him. He probably had a heightened sense of smell to go along with his other superpowers.

"Ah." Seemingly appeased that Winston's jaunt hadn't been a personal insult, Christian hurried off down the hallway, the wet scarf and hat held out at arm's length.

He heard Kyra's laughter coming from the kitchen.

"You ladies make it back safely?" he said, poking his head through the door. "Kyra, maybe you should bring a compass next time. In case you get lost."

With a giant muffin covering most of her face, she shook her head. "I don't get lost."

"First time for everything."

Rebecca appeared half asleep, head propped up on a palm, a vigorous redness to her cheeks. She showed him a toothy smile, the only animated thing about her. After sipping from a steam-topped cup, she gestured toward the counter. "Pot's nice and hot."

He rubbed his hands and blew into them. "Don't mind if I do." The coffee smelled good and strong, the mug thawing his hands. Then he noticed the snow on the rug by the kitchen door. Boot treads marked several clumps, very little of it melted. Someone had just been there. "Where're the Dandys? Haven't met them yet."

"Dunno. Maybe sleeping. Seems to be the thing to do on a day like this. That's where I'm headed soon as I warm up."

"Sounds like a good idea all around. Everyone hibernating like bears." Kyra giggled, then continued on her dog-minded muffin obsession.

"So you sell insurance?"

"Yep."

"Like it?"

"Nope."

She snorted, her mouth full of coffee. Very unladylike, and very endearingly human. He thought she no longer perceived him as a threat; he just didn't want to add memorable to the list, so no more humor. "Sorry." He sat down across from Rebecca.

"Then why do it? I mean, why sell insurance if you don't like it?"

He shrugged. "Pays the bills. Living the American dream."

"'The American Dream'. Like to experience that someday. I feel like an immigrant just reaching the shores."

He hefted his mug her way. "Keep hope alive." She glanced at his ring finger, at the indentation his wedding ring had left. He always took it off while on a job. Wearing it felt like a betrayal to his wife and daughters, their not knowing about his "work." It probably really didn't matter; only to him.

"To hope." She drank to his toast. "Have any kids, Dave?"

"No. Just an ex-wife."

Rebecca gave her daughter a sad look, so mournful Winston suspected Kyra'd been put through life's wringer. "I guess everyone has their problems."

"I guess."

Kyra, having destroyed the muffin, had long lost interest in their conversation. She stretched her arms, reaching for the ceiling and delivered an award-winning yawn. "Mommy, can I go take a nap?"

Stress lines marked Rebecca's face as she hesitated. An easy question like that shouldn't be that hard to answer. Finally, she said, "Sure, honey, I'll be along shortly."

"Pleasant dreams, kiddo."

Kyra trudged out of the kitchen, smiling contentedly, on her way to recharging her high spirits.

"I worry about her." Rebecca looked down at the coffee cup, then at Winston with sad, full eyes. Winston knew the look well. Confession time.

Winston didn't want to get involved, didn't want to absolve. He offered something innocuous, the best solution to avoid a tough problem. "You won't let anything happen to her. Don't worry. You seem like a good mother."

"If only," she replied, her voice hushed.

❋ ❋ ❋

*Bitch. Goddamn cheating, lying bitch!*

Brad knew it. As easy to predict as to what his partner, Steve, brought for lunch to the job on any given day. She lied to him, cheated on him. Shacking up in a bed and breakfast with some low-life scuzzball.

He supposed he knew it all along. His detective instincts had never let him down. Should've listened to the inner voice earlier. And it made everything clearer now, all the puzzle pieces locking together, his mind focusing like a microscope.

The proof he'd just witnessed sealed the deal. Frolicking with some bearded bastard, her lover. Taking his daughter along for a romantic stroll in the snow. *His* family.

*Son of a bitch*!

After the punk-ass deputy — whose invitation to meet he fully intended on accepting once he cleared the air with Rebecca — had hung up on him, it was a snap to find her location. No hotels in Hilston, but three B&Bs. After checking out the first two locales, he arrived at the Dandy Drop Inn. The biggest, nicest looking one of the bunch. And no doubt the most expensive. Her choice, so obvious. She thought he owed her the world and damn near took it out of him, dollar by dollar.

How long had it been going on? Did they screw in *his* bed? Laughing at him behind his back? He'd show them how to laugh soon. Even his daughter was in on the little tryst. No one could be trusted, not a damned soul. And now he had a third member to add to his list.

*Fuck*!

He drew back a fist and slammed it onto the dash. Then he did it again. And again. He didn't stop until the dashboard material cracked, a jagged line of lightning. He needed that. Didn't give a damn about the dash either. As he sucked at the blood on his knuckles, he stared at the inn, every light ablaze on the lower two levels. The party raged inside, while he suffered outside, a goddamn, frozen cuckold.

*Bitch, lying whore* ...

He needed to settle down, let his anger simmer from the boil. Something he'd use later. When the lights went off, he'd make his move. The fewer witnesses, the better.

❋ ❋ ❋

The house was cool; big, dark, and fun, like a carnival ride. The kind Mommy wouldn't let Kyra ride.

She had every intention of taking a nap, she really did. She didn't like lying to Mommy, especially after the way Daddy had treated her.

But the stairwell rose before her, practically inviting her. She'd never even seen a stairwell like this before. Certainly, she'd never climbed one.

The adults were talking boring stuff, leaving her out of the conversation. And Mommy was taking her secret buddy away from her. She didn't mind, though, not too much. She knew Mommy was lonely, heard her cry at night sometimes. Unlike Kyra, Mommy didn't have many friends. Didn't even leave the house very much. So she really hated lying to her.

But the *stairwell*. Like a ladder leading to something exciting, something unknown; each stair big enough that she could sleep on one.

She listened. Mommy and Dave were still talking. Probably would forever, the way adults do. So boring.

Exploring was fun. Her teacher, Mrs. Tidwell, had told her class it's good to explore; you never knew what you might discover. Kyra decided to do it for Mrs. Tidwell. Maybe even talk about it during Show and Tell. If she ever went back to her school. Sometimes she didn't think she would. Mommy hadn't told her much about what would happen after Christmas vacation.

Actually, she'd already discovered something cool in the house. Something secret, so secret she hadn't even told Mommy or her new pal, Dave, about it. It felt more special that way. And it made her wonder what other cool stuff she might find.

The first stair groaned beneath her boots like a sour tummy, her soles still wet from the snow. With a hand on the railing — how fun it would be to slide down it, the way she'd seen kids do on TV — she climbed the steps to a landing that twisted up to yet another floor. Darkness threatened to swallow her. Who knew what might be hiding in the shadows? She'd actually seen parts of spooky movies before. Sometimes when Daddy came home and fell asleep in front of the TV, she watched them. She knew about vampires and masked killers; oddly enough, they never scared her. What happened in her home scared her more. Watching Daddy hit Mommy. Hearing them fight, always ending with Mommy so sad, always crying. So whatever waited for her on the second floor didn't frighten her at all. Not like Daddy. The kids at school thought she was brave; she thought she was, too. Going up the stairs felt like a test of courage, like the boy in the civil war book her teacher had read to them.

It was so dark she couldn't see where the stairs ended. At the top, her foot lifted and came down hard. *Clump*. She froze, making sure she hadn't been heard. Then she continued down the hall. More sconces — she thought that's what Christian had called them — lit the walls like glowing crystal balls, not very bright. Light peeped out from beneath Room Number Four, the weird guy's room. Everything else was shrouded in darkness.

What really intrigued her was the next flight of steps up to the third floor. If the first set had been a challenge, this was like the next level in a video game. No way she'd back down now, not when adventure called.

A cold draft kissed her face as she mounted the last step, a soft whisper like leaves whipping in the wind. No lights on the walls here. Just darkness, complete nighttime darkness. Shadows hiding within darker shadows. She gripped her shoulders, shivering, fighting the chill.

Her hand slid against the wall. Beneath her touch, the wallpaper bubbled up, dusty and gross. The light from downstairs vanished behind her, leaving her alone in the inky blackness, so awful and hungry. But she couldn't stop now. Down the hall she moved, her fingers walking the wall like a spider. The wall ended, her fingers slipping into a recess. She felt a frame, found a doorknob. She twisted it, meeting with resistance. Locked. She continued traveling down the black tunnel. She sensed a stillness before her, the end of the line. Her breath bounced back, halted by a wall. To her left, she found another doorknob. This one opened with a simple turn.

Immediately, the room warmed her, less chilly than the hallway. The air tasted old and thick, kind of like at Grandma's house. And something stank, a smell like rotten oranges, strong and bitter. Her fingertips brushed beside the doorjamb, searching for a light. Nothing. She closed the door behind her with a click that sounded thunderous, much too loud. With her hands out, she moved into the room, shuffling her feet so not to trip on anything. Her fingers grazed something, hanging clothes maybe. The clothes swung back and forth, the ceiling creaking above her, chattering like a cricket. Something draped over her arm, soft and scratchy. A spider web? She shrugged it off. Her knees hit something, stopping her. Like one of the blind people in that story about the elephant, her hands explored it, guessing what it could be. A bed! Covered and made. Navigating her way toward the head of the bed, her hand hit something. *Tunk*. It fell to the floor but thankfully didn't break. Next to her, a lamp wobbled, its pull chain clanking against its body.

She tugged the chain and an oval of light opened the darkness. Millions of dead eyes looked at her. She gasped, then smiled. One of the coolest things she'd ever seen. Dolls, more dolls than she'd ever seen in her life, more than even her friend, Brittany, had in her bedroom, more than the world's biggest toy store. They sat in baby-like chairs, some sharing a small bench. There were even a few in miniature beds next to the big bed. What she'd bumped into had been dolls hanging from the ceiling by ribbon, now twirling around in circles like ballerinas. Sort of like Geppetto's workshop. Dolls filled the shelves in an old, white bookshelf. Some sat on the windowsill, dust on their faces and arms. But these weren't like the dolls her friends collected. They looked old, with hairstyles from the movies Mommy watched. More ribbons tied their hair. Lots of pigtails, too, something Kyra had always wanted to try. Their eyes were big as marbles, their eyebrows even bigger, raising like rainbows. Some wore dresses that poofed out at the bottom, covering their feet. Others had on wedding dresses, ready for their special day. Many of them wore hats bigger than their heads. All dressed in lace and grandma-like stuff. And not one of them smiled.

Instead, they stared sadly at the empty bed in the middle of the room. Kyra wondered who the lucky girl was who slept here. A comforter with different shades of sky blue and cotton candy pink covered the bed. The sheets were turned down, just a corner, like an envelope flap. It didn't look like anyone had slept in the bed for a while. Enormous pillows sat fluffed up like gigantic marshmallows. And the bed looked perfect, the sheets tight as the top of a drum. Thinking of Goldilocks, she giggled. She imagined three bears finding her in their bed.

So she just had to sit on the bed, she'd be mad at herself if she didn't. When she jumped onto the bed, a tiny cloud of dust flumped up, dancing in the lamp's rays. As she bounced, the springs squeaked. It reminded her of mice. Or how she imagined they might sound, kinda gross, kinda cute. Now all the dolls stared at her. The way her shadow moved across the room, almost alive, gave her a chill. It looked like the dolls were ducking into her shadow, escaping the light.

Next to the bed stood a nightstand. On top, she saw a hairbrush with icky gray hairs curling out of it, lots of 'em, too. Water filled a glass, maybe more of a jelly jar without a label. Dust covered the glass, and little black dots swam on top like bugs. But it was the box that really hooked her attention. Pretty drawings of circus people decorated it — a ringmaster; marching men wearing tall, furry hats like honey-combs; an elephant with a quilt on its back; pretty ladies in tutu's spinning, spinning, spinning like the still-twirling dolls dangling from the ceiling. All painted in light blues, pinks, greens. She blew the dust off the top, lifted the latch, and opened the lid. A toy ballerina no bigger than her thumb popped up, jolting her. The figurine held one foot to her knee, her arms raised, hands together, and moved around in a circle. Dancing to music, beautiful music. Tinkling bells, sweet as candy and softer than bunnies.

Mesmerized, Kyra brought it closer. And hummed along to the melody.

Then a woman's voice joined her. A shriek stuck in Kyra's throat. Her heart knocked, knocked, knocked. Scared, she kicked back on the bed, mussing the bedding. The box dropped to the rug, the lid snapping shut and chopping off the music.

The woman stopped humming. Then stepped into the circle of light. Smiling like sunshine, lines wrinkling her face like golden rays.

"Missus Dandy! You scared me!" Kyra knew she shouldn't be in the room, knew she was in trouble. But Mrs. Dandy didn't look mad.

With a gentle chuckle, Mrs. Dandy moved toward the bed and sat next to Kyra. She moved stiffly and slowly, as if her bones hurt.

"I'm sorry I gave you a fright, child. But you know better than to go off into other people's rooms."

"Sorry." Seemed like Kyra'd been apologizing a lot lately. Something kids always had to do. She couldn't wait 'til she was grown up so she could stop apologizing. Still, she knew how to act. She rested her forehead down on her drawn knees and wrapped her arms around them. Her best "sorry" look.

Mrs. Dandy laughed again, nice and soft. "It's fine, Kyra. You like the room?"

Kyra raised her head, bypassing the tears stage. "It's so pretty! Like a dream."

"Yes, that's what Jodi thought, too." She placed a hand on Kyra's back while she bent down to retrieve the music box. "This was her favorite." Mrs. Dandy twisted a key in the back, then opened it. When the music started, she hummed along, eyes closed, her head swaying back and forth. "*La dee dahhhh, dah dee dahhhh ...*"

Kyra joined her, trying to mimic her silly words. Mrs. Dandy's hand crawled across Kyra's back and gripped her shoulder, pulling her into a nice, warm hug. Together they sang. Kyra could've done it all night.

When the music stopped, so did Mrs. Dandy. Holding the box in her hands, she stared at it, looking as if she might cry. Kyra knew the feeling. She hugged the old lady, burying her face in her arm. Hugs always make things better. Mrs. Dandy stiffened, then relaxed, patting Kyra's head.

Kyra released her, then asked, "Is Jodi your daughter?"

"Yes."

"How old is she?" For a moment, excitement stirred Kyra like static. She thought she might have someone to play with, making things a little less boring.

"Oh, dear, she's long since moved on. She'd be 'bout your mother's age, I reckon."

"Oh." Kyra couldn't keep the disappointment out of her voice. But she was being selfish. "Does she come to visit? Does she still like her dollies?"

"My, you are an inquisitive cuss, aren't you?" Suddenly, Mrs. Dandy didn't seem so sad. She smiled at Kyra again, laughing. "Yep, we keep it ready for her. Someday, someday."

"Huh. I'd like to have lotsa dolls like these when I'm Mommy's age."

"Well, maybe you will, Kyra, maybe you just will." She grinned at Kyra, so happy. "But, what do I know? I'm just a silly old woman. Don't mind me none, child. Anyhoo, anyhow, does your momma know you're up here?"

Again, guilt ate at Kyra, kicking her off her cloud of enchantment. "No. Are you gonna tell her?"

"I don't reckon there's a need for that, do you?"

"Nope. But I better get going." She bounced off the bed and turned back. "Jodi's so lucky. Her room's wonderful."

"Thank you, child. That means a lot to me."

"Bye." Kyra skedaddled, running quickly down the hallway toward the light coming up the stairwell. She hoped Mommy wasn't looking for her. So she hurried, breezing down the steps, almost like in her dreams of flying across the sky. As she chugged down the second stairwell, she remembered something. Something kinda weird. She hadn't heard Mrs. Dandy come into the room.

\* \* \*

Rebecca said goodbye to Dave and left the kitchen. Not that she hadn't enjoyed her chat with Dave; she had, very much so. It felt nice talking with someone about nothing, almost like a friendship. They'd carried on about the weather, cars, and Omaha steaks. Such mundane things felt so new, so different, so alive. Of course, she'd purposefully kept her personal trauma out of the conversation. Dave didn't want to hear it, she knew, and she certainly didn't want to burden a stranger. Her concern, her problems, her mess to clean up. Been there, done that. She shook her head at the joke her life had been; she might've laughed, but she hadn't yet reached her life's punch line. She just hoped it would be an uplifting one, a happily ever after.

Still, she'd spent longer in the kitchen than she'd intended to. She needed to check on Kyra. Although dog tired, she rounded the stairwell, picking up her pace. Sleep on the agenda; a quick catnap would be just what the doctor ordered.

Actually, she half-way suspected she might find Kyra gone. Hell, for her daughter's benefit, Rebecca sorta wanted it to happen. Then Kyra would learn her lesson once and for all, learn to stay close where Rebecca could always find her.

As she entered the hallway, she thought about how awful that sounded. But it's hard to be a good parent. These days it pays to be wary.

She pushed open the door slowly, which just made the hinges screech louder. She stepped into the dark and heard her daughter breathing. Peaceful, long breaths spread out evenly. She grappled at the end of the bed until she found Kyra's foot. Just to be sure, she turned on the lamp, tilting the shade away from Kyra. Fast asleep, curled up into a comfy ball of love and warmth.

She chuffed out a sigh and crawled into bed next to her daughter. She shouldn't have doubted Kyra. Maybe she should quit doubting herself as well; perhaps that was the key to solid parenting. She turned out the light and her light of consciousness soon followed.

\* \* \*

In front of the altar, Tommy asked, "Babe, you think we oughta take it down?"

"No. I want the Dandys to know why we do it." It didn't bother Heather that Tommy questioned dismantling the altar. Rather, she didn't like how he stared at it. Not out of reverence, but rather, he looked puzzled, sort of nonchalant. Like sometimes he just pretended to be into their righteous cause, not truly believing in it. "You're not *ashamed* of our Lord God, are you?"

"*What?*" With a jerk of his head, he gave her an "are you crazy" look. "Course not, babe. I mean, it's what we're all about." Arms extended, fingers wiggling, he beckoned her.

As his bride, she dutifully fell into his waiting arms. "No, I know better. I'm just bein' silly. Guess I'm still riled up about that … that woman and her child."

His hug felt tight, secure. God's helping hands around her. "Don't you worry 'bout that woman. She'll get hers. Soon." Tommy's eyes grew dreamy, the way they did when they'd sent her parents on their journey. Although relief swelled in Heather's bosom, she also questioned why Tommy enjoyed their work. Not for the first time. The Good Book says to take pride in one's work. And it's not a sin to enjoy one's livelihood. But she experienced no greater joy than being the right hand of God. She just hoped Tommy was the God-anointed left hand. Then she let out a snort, mostly muffled into Tommy's chest. Of course, God wouldn't let her down. He'd sent Tommy to her for a reason.

"I know, babe. Can't wait." She pushed him away before his body grew some other ideas. No time for that now. Besides, she'd begun to feel saddle sores. "We need to get everything prepared. They'll be here in … 'bout twenty minutes or so." They'd skipped dinner in the big house, clearly too excited to eat. Besides, God's nourishment of her soul was all Heather really needed.

Like a finely tuned machine, they completed their work in minutes, dancing past one another on different chores, never once questioning the other's moves. And it made Heather hate herself for having questioned Tommy's motivation. Dumb, so dumb of her, and shamefully showing little faith.

A knock on the door announced the Dandys' prompt arrival. A tingle electrified Heather's hidden parts, working its way up to her brain. She imagined a mental lightbulb snapping on, sorta like in the cartoons. Tommy smiled at her, grabbing her hand. Their fingers entwined, a human bridge to the Lord. Reluctantly, she pulled away. He had to greet the guests, a man's duty after all.

When Tommy opened the door, Mr. Dandy ducked his head and entered, holding a small picnic basket. "Howdy, howdy, howdy, folks! Jim Dandy to the rescue with a few of Dolores's goodies to fortify on a cold night." A light dusting of snow breezed off the top of the basket.

Bundled up in a heavy coat that added an extra layer of fat to her appearance, Dolores strolled in behind her husband. Her shoulders shook, warding off the brutal night's chill. "And I've got the Spinner Dominos."

"Let me get your coat for you, Missus Dandy." Tommy was nothing if not a gentleman.

"Why, that's mighty kind of you. And, pshaw." She trumpeted her lips and flagged a hand down. "Let's not stand on formalities. You are, after all, guests in our house. It's Dolores."

"Gotcha." Tommy took her coat, then slung it on the bed. Manners count.

"And you know to call me Jim." While Jim had come in coatless, he had warmed his head with a John Deere cap. He swooshed it off, held it to his belly, and bowed. "At your service."

The Dandys practically glowed. Red patches stood out on their cheeks and the tips of their noses, cherub-like almost. But their auras — their souls — flickered around their bodies, a green ring of burning fire. Demanding to be released.

When the Dandys saw the altar on the wall, their festive mood fizzled.

"What's this?" Dolores said, pointing a finger. Jim remained quiet, slack-jawed.

"Oh, I hope you don't mind. Heather and me, well, we're Christians. We like to practice our faith no matter where. Just doin' God's work." Tommy flashed his warm grin at them, then turned to Heather with a secret wink. "We took special care not to damage the walls." Not entirely true, but Heather knew God would understand.

Finally, Dolores's face loosened with a smile. "I think that's fine, just fine. Religion's a special thing, something more folks oughta take time out for. Isn't that right, Poppa?"

"Took the words right out of my mouth." Jim chuckled, a hearty, good-natured growl.

Exhilaration washed over Heather like baptismal water. She knew the Dandys would embrace their sweet departure, rapturous over their promised afterlife. And she had no doubt they were bound for Heaven. With folded hands, she closed her eyes and prayed where she stood.

Across the room, Tommy said, "Amen," and clapped his hands, anxious to get started. So was Heather, more than ever. She beat everyone to the table.

"What a spitfire, 'ey, Mother?" Jim dropped an arm across his wife's shoulder. So cute the way he pulled her into him, their auras joining as one. "Reckon they don't know we're the Spinner Domino champions of Hilston, Missouri." Dolores laughed, swatting at her husband's chest.

"We'll just see 'bout that," said Tommy, swinging into a chair. "Even though I never played it before, I'm purt near good at any sport." Definitely true, thought Heather, not just boyish bragging. There didn't seem to be a thing her husband couldn't master.

The Dandys claimed their seats at the compact, four-chaired table. The group filled it out nicely, the men seated across from one another. Tommy wore his elation like his tight jeans — every secret showing. Owl eyed and ready to hoot, his gaze bounced between the older couple. He breathed loudly through his nose, the way he sounded during love making. And for the first time — outside of their marital bed — she saw drops of sweat boil across his forehead.

As Jim flipped a number of dominoes face down, Dolores fussed with the picnic basket on her lap, her face hidden behind an open wooden flap. She pulled out a plastic-wrapped plate of cookies. Carefully, she took the plastic off, keeping it remarkably unwrinkled and returned it to the basket. "Here we are. Chocolate peanut butter cookies."

"Wait 'til you kids taste these."

Apparently, Tommy couldn't wait. To Heather's shame, he grabbed one, stuffed it into his mouth. Before swallowing, he repeated his foul table manner. Crumbs speckled his lips, a few dropping to his shirt.

"Tommy Goodenow! Where are your manners?"

He swallowed and issued a mumbly, "Sorry, babe. But they're mighty tasty."

"Ah, it's fine, girl," offered Dolores. "I like a man who shows his appreciation through his belly."

Patting his stomach, Jim said, "Must be why she's head over heels for me."

Everyone roared except Heather. It seemed Tommy valued his own craven physical needs before their duty. When Tommy finally noticed her glaring at him, he gave a little boy's nod and wiped his mouth with a napkin. Then he tossed the napkin onto the red and white checkered tablecloth. How his awful manners had escaped Heather before, she couldn't tell. Still, that's what marriage is all about, she supposed, learning one another's weaknesses and accepting them. For better, for worse.

"Okey dokie. The object of the game is …" While Jim explained the game's rules, Heather drifted to her special place. Sometimes she thought she actually left her shell of a body. Maybe not. But it was a quiet place, a place to meditate on God made especially for her. Well, she shared it with her Lord and Maker, of course. She prayed, gave thanks, offered her services. Felt downright privileged to be sending worthy souls to Heaven. And to the other place, reserved for people like her parents and the woman and child across the driveway.

As if from a distance, she heard chatter surrounding her, hollow echoes of voices. Tommy asked questions, the Dandys belted out laughter, none of it mattered. God had sought her out, ordained her to carry on His work. Again, she thanked Him. As if chasing her body, she slowly reclaimed it, feeling God's light filling her from head to toe.

"Amen," she said. The party talk had stopped. Then she noticed everyone looking at her.

"Heather? Heather, you all right, girl?" Jim loomed close to her face, his breath fetid smelling of pickles. "You don't look so good. Your eyes. They're … well …"

"Do you need to lay down, honey?"

Tommy said, "No, no, she's all right. Just how she gets when she prays."

"You sure, son? Them pupils of hers look big as saucers."

She smiled, comfortable in her serenity. "I'm fine. Better than I've ever been." She looked at Tommy, nodded. God told her the time had come.

Tommy's grin grew into a shark's bite. From his boot, he retrieved a knife, his favorite. Slowly, he twisted it, letting the lamplight catch the blade. He admired its sleekness, its salvation-bringing quality. Then he rested his arms on the table, knife pointing up. "Well now, Jim … Dolores … I'm afraid we didn't just invite you over to play —"

Jim yanked the tablecloth toward him. Tommy fell forward, his chin banging onto the table. Faster than Heather could track, Dolores's hand flew out of the basket. Her arm whipped over her head, coming down lightning fast. Holding something glinting in the light. *Whack*. The hatchet separated Tommy from his hand, the blade buried into the table. His stump raised, blood spat out of it. He stared at it, stunned into silence. Except for the awful mewling. His jaw wobbled, tongue bobbing, but no words escaped. God, no words.

"Get back, Mother."

Dolores's chair scraped back across the floor with a teeth-grinding crunch. The table flew up and over, Jim driving it. Tommy crashed to the floor, cookies and dominoes *clack-clack-clacking* onto his pale face, his bloodless face.

Heather sat frozen, her arms dead weight at her sides. It'd happened so fast, so horribly. Yet it didn't happen. A hallucination. God wouldn't *allow* it to happen.

Jim ripped the tablecloth away from the hatchet. He lassoed Tommy with it, a red and white checked ghost, quiet and lifeless. Blood spread like an inkblot through the cloth. His hands around Tommy's neck, Jim kicked at the table. It skidded across the floor and banged into the altar. Jesus dropped.

Heather sucked in a deep breath, ready to scream. A hand clamped over her mouth. Tommy's favorite knife, the one he had finished Heather's parents with, touched her throat, the steel ice cold. It drew a nick, a tiny one, but Heather felt the warmth of her soul seeping out. Tears of life, of fear, dropped down her cheeks.

"Well, I'll be hogtied and dipped in spit, Mother!" Jim let up on Tommy, who slid to the floor. "What in the world do you make of *this*?" His smile never changed, the only one he knew: cordial, relaxed. As if nothing had happened.

Behind Heather, Dolores laughed and released a big "Hoo-whee!" Then she said, "I reckon this is gonna be our best date night in a *long* time."

A dark pool blossomed across the floor beneath Tommy. His legs kicked, the way Heather imagined a hanged man might jerk his soul away. Before she passed out, the last thing she saw was her loving husband's soul drift away. It didn't rise, just ate itself up, folding inward, then vanished into blackness. The last thing Heather heard was the Dandys' good-natured laughter.

# Chapter Six

Rebecca had no idea if she'd slept, the line between waking and sleep muddied. She certainly didn't feel rested. She sat up, stretched, her sweat-drenched shirt clinging to her. The radiator hissed, a comforting sound. A hint of a dream struggled to surface, one where she was asleep while oddly aware of her surroundings. She remembered sensing an intruder's presence, felt their warmth, their body occupying space. Someone watching her, unmoving and quiet. She'd struggled to open her eyes, but something kept pulling her down, a rock anchoring her to sleep's ocean depths.

She forced a dry swallow down her parched throat. Kyra, still curled up like a potato bug, hadn't budged. Rebecca checked her phone. Of course there wasn't a signal; she'd pretty much resigned herself to not getting one until the storm passed. But the time read 8:47, proof that she'd slept. For a little over two hours.

Rebecca inched out of bed, careful not to disturb her daughter. No doubt Kyra would be hungry when she woke, so Rebecca thought she'd scavenge the kitchen for a snack. Better go alone, too, in case the strange young couple was there again.

She slipped into her shoes and bypassed the mirror, afraid of what she'd see. Carefully, she removed the chair from the door and stepped into the hallway.

* * *

Bright light warmed Heather from head to toe. At first she thought she'd been lifted straight to Heaven. A voice — God's voice — spoke to her. Of course she didn't see Him; more like *felt* His voice, heard it in divine stereo. She couldn't make out the words, not exactly. But the message came through strong and clear. A beautiful sensation saturated her mind, her body.

Her work had only just begun. Tommy's passing now felt like a minor setback on her path, her mission. He'd gone to a better place, happier now than he'd been in life. And he'd wait for her, this she knew. With God's shining light showing her the way, she clawed her way back to the sinful, material world.

Voices echoed as if from across a body of water, hollow and distant. The dull lamplight in the room crushed her with despair, a dismal reminder of the brilliance she'd just left behind. But it didn't last. If anything, she felt renewed, energized. Ready to continue her work.

Across the room, Jim Dandy rolled Tommy's soulless husk up in the plastic she and Tommy had planned to use for the Dandys. Taking out the trash and, really, that's all Tommy's body was now. So Heather didn't mind all that much; a body without a soul seems as pointless as life without faith. It bothered her more that her wrists ached, bound behind her.

Next to her, Dolores said, "Father, she's awake."

Jim straightened with a double crack of the knees. "Welcome back, young lady." He dropped a chair in front of Heather and sat. Leaning over, he said, "Doin' all right?" Tiny blood vessels crisscrossed through his eyes. One long, gray nostril hair dropped and retracted with each breath. And all she could think was how she couldn't wait to release the Dandys' souls. She just might enjoy the job as much as Tommy would've.

"I asked you a question, girl. Doin' okay?"

Heather nodded.

"Now why don't you tell us what in the world y'all thought you was doin'?"

Heather cleared her throat, her mind. "God's work."

"What? Never seen no God's work that involves knives," said Dolores.

"I'll say, Mother. Why, I think these young 'uns were fixin' to kill us. Is that about right, girl?"

"No. Not kill. *Release* you." Heather spat the words, demanding to be heard. Long ago, she'd learned the devil uses ridicule as a tool, a hurdle the righteous need to jump often and with grace. *Bring it.*

"What do you make of that?" Jim looked at his wife, his eyes dancing with amusement.

"Land's sake! I don't care how they try to gussie it up, they was fixin' to kill us. All our years doin' this, we've *never* had someone try and kill us. *Us!* Can you imagine? Lord a'mighty —"

"*Yes*, he is!"

"Girl, you talk when spoken to, got that?" Jim's good-natured act vanished, replaced by an anger reserved for sinners. Heather had woefully misread the Dandys. Sometimes the devil wears sheep's clothing. "Now ... am I to understand you wanted to kill us 'cause God done tol' you to?"

"I'm his righteous soldier, delivering souls, good and evil, to their just —"

"I've heard about enough, Poppa," Dolores said. "Let's carry on. I'm feelin' mighty vital tonight."

"You mean 'frisky,' Mother?"

Crimson shades blemished Dolores's cheeks. With a smile, she said, "Don't be that way in front of young 'uns! I declare."

A knock on the door kicked Heather's heart into her throat. God's cavalry to the rescue.

With a glimpse at his watch, Jim said, "Ah, right on time as usual. Come in!"

Snow swirled behind the host, Christian, as he entered. "Good evening again, Missus Goodenow." To the Dandys, he said, "Are you ready for my services?"

"Yep." Jim jerked his chin toward the body on the floor. "Got one to get rid of. Need your help with the girl in a shake of a coon's tail."

At first, Heather took it all in with a sense of invulnerable serenity, knowing God had her back. Yet it became clear the Dandys meant to kill her. And the worst part? At the hands of an abomination, a queer. *Unacceptable.* God had given her all the time in the world; two worlds, actually. Now was not her time to move on, not by God's choice. So why hadn't He come to her aid? The answer seemed so simple, it shamed her that she doubted Him. *Of course.* Another test to see if she's truly worthy, one of the faithful. God wants her to fight. And fight she would, too, like a warrior on Heaven's front lines.

"*Wait!* Don't you let *him* near me." She snapped her hands apart, the rope pulling taut. "Don't let him touch me!" She averted her eyes, unable to look at the homosexual.

"Now, what do you got against ol' Christian, young lady?" asked Jim. "Why, he's like a son to us."

"That he is, Poppa."

"He's a sinner! A foul thing from hell! He's a ... a *gay!*" Even the word tasted bitter on Heather's tongue. She spit, clearing the repugnant taste.

"What? A ... gay?" The host blinked at Heather, his eyes moist behind his glasses. "I'm not gay. *Why* does everyone always *think* that?"

"Now, missy, you done hurt Christian's feelings." Dolores jumped out of her chair, prodding a finger at Heather. "*You* consider yourself a Christian. Not very Christian-like, I don't think, callin' him names. And even if he was a homosexual, don't you think your God would accept him?"

Fire flared through Heather, her mind on the verge of exploding. Never had she heard such profanity. It wouldn't go unpunished, either. "Of course not! God *hates* queers! Don't you *dare* —"

"But I'm *not* gay."

"Shut up, *queer*! And your name ... the ultimate blasphemy!" Her chair rocked as she wrenched against the binds. The rope loosened, just a bit. Fury drove her, righteousness pushing her over the top. "You're *all* goin' to hell! You hear me? *All* of you!" With a surge of energy, she shifted to the left. The chair hovered on two legs, tottered, then fell. Pain knifed through her shoulder. She growled through clamped teeth. Soon, very soon, the three of them would pay for their sacrilege. "And I'm gonna send you *all* there."

"Shut yer *yap*, girl." Dolores waddled toward the queer. She reached up and stroked his shoulder. "Shhh, Christian, don't listen to the girl. She don't know nothin'. We know you're a healthy boy with—"

"But I'm *not* gay." His lies sounded weaker than his pathetic voice. On the floor, Heather writhed, her stomach roiling from the nightmare surrounding her.

"We know you're not, son." Dolores turned toward Heather, her eyes narrowed. "I've had 'bout enough of this. Damn lil big-mouthed *bitch*. Let's put her out of our misery." She approached Heather, the hatchet raised above her.

Heather twisted, pushed, the chair scraping over the floor. Her foot swept at the woman's ankles, her only weapon. Dolores hopped back, studying her weapon. "Poppa, you want the honor with this one?" With a smile, she offered the hatchet to her husband.

"No, you go on ahead."

"But I took care of the boy."

Jim smiled. "Well, now, that's an argument I can't rightly pass up. How 'bout we take turns?"

"Sounds dandy to me, Jim Dandy." The tip of her shoe smashed into Heather's nose. Spikes of yellow and orange pain distorted Heather's world. Above her, a twin image of Dolores prepared for a killing blow. Time for Divine intervention.

"Wait," screamed Heather. "Stop! I'm with *child!*"

Dolores lowered the hatchet, blubber jiggling on her underarm. The room hushed, quiet as death.

Jim's boots appeared in Heather's line of sight. "You mean to tell me, young lady, you and your fella were havin' premarital sex?" He said it as if the notion disgusted him, ironic coming from a sinner.

"What? No. *No.* Tommy and I just ... *consummated* our marriage yesterday." She hated telling the Dandys about her marital bed, absolutely despised it. It made sex seem so dirty again. But she had to survive, no matter the cost.

"Then the baby's another man's?"

Bile raced up Heather's throat, the horrendous implications sickening. "Of course not! I was ... *pristine* until we got married!"

"Then it just ain't possible, girl." The old man slapped a knee, chortling.

*Just keep right on laughing, devil spawn, you'll get yours. Soon.* Heather heard her very own Judgment Day calling.

"But it is! I swear to you ... absolutely *swear* ... I *know* it happened. *Felt* it happen last night. God *showed* me." Disgust crawled through Heather. She felt her soul dirtied by pleading with the sinners.

"'Spose it's possible, Poppa. Stranger things have happened. Either way, I don't wanna take any chances. Not if there's a baby on board. Not like ... like ..." Dolores moaned, just once, a train's diminishing rattle. Wrinkled hands covered her face.

Jim folded her into a strong hug, so intense Heather expected to hear bones break. "I know, it's all right. Shh. Don't go there ..." The queer dropped his chin, closed his eyes, and folded his hands. As if praying. *Praying!* After Dolores settled, Jim turned toward Heather, anger in his eyes. "Well, now, this changes everything. You'd best not be lyin' to us ... for your *own* sake."

Heather saw hope, jumped at the opportunity. "I'm not. I'd never lie about God. I'm pregnant."

"All right ..." Jim dragged a hand down his jaw, appearing skeptical. But Heather knew one thing he believed in — his wife. Something to remember, something to exploit later in her war. "... then I reckon we got different plans for you, girl. We had our hearts set on the other woman and her adorable daughter, but now ..."

Dolores finished his thought. "Looks like our family might be growin' more than we ever thought." Her smile swam back. "Christian, please take care of Miss Heather."

Heather cringed at the thought of his touch. "No, wait! Don't let him —"

Christian slapped a hand over Heather's mouth. Then he squeezed, his fingernails digging into her flesh. She bit his palm, his filthy, disease-ridden palm. Tart, poisoned blood trickled into her mouth. She struggled, spitting against his hand. When he punched her temple, her teeth bit into her tongue. Effortlessly, he pitched her over his shoulder. "My pleasure," he said, service with a smile.

❋ ❋ ❋

"Stop. Stop, *dammit.*"

Domenick's nephew punched the brakes. The Humvee's back end slid, drawing closer to the parked cars along the road. Once the vehicle rocked to a halt, Domenick's heart kept knocking.

"Dumb ass! Who taught you to drive? The blind?"

"Sorry, sorry." Calvin threw his hands up like a surrendering man.

Domenick shook his head, his patience tried. Nothing penetrated his moronic nephew's skull, so why even bother? He pointed at the car inches from the passenger window. "There. Bet that's it. Shitty Chrysler. About the right size, but who can tell for sure with all this damn snow? Make sure it's the right one first. Then flatten the tires. Don't want him goin' nowhere."

Calvin stared at Domenick, his lower jaw working beneath the mask. "But ... Mister Domenick, it's cold out there."

"Cold. Shit, I'll show you cold. How 'bout six feet under's worth of *cold?* Just get out there and *do* it, for Christ's sake. Buncha little girls!"

Calvin snagged a switchblade out of his coat pocket. The blade flipped out, Calvin studying it by the dashboard light. Buying time. Domenick tossed his hands up in despair, tired of having to explain everything. Twice.

"Okay, okay, I'm goin'." Calvin took a deep, germ-ridden breath and slid out. He swiped snow off the side, the hood, nodded satisfactorily toward Domenick. Then he dropped out of sight, and the accountant's car lowered, more snow tumbling off the roof. He sprang up, smiling, a damn school kid waiting for a golden star. Domenick waved him back.

"All right, you ready?" Calvin nodded, wisely keeping his mouth shut for once. It only took about ten hours of on-the-road lessons. "Pull up in front of the inn."

Calvin slowly idled the Humvee a few car lengths down, the short trip taking forever. With anticipation gnawing at him, Domenick was more than ready, the waiting game long played out. He wanted his money back, a few deserved deaths at his hand. Small desires, and it was taking a long time to get there.

"I'll stay here. Keep the engine running." Rubbing his hands in front of the heater didn't warm him much, not through his layers of gloves, but he'd learned visual cues work best on his nephew. "Take the automatic and get things done. That's all I'll say."

"You mean ... you're not goin' with me?"

Dumbfounded, Domenick glared at his nephew. "What? You some lil kid needs hand holdin'? I pay you, don't I?" A stupid, bobble-headed nod. "I'm the boss. Do your damn job and quit bitchin' about it."

"Right." Calvin grabbed the rifle from the backseat. Then he gulped, *gulped* for God's sake! "Um, should I still wear my mask?" He pinched it away, letting it snap back into place.

"Think about it, *dumb ass*. You might need it."

Realization appeared to slap Calvin upside the head, something Domenick considered making a physical reality. Yet he continued staring blankly at Domenick.

"Just get it done, already. Don't come back without the money." He gave him an imperious wave of the hand, dismissing him.

Domenick watched as Calvin hopped over a snow drift to where the sidewalk presumably lay. With ginger steps, he leaped through the snow, hopscotching toward the inn. Afraid of getting his feet wet, the world's worst enforcer. Domenick seriously needed to think about doing some downsizing, nephew or not.

Finally, Calvin climbed the steps to the wrap-around porch, reached the door, rifle hidden behind his back, and knocked. *Knocked, for God's sake.* Domenick never knocked, wouldn't even consider it, his reputation a skeleton key to the world. He went where he wanted, took what he needed, no invitations necessary. At the doorstep, Calvin lifted his hands and shrugged.

Domenick jabbed at the window release, missing it the first few times in his fury. With a whir, the window lowered. "Idiot! Don't fuckin' knock! Just get in there! Whatever it takes!" Frustrated, Domenick sat back and turned up the radio. Then his nephew vanished into the dark mansion.

❄ ❄ ❄

Headlights swept up behind Brad, the Humvee careening down the road. As he lowered into his seat, he watched two men drive by. Based on a quick assessment, the guys looked out of place — not the sort of yokels he'd expect to find in Hilston, Missouri — dressed in expensive outerwear.

*Grand Central Station in a snow storm.*

The driver got out and staggered toward the car next to him. By his unsteady gate, he looked drunk, maybe just a pussy afraid of the snow. Suddenly, he jabbed a knife into one of the tires. Then flattened another.

*What the hell?*

Then the Humvee moved forward a bit and stopped. The driver exited carrying what looked like a rifle. Brad thought things were about to get interesting.

*Just what kind of inn is this anyway?*

Maybe these guys were after Rebecca's new boy-toy, also; one of those serial, love-'em-and-leave-'em assholes. At first, the idea tickled Brad. Then not so much. It had to be his kill, by his hand. Nothing less would satisfy. Probably the only thing that would make his night worse was someone wasting Rebecca and her lover before he had a chance to.

*Dammit. One thing after another.*

He'd been about ready to make his move, too. The inn's lights had gone out; not much action since he saw the old couple leave and go around to the eastern side of the house. A jolt of pain reawakened his headache, a sure sign he needed to be proactive instead of waiting for shit to happen.

He popped open the gun and counted the brass casings through the clip's holes. Loaded and ready to go, something he already knew. But it pays to be careful. Braced for the cold, and fully embracing what lay ahead, he opened the car door ...

❋ ❋ ❋

Almost 9:00 and Harold couldn't stand it any longer. He'd listened carefully, waiting as impatiently as a man on death row. There were no moans of ecstasy, no beds rattling. Honestly, he had no idea how an orgy sounded, just his rich imagination at work.

But the thought of exclusion hurt. Even though he didn't particularly care for people, he still wanted to be invited. *Something.* Right under his nose, people were swapping sex partners, not giving him a second thought. Well, hell, if they weren't going to invite him, he'd just find the party himself. He'd already loaded several condoms — ambitious thinking, maybe, but he thought he might rise to the occasion, so to speak — into his jacket pocket.

And he'd been waiting for hours. Alone with only his fantasies to keep him company. No more. Time to take the bull by the horns, as his ex-wife always used to say.

He yanked off the confining power tie and tossed it to the floor, a small act of defiance. And one less article of clothing he'd have to remove later. Really, didn't he look better, *hipper*, without it? Less uptight and ready to roll, his new lifestyle. At least the one he wanted to project.

Surely the hot woman had gone back to her room by now. Unless she was screwing his neighbor. The thought boiled his blood. But he hadn't heard anything down the hall. A tigress like that wouldn't come and go without growling.

Fortified, Harold left the room, his constant companion, the briefcase, at his side. It bothered him what to do with the briefcase while having sex. Hold onto it? Maybe the woman would see it as a kink, the sorta fetish swingers are supposed to love. Either way, it wasn't going far. He'd clutch it between his naked knees if he had to.

The inn sat in silence, disappointingly so. The earlier carnival of lights had traded down into darkness. Very few lamps lit the lower level. Beneath the stairwell, the hall looked even blacker, the sconces (always sconces!) barely registering above a spark.

Self-doubt trailed him down the hallway. What if he was being overzealous, letting his imagination take charge as so many others tried to do with his life? Swingers during a snowstorm did seem unlikely. Even big libidos might be tamed by a storm. Still, whatever, you only live once. And he planned on living to the fullest now; unlike he had before with his sad, wasted life. Live large and take charge.

He rushed down the hall, the woman's door dead ahead. He imagined her waiting in bed, only a thin silk sheet separating her skin from his. What about the kid? Send her to the kitchen? Surely, there was a TV somewhere in the damn place.

With his hand poised above the door, a knock at the front door stopped him. His testicles retracted along with his hand. Another round of knocking. Then someone entered. Quietly.

*The police? Or maybe someone far worse?*

❄ ❄ ❄

Something didn't seem right. Not that Winston knew anything specific; rather, he intuited it. Call it instinct. Survivor's luck. He hadn't gotten this far in the "security" business without developing a sixth sense for trouble. Minutes ago, he'd heard Carsten stomping downstairs, unusually loud. Winston considered the accountant a quivering wallflower, the sort who floats lightly in the breeze. Then his stomach pitched when he thought Carsten might be making a run for it.

Winston swiped his car keys up from the bedside table. As an afterthought, he knocked on the wood three times, never more than three. Like an echo, he heard a faint knocking at the door downstairs.

Shoeless, he scurried down the hall and knelt on the landing. The door opened, and a figure quietly stepped inside. Once the man sneezed, he may as well have announced his entry with a bullhorn.

As if on cue, Christian stepped out of the shadows as he always seemed to do, the prince host of darkness.

"Can I help you, sir?" Christian flicked on the foyer light.

*Shit. Domenick's goon, his strong-arm, Calvin.*

Clearly startled, Calvin jumped, but his hands remained behind his back. He appeared jumpy, fidgety, a man peaking at caffeine's trail. Winston had no doubt what he hid behind him.

"Ah, yeah, I'm looking for a guy. Harold Carsten." The blue mask he wore muffled his words. But Winston filled in the blanks easily enough, as Calvin was hardly a locked diary. "Maybe another guy, too. Winston Ashford. They stayin' here?"

Christian folded his hands. He straightened, adding a couple inches to his already formidable height. "I ... see. And may I ask who you are? And what this pertains to?"

Attempting intimidation — something Calvin never could achieve — he stepped toward the host. "No. Look, just tell me what room they're in, go hide somewhere, and maybe I'll let you live."

Unbelievably, Christian threw his head back and laughed. The sound echoed off the rafters, traveling into Winston's spine. "That's a generous offer, sir. But I think not. Now, how about you get in your car and leave?" Reaching around Calvin, Christian pulled the door open. Calvin shuddered in the draft.

"You're not listenin' to me, asshole! I'm the one givin' orders here!" Calvin whipped his arm around. His gun banged into the wall, bouncing back against his leg. Christian snagged a hand around Calvin's wrist and raised the rifle. Calvin's eyes widened, his shock evident. With his free hand, Christian grasped Calvin's neck, his massive fingers nearly closing around it. Steering Calvin by the neck, Christian drove him outside into the storm. The door slammed behind them.

*Goddammit!*

Time for emergency measures, mission aborted. Winston tore back down the hallway and flung his door open. He jammed his feet into his loafers, every second urgent. Quickly, he looked at his belongings. Toothbrush, new underwear, fresh shirt, nothing traceable. They stayed. He snatched his winter coat and left, his gaze flitting between his feet and the front door.

*If Calvin's here, Domenick's no doubt close.*

He thundered down the stairs, manipulating his arms through his coat.

Rebecca stood at the bottom of the stairwell. She gasped, then smiled, opening her mouth to say something.

Winston forced a hand over her mouth, picked her up around her waist, and pushed her through the kitchen's swinging door. No time for explanations.

It'd only been minutes, but they lasted an eternity. Domenick's neck hurt from constantly craning his head. He'd heard no gunfire, saw no flashes in the darkened windows. No screams, nothing. Not at all what he expected. Or wanted.

The front door flew open. Two men slow danced out beneath the porch light, one his nephew, his partner a large blond guy. They grappled for control of Calvin's gun. Calvin's mask slipped down. The blond squeezed his nephew's neck. Calvin's tongue lolled out.

"Jesus Christ!" Domenick reached under his seat, frantically scrambling for his pistol. Sanitizer, boxes of tissues, vitamins. His fingers grazed the gun's grip. He cocked the hammer back and grabbed the door handle. *Locked.* Goddamn baby-proof doors, something he'd insisted on for safety.

Shots rang out. Domenick ducked, his head smashing onto the dashboard. Silence followed. He scooted over to the driver's side, then peeked out the window.

The blond's stranglehold on Calvin loosened as his nephew slumped down. The big man pinched the gun out of Calvin's grip and tossed it into the snow. Then he took Calvin's head beneath his armpit and gave it a sharp twist. Calvin's last look of life was his most common — dumbfounded.

Domenick slipped out the door, his heart thudding. He ducked behind the Humvee and risked a look through the window. The blond man stood over his prey, hands clasped together in an oh-so-dainty manner.

For a moment, Domenick considered jumping back into the Humvee, getting the hell outta there. But he didn't have his money. *His* money, not anyone else's. He waited until the blond dragged Calvin back into the house, then he counted slowly. Tried to find the goddamn center his wife always rattled on about. Sweat froze across his forehead. Arthritis dulled his knees. He dropped into a squat and maneuvered around his vehicle, avoiding touching the dirty Humvee.

"Howdy."

Domenick shot up and twisted. An old guy grinned at him, a shovel casually pitched over his shoulder. Domenick yanked his gun up, but he wasn't fast enough. The shovel swung toward him. Metal crushed his nose. A dull sensation numbed his face, not the immense pain he expected. As he dropped to his knees, he thought about the shovel. The filthy shovel that struck his face.

Then he fell into the snow. The soiled, polluted snow …

\* \* \*

Rebecca kicked her legs, Dave's hand silencing her screams. Random, horrid thoughts zipped through her mind.

*Kyra, oh my God, Kyra. Not another one. Another man, another violent bastard!*

He shoved Rebecca through the kitchen door, carrying her, his grip firm and threatening. Her fingernails dug into his hand, drawing drops of blood.

"*Rebecca, quiet,*" he whispered. "I'm not gonna' hurt you. I'm tryin' to *save* you."

Less than convincing. Saviors don't abduct.

She tugged at his hand, his arm rock solid. He pushed her against the counter, pinning her with his body. *A rapist.* When he spun her around, he barely sidestepped Rebecca's knee meant for his crotch.

"Rebecca, you *need* tó be quiet." He pressed his finger to his lips. "We're in trouble. I'll get us out of here. *Trust* me."

*Trust.* An easy word to toss around, not so easily earned. The fact he asked for trust after grabbing her nearly pitched her into a laughing fit. But she saw an opportunity, a small one. Play along, get the drop on him when he least expects it. Beneath his touch, she tensed and shuddered.

"Don't scream when I take my hand away. Okay?" She nodded. He dropped his hand down to her shoulder. Holding her captive, something she knew well. "There're men out there. *Dangerous* men."

"What? *Who?*" It sounded like a ploy, something to wear down her defenses. What he said made no sense, something out of a thriller. Then three rapid explosions cracked outside, gunfire.

*Kyra!*

Dave jolted, the fear in his eyes unsettling. "Hear that? I'm *not* fucking around. Go —"

"I'm not going anywhere. Not without Kyra, dammit."

He dropped his head, sighing. "If you go after Kyra, you're gonna get us both killed. You're not equipped to deal with these men. I am. I'll get her. I *swear* I will. But now I need you to go to my car. It's our best chance. There's a gun in the —"

"A *gun?* Why do you have a gun?"

"Protection. I travel a lot, sometimes to bad places." His eyes shifted slightly, an obvious lie. About the only good thing her husband ever taught her. "Just … get it, okay? It's a silver Camry, parked a block and a half down, facing this way. The gun's in the glove box. Pull the car up, leave it running. Don't talk to anyone, don't stop. Have the gun ready." He slipped the keys into her hand.

Cautiously, she worked the keys between her fingers, sharp edges sticking out. "I'm *not* leaving Kyra."

"*Listen*. She's still asleep. Or you'd hear her. Right now it's the best place for her. But *none* of us are getting out of here alive unless you do as I say. If I meant you harm, I wouldn't have given you my keys."

She considered, realized he had a point. But after she pulled the car up, she was coming in, gun in hand. And she planned on keeping the weapon, too, and had no qualms about using it. God help anyone who kept her from her daughter. "*Get* Kyra. Don't let *anything* happen to her. Then we're having a nice, long chat."

"Fine. Just *go*."

He released her shoulder. She brought her hand up, thought about ramming the keys into his throat. But something in his manner, his resolve changed her mind.

"*Go*."

At the kitchen door, she stopped. "You bring Kyra to me. Get her. I mean it. If you don't … I'll get *you*."

He nodded, looking weary and tired. "I believe you. Take my coat." He tossed it to her.

She locked eyes with him, demanding he understand her intent. She'd make good on her threat and he damn well better believe it. The coat swam on her, slipping off the shoulders. Then she opened the kitchen door and stepped out into the eye of the storm.

※ ※ ※

*Dammit.* Winston should've just taken off. Forget the woman, forget the child. Fight the storm to reach his family. Take them away, far away. Where, exactly, he'd work out later. It seemed unavoidable that he'd have to tell Julie the truth, at least part of it. And that scared him more than angry mobsters.

But he also couldn't leave a six-year-old girl at the mercy of bloodthirsty killers. Domenick's crew didn't care who stumbled into their path. Nothing mattered to them except money and vengeance. And the entire situation was partially his fault. He should've taken care of business upfront, damn the weather. Okay, maybe not his fault, but he had to share a little culpability.

He thought Rebecca would never leave, another obstacle he'd have to clean up. Frankly, it surprised him she did. But he knew his wife would respond the same way given the circumstances; hell, he would, too.

Winston opened the kitchen door a crack and listened. The front door squeaked, then banged back against the wall. He saw Christian stomping in backward, dragging snow along with him. Not to mention Calvin's body. Once the host cleared the door, he dropped Calvin's arms with twin *flumps*. He rubbed his chin, considering the corpse at his feet. With casual precision, Christian rolled Calvin into the Persian rug, a pig in a blanket for the murderous palate. All the while humming, just another mundane aspect of his job.

*Jesus. What the hell's going on here?*

Clearly, this went beyond Christian's usual fastidious fussiness, not just a matter of avoiding blood spilling onto the pristine hardwood floors. A murder cover-up, plain as day, no self-defense involved. What chilled Winston even more was how the host appeared to be enjoying his work.

Christian dragged the body out of Winston's line of sight, back toward the stairwell. Right where he needed to go to save Kyra. He waited. The soft sound of the body swishing across the floor receded. A door opened, then gently closed. Then he heard nothing.

❊ ❊ ❊

Harold's heart threatened to explode, a warning from his body to take better care of it. From beneath the stairwell, cloaked in shadows, he watched as the gay host escorted Domenick's nephew outside by the throat.

*They found me. Good God, they found me!*

As he rushed back down the hallway, he rattled each doorknob, all of them unmoving. The final door, the woman's room, opened. When he jumped inside, a lamp popped on, sending his heart into overdrive. The rugrat sat up, blinking at him like Santa'd just entered her damn dreams.

"You're not supposed to be here."

"Shut up, little girl." He forced a harsh whisper, not an easy thing to do without volume. He searched the room, spilling cosmetics off the dresser. Yet he had no idea what he hoped to find. A solution to his problem, a way to stay alive. All the money he carried hardly mattered. Then he reconsidered. Hell, yes, it mattered.

"I'm telling Mommy." The girl's threat rang hollow. She appeared indifferent at best. "What're you lookin' for?"

Gunfire ripped in the distance. Three shots, a commonplace happening in Domenick's world. Not so much Harold's, and he preferred to keep it that way.

"What was *that?*" Now fully awake, she bounced off the bed.

"Shut *up.*" Jealousy struck him as he looked inside the bathroom, an amenity not afforded him; always destined, it seemed, to be traveling second class. He saw nothing of use, although a pair of the woman's underwear momentarily distracted him. But he had to focus. He turned to the girl and said, "Gunfire," hoping to shock her into silence.

Still no emotion. Obviously, another kid weaned on the teat of TV, murder reduced to entertainment in their boob-tube world.

Then her eyes widened. "Really?" She scuttled toward the door, the back ends of her slippers slapping at the floor. Her grubby little paw reached for the knob.

"*No!* Stop, *dammit!*" He raced across the room and wrenched her hand away.

"Ow! That hurt!" She shook her hand, exaggerating it the way kids do. "And you shouldn't *cuss!*"

Exasperated, he deliberated who he'd rather try his luck with, the kid or the mobsters. The kid inched ahead, just by a runny nose. "And you know what *you* should do? If you know what's good for you? Go lay down in the tub. Wait there. And shut up."

"Don't wanna. You can't tell me what to do."

"Little girl, there're men out there with guns. Shooting them. You know what a gun can do? Tear your body apart. Rip your arm off and —"

*Shit.* Tears. Something Harold felt vastly inadequate to deal with. With a deep breath, he tried to bring his anxiety down a notch. "Look, that won't happen if you just go lay in the tub, okay?" He'd try it her way, folding her reality into the situation. "It works in the movies. You'll be safe there." *And blessedly quiet.*

"No. I'm not gonna get in the tub. I already had a bath. Only Mommy can —"

"*Fine*. Have it your way. Just please shut the *hell* up."

This, of course, unleashed more tears. Worse than a baby, all he needed. "Sorry, sorry, shit, sorry ..." Everything he said just poured gas on her fire, the brat's tantrum rising. Maybe he better leave before her bawling gave up his location. On the other hand, he could hide out here. Domenick would probably just check his room upstairs, not look down here. He fiddled with the knob, searching for a lock. Nothing.

The kid settled down long enough to string together a few coherent words. "Where *is* my mommy?"

Harold sat on the bed and mopped sweat from his forehead. "I dunno, little girl. I'm sure she's all right. But outside here?" He gestured toward the door. "There're evil guys. With guns. Wanting to kill us. So you've gotta be quiet. 'Cause that's the only way out of this hell house. And I —"

"It's not the only way out."

"Say that again?"

She stood in front of him, now more angelic than a Christmas tree topper. "I know a secret way."

He didn't believe her. Kid games and all that crap. Still, desperation loosens ears sometimes, wishful thinking abides. "Show me."

"Only if you help me find Mommy."

*Great*. A deal with the devil. Of course, he knew contracts were made to be broken. "Fine. Where's this other way out?" He used finger quotes, the sarcastic nature lost on the kid.

"You promise?"

"Yeah, fine, promise, pinky swear, all that."

Her little face scrunched up as she studied him, a miniature gargoyle. Finally, she must've deemed him worthy. She hurried across the room, her long gown billowing behind her. An open expanse of wall sat next to the bathroom, no hangings, no furniture in front of it. Which struck Harold odd, as cute crap overloaded every little nook and cranny in the damn house. The girl felt the wall, running her fingers along it. When she gave the wall a solid fist *thunk*, a hidden door popped open. *Unbelievable*. He never would've seen it. The paisley wallpaper had been perfectly plastered over it, no seams visible.

Harold wasted no time. He poked his head inside and grimaced. Webs hung down, draping like broken chandeliers. The passageway looked narrow, barely enough room for a slender man to clear. Planks of rotted wood lay across the floor, green and moldy bracing at the top, none of it too sturdy looking. And dark, so dark he couldn't see but a foot down the length. A servant's entrance, a leftover from the days of slaves condemned to less-than-human accommodations. The way he felt most of the time; a fitting escape tunnel to his new life.

He reached inside. To the right, his fingers thumped against a wall. On the left side, he wagged his arm about, feeling a cold breeze.

"Where's it go, little girl?"

"Not sure. Haven't explored it all yet. But I know one door comes out by Christian's desk."

That didn't suit Harold's needs, not one bit. If at all possible, he wanted to avoid everyone at this point. He certainly didn't need to end up back in the center of the action. He needed to find a way out of the house. Should be easy enough; just follow the draft. The servants probably had their own outside entrance. *Somewhere.* "Got a flashlight, little girl?"

"No! Why would I have a flashlight?"

*Yeah, stupid question*, Harold thought. Back when he was a kid, flashlights were considered fun. Whatever. Darkness bothered him; another less-than-fond memory from his childhood. He'd have to make do with the light from his phone. Not ideal, but it offered something at least. He just had to remember paradise waited at the end of the dark tunnel. A light, sunny paradise with days so long, nights seemed like God's afterthought.

"Okay, gotta go."

He ducked, sticking one leg inside, the briefcase banging against the wall. Little fingers clutched his arm. "Wait! You promised me you'd find Mommy!"

"Might be dangerous for you, little girl. Just go lie down in the tub, best place for you." Then she coiled her hands into fists, tightening up like a flexing bodybuilder. Ready to blast off a scream. *Good God.* "*Fine.* Whatever, little girl, just ... be *quiet.*"

Quite the actress, she immediately changed face. "Okay. But I'm *not* a *little* girl. My name's *Kyra.*"

Harold groaned. Everything the girl did amped up the drama. Just like his ex-wife, Barb. They start training 'em earlier and earlier. "What did I say about shutting *up*?"

With an excited grin, she twisted an imaginary lock on her lips and pitched the key. Too bad it wouldn't take for good. It might not all be a loss, though. He'd use her as a scout, find their path through the darkness. Hell, she knew the passageway already. If they stumbled onto her mom, fine. But he wouldn't go out of his way to look for her. To his car and gone, his immediate goal, done in one. His mother always told him he needed to set goals in life. Too bad she spent so much time acting as a goalie by blocking his progress.

Harold considered what to do with the girl once they reached the safety of outside. Maybe he'd drop her off with a neighbors or something. But in the meantime, he needed her.

"Fine, Kyra-sabee, you act as my guide." Clearly, she didn't understand his reference. What *did* these kids know these days? "You're leading." Which seemed to suit her just fine. In less than a minute, she slipped into her coat.

With Kyra in the lead, Harold popped his cell phone on, using the meager light to navigate the dark path.

# Chapter Seven

Well, hell, on a night like this, Deputy Randy Gurley didn't want to venture out. Colder than a nunnery and whiter than his hind end, the storm looked even worse than it did last night. The sheriff's office felt nice and cozy. His feet were quite comfortable kicked up on the desk, a space heater warming his back. Truth be told, he wasn't exactly patrolling last night when he stumbled across the Stansfield woman. He'd been on his way home, playing hooky more or less. With the sheriff out of town and even crime taking a break during the storm, it seemed pointless to patrol.

But he couldn't ignore a damsel in distress. Particularly a hottie like Rebecca.

As he nibbled a pencil, he thought about her. Hadn't given her much consideration earlier because he knew he'd never see her again. But there'd been a moment where he had second thoughts, nearly asking her to come to his place. He thought she just might, too; he could be pretty irresistible at times. But it wouldn't have been very professional of him, not at all. If a man doesn't take his livelihood seriously, then he's not a man worthy of respect.

Of course, Rebecca's husband showing up changed everything. Nosing around like a bloodhound, looking for his wife. Tempestuous fella, too. Rebecca didn't need to tell him about her husband; between the clues she let slip and the way the guy acted on the phone, Gurley immediately had his number. Wife beater. *Very* uncool. Gurley half-way hoped he'd succeeded in taunting the asshole into coming down to the station. Lock him up in the drunk tank for a while. Let him cool down. But, nope, sounded like he didn't plan on giving up.

A wrench in the works. Soon enough, things at the Dandy Drop Inn might go belly up. Course it also meant he might get to spend a little more time with Rebecca.

While he hated leaving the office's warmth, body heat sounded mighty nice as well. He launched the pencil up. The sharp point lodged into the dropped ceiling with a thump. White particles floated down. Deputy Gurley couldn't escape the snow, indoors or outdoors.

He took a few more minutes, enough time to finish a rancid cup of coffee, then he swept his boots to the floor, donned his hat, tipped it until it felt just right, and left for the inn.

❊ ❊ ❊

*Jesus Christ and what a night*, Brad thought.

He couldn't believe what he saw, couldn't be absolutely certain either. He'd give his right nut now for a pair of night-vision goggles. Parked a half-block away, the relentless snow made things hard to see. The moon and stars had packed up as well, so he couldn't trust his eyes, not entirely. What he thought he saw, though? A huge guy breaking the neck of the rifle-carrying guy. No doubt about the rifle; he'd heard the shots, watched three flashes. Then the shorter guy, the dapper one from the Humvee, took a shovel to the head.

The night's events gave him a toasty holiday feeling, one of sheer joy and anticipation. Not so much for Rebecca, of course. But a plan bubbled in his mind, a real beaut. Obviously, there's some bad shit going on at the Dandy Drop Inn. Why not use it to his advantage? He'd witnessed, what, two deaths? Why not add Rebecca to the pile up? Kyra, too. They both deserved it. And he'd just been handed a get-out-of-jail-free card.

Honestly, when he set off earlier, he didn't *think* he planned on killing them. Just teach 'em a lesson or two, one they wouldn't forget. At least that's how hindsight saw it. But that was beside the point. Once he saw his so-called "wife" with the other bastard, that's when it clicked. As sure as a gun hammer clicks when pulled back. He just hadn't been sure how to pull the trigger at the time. Now he'd been handed a golden opportunity, one he'd be foolish to ignore. It's like God or whatever handed him the murder weapon and was telling him,

"Go ahead, Brad. Bitch deserves it."

Even better? How 'bout he swoops in, takes the bad guys out, too? Might get a commendation. Press would be all over it, too. *Grieving Hero Brings Wife's Murderers to Justice.* Absolutely beautiful in its irony.

And he couldn't believe how his night just kept improving. A figure struggled his way, attempting to run through the snow with a sideways kicking gesture. But he recognized the way those hips moved, snowstorm or not. *Rebecca.* And she had the gall to wear her lover's coat, way too big for her, clenched beneath her chin with whorish hands.

Yes, sir, things were looking up.

She didn't even look his way when she passed, her gaze glued to her path. He gave it a few minutes, then quietly slipped out of the car, his gun leading him to his prey.

❄ ❄ ❄

The minute Rebecca stepped outside, she wanted to turn right around. To hell with what Dave had said, she needed to save Kyra. From whom she had no clue; only her daughter's safety mattered. Reason overruled her mother's instinct, though. With a gun and a car, they could get away. But trudging through the snow felt like wading through cement, a nightmare where she couldn't will her legs to move fast enough.

*Hold on, baby, Mommy's coming for you.*

Behind her, she heard a vehicle crunching over the snow. A Humvee slowly pulled away from the inn, the red taillights blinking in the falling snow. The men with the guns? Again, she thought about going back in. Especially if they'd left. But she knew, absolutely so, she'd better not go back in unprotected.

And she meant what she'd said about having a talk with Dave. Obviously, he'd been withholding the truth from her. He appeared to know these gun-wielding men, hardly the company an insurance salesman keeps.

She unburied a leg, stepped high, and plunged it down again. Rinse, wash, repeat. Getting nowhere. Her anxiety booted into the stratosphere.

The snow overlaying the land acted as a sonic amplifier, every sound intensified, every frozen branch cracking like knuckles. She listened, half-expecting a scream from Kyra, more gunfire. Wind blew snow into her face, slipping down inside the loose-fitting coat. By necessity, she kept her head down, watching her feet. She alternated hands, keeping one in the pocket, one holding the coat closed. Even though she knew she hadn't yet traveled a block-and-a-half, she pressed the key fob often, pointing it at random cars. More like misshapen snowmen, mounds of snow covering every inch of the automobiles. Why the hell did Dave park so far away anyway? She saw plenty of open parking spots closer to the inn. He had a lot to answer for.

Snow soaked through her jeans legs, cold and chafing. She took to the street, hoping plows had cleared a path. No such luck. A recent tire rut — possibly from the Humvee — provided a faster, albeit narrow, passageway. She picked up speed, constantly clicking the fob.

A muffled horn bleated. She pressed the fob again. Several cars down, a hint of light powered through the snow. *Victory.*

Once she reached the car, she swept snow from the headlights, then cleared an opening over the windshield. Snow drifts leaned up against the car. She kicked some of it away, hoping the car could power through the remains of the miniature wall. Her hand found the handle. She groaned when it didn't open. Using her hip, she bumped into the door, loosening it. Every little thing seemed to detain her, every detail of her short trip agonizing. As she struggled with the door, awful scenarios of Kyra's fate ran scattershot through her mind, bleak and violent images.

The door wrenched open. Elated, she slid in. The car sputtered at first, dwindling along with her hope. She closed her eyes, tossed off a speed prayer, and twisted the key again. The engine turned over. Cold air roared out of the heater. She rolled down the window, scraping away snow. A dusting blew in, alighting on her face. Her teeth chattered like maracas. Quickly she rolled the window back up.

She dropped the gear into first and prepared to gun out.

The window next to her shattered. Glass shards showered her. Instinctively, she hunkered down, shoulders bunched to her ears.

"Hey, baby, miss me?"

Her pulse tripled, her heart leaping a beat. A scream lodged in her chest. Hunched over like an ape, Brad stood outside, a tire iron in one hand, a gun in the other. Smiling ear to ear.

Rebecca cranked the steering wheel, stepped on the gas. Quick as a jack rabbit, Brad snaked an arm in, knocking her back. He snagged the keys from the ignition and hurled them. The keys turned in the air, a weak lamp catching the silver. They dropped silently into the snow.

"Leave us the *hell* alone, *Brad*!" She slid across the seat, knowing she couldn't overpower him. Her knees bumped into the glovebox. The cover slipped down, exposing Dave's gun.

Brad leaned back in, his gun aimed at her chest. "Don't think so, bitch." His words sounded calm, more restrained than usual. Yet the fury in his eyes she'd seen before. Just not at this level. "I'm gonna make you pay for what you did. I'm —"

"What the *hell* did I *ever* do to *you*?"

"You know what you did, bitch. Don't lie. Too late for lies. When I'm done with you, I'm gonna get that bitch of a daughter of yours and —"

The threat against Kyra ramrodded her into action. She yanked the gun out, pulled back the hammer. The gun training Brad had subjected her to — back in the early, "good" days — was about to pay off. In buckets of blood.

She didn't hesitate to pull the trigger. Neither did Brad.

Two shots disturbed the snow-silenced night.

❄ ❄ ❄

Before Winston left the kitchen, he found a knife, long-bladed and dull. Perfect for chopping vegetables, maybe, but hardly a worthy defense against guns. Better than nothing.

Years of practice taught him how to move. Using fast, quiet strides, he stopped at the stairwell and looked around the corner. The door behind Christian's counter stood ajar, orange light trickling out. A constant drumbeat accompanied Christian's diminishing humming. *Thump, thump, thump.* No, not a drum beat. Calvin's body dragged down wooden stairs.

Once Winston rounded the stairwell, he raced down the corridor. He slipped the knife into his belt.

The door opened, unlocked. "Kyra?" he whispered. No answer. A bedside lamp lit the unoccupied room. Blankets twisted in a white pretzel on the bed. He crossed to the bathroom, gave the door a knock and peered inside.

*Shit. Where is she?*

He sat on the bed, shut everything out, and concentrated.

Christian was accounted for, tending to Calvin's remains. Domenick couldn't be far away, but remained unseen and unheard. Which left the Dandys and Carsten. The silence sent a chill down his back. With everything going on tonight, the inn should've been alive with chaos.

He stared at the wall next to the bathroom, his eyes blurring at the paisley patterned wallpaper. But something seemed off. A trick of the light perhaps, yet the pattern seemed to move, angled at a slight distortion.

As he approached, his toe kicked into the wall, closer than it looked. A hidden door, wide enough for an ironing board and not much else. The door swung open on silent hinges. Obviously an old servant's hallway, and by the looks of it, not used in years. Kyra had entered the passageway, irresistible to a child. Maybe the safest place for her. Unless she bumped into Christian.

His cell phone's battery long dead, he plucked out his lighter; it, too, was on its last legs. Hesitantly, he closed the door behind him. No sense leaving a trail. With the knife in one hand held out in front of him, the lighter in the other, he entered the darkness.

✳ ✳ ✳

Chains jangled at Heather's back. Her hands strained in the metal cuffs, her arm muscles reaching their limit. Hooked to the wall, the chains unbreakable, no escape. But Heather wouldn't let it break her spirit. Lord knows the sinners had been trying to break her, a true test of her belief.

After the homosexual had carried her outside into the snow and down through a cellar door, he dropped her in the dank basement. She felt like the devil himself had carried her to hell. While he'd shackled her, she lunged at him, teeth bared. The chains snapped her back against the wall. She managed to spit on him, though, just a taste of what she had planned. Frankly, it surprised her he didn't retaliate. But he stood alert, head cocked like a dog, as if hearing something. He disappeared through a door, faster than she thought he could move.

She sat on her haunches, not wanting to dirty her dress. Her thigh muscles ached, a good ache, a martyred pain. The key to her freedom hung on the stone wall ten feet in front of her. Literally. That's where the gay had hung the key. So close, yet so far. Just like her unfinished work here in the House of Satan.

Goose pimples rolled across her arms. It was dark, so very dark, and cold. No lamps, no overhead lights. But a splintered door stood at the opposite end of the cellar. Green light rimmed the door's outline, unhealthy and hellish; it looked ready to drop at a hearty knock. The same door the Dandys had entered a little while ago. The old man had carried another man in his arms, just like Tommy had carried her over the carriage house's threshold. A constant thrumming drowned out their hateful voices. A pulsing sensation moved the earth below her feet.

*Tum … tum …* A generator's heartbeat? Or the devil coming to collect his due from the bowels of Hell?

The green light didn't illuminate much, told nothing about her prison. Her chains bound her two feet to the wall, that much was obvious. But just because she couldn't make out anything in the darkness, didn't mean Heather couldn't *see.*

She saw plenty. Broken souls dissipating, flitting away like bats in a suddenly lit barn. Souls searching for a way out, trapped in an eternity of limbo, suffering. Suffering like her. For the first time, she heard them, too. Anguished howls, mournful moans, disembodied pleas for deliverance. The basement had been a charnel house, a killing room. Yet unlike her good work, the Dandys doomed these souls to an everlasting afterlife of nothing. *Sinners.* And she'd make them pay, yes she would.

She swiped her hand in the dirt, expecting to feel rough granules sift between her fingers. Instead, she pulled away mud. She pinched a bit, held it in front of her, straining to see the color. But she didn't need to. She knew it was blood.

More blood would be spilled tonight. Just not hers.

With a growl, she threw her weight forward, the chains again yanking her back. Her chin bit the ground. Her beautiful hair splayed out on the dirt, angel wings attempting to fly. She screamed, not because she feared for her life. Rather, to unleash her anger.

When she heard voices coming her way, she silenced. And prayed.

❅ ❅ ❅

Harold kept three fingers lightly perched on Kyra's shoulder, afraid to touch her too much (one can never be too cautious in today's litigious society), yet just enough to maintain his lifeline through the dark corridor. As they scooted down the narrow hall, the brat wouldn't let up on her running commentary. Every time Harold shushed her, admonishing her to use an inside voice. She complied at first, but one minute later would raise her voice to the rafters again.

"This door goes into Christian's room. Then out to his desk. That's where I went last time." She placed a hand against the wall to the left, a welcome scrap of light living beneath an unseen door. A passageway, no doubt, leading right to Domenick.

"Yeah, no, we're not going out there. And *please* be quiet."

He'd had about enough of the girl. But like a rat in a maze, he was stuck for now. The walls closed in, suffocating in the worst kind of sense, the air still and musty. It concerned him he no longer felt the draft. There had to be a way outside, just had to. Slave owners didn't want the hired help tramping through their mansion.

He presumed the corridor led across the complete backside of the huge inn. But it felt twice as long, tepidly stepping toe to toe through the blackness. Occasionally his hand slipped onto web-covered glass, windows presumably shuttered on the outside, capturing them inside and keeping any light from entering.

"Keep going." With a little shove, he redirected the brat along their straight path. She seemed unfazed by the blind maze, enjoying it almost. A web entrapped Harold's face, tight and sticky. With a yelp, he clawed at it. Something crawled over his scalp, small legs skittering at a clip. "Get it off, get it off!" He bent, offering his head toward the girl.

"There's nothing there," she said with a giggle. Her clammy hands patted down his dome. His comb over unraveled, a long strand falling beside his cheek.

"Let's just get out of here." Embarrassed, Harold straightened. He tossed back his shoulders, attempting to man up. *Just keep remembering the pot of gold at the end of the rainbow.* He gave the briefcase a shake for extra reinforcement.

"Where do you think my mommy is?" Again, she said it too loudly.

"Probably looking for you, little girl." He knew she hated being called "little girl." Too bad. His sadistic side enjoyed the small pleasure. Call it punishment for her bratty behavior.

Harold shuffled through the darkness, too afraid to lift a foot. His shoes slid across the dirt-covered planks, every squeak threatening to drop him through the boards. Sweat slipped down his spine, his temples, his thighs. Then cool air enveloped him like someone had just tossed open a window. But something stank, bitter and full of decay. Harold lurched, his gag reflex drawing in his stomach.

"What's that smell?" When the girl pinched her nose, her voice raised higher.

"Shhh!" Harold followed the draft. His foot tapped into something hollow sounding, a throaty *chunk*. Startled, he fell back, flailing his arms for balance. He dug a toe in, ensuring solid footing. His phone went back up. The light flashed on rising wooden steps, even narrower than the passage. Another very thin passageway ran alongside it. He lowered his head and leaned in. More stairs going down, directly beneath the ascending steps.

Clearly excited, the girl hopped up and down. Harold wondered how thrilled she'd be if she knew a happily-ever-after wasn't guaranteed. "Stairwells," she exclaimed. "We shouldn't go up. That's what people in scary movies do."

While Harold hadn't seen a "scary movie" in years, he had to admit the girl had a point. And their way out of this nightmare certainly wouldn't be upstairs. "Fine. Lead the way."

On the top step, he pinched her shoulder. "Slow *down*. We don't want to fall." *We*, of course, meaning Harold. "One step at a time."

Splintered and rough, the handrail vanished after a foot. Harold teetered, his hand flattening against the stone wall to the left. Something adhered to his fingers. Afraid to look at it, he wiped his hand against his slacks. The gummy substance remained, worse than if he'd stuck his fingers into a honey pot.

As they descended, the phone's light played with their shadows, bobbing and dipping like cartoons. The darkness surrendered into a color beyond black. When Kyra stopped at the foot of the stairs, Harold bumped into her. Now the draft drew rushing air by them, a constant stream. He stepped onto blessed solid dirt, no unsteady planks to walk, the space opening up. Only one way to go, down another long hallway. But this one appeared wider, even scarier than the tight confines of the servant's corridor. The dim light couldn't hold the width of the underground tunnel. Anything could be lurking at the sides. Harold gulped, fears sneaking up behind, crushing from the sides.

He reclaimed the girl's shoulder and said, "Okay, let's go faster."

The girl nodded, her eyes sunken into darkness. As if she owned the damn place, she marched along the corridor. Harold struggled to keep up. The cold draft increased, an active breeze, the rancid smell riding it.

The phone's light weakened. Within a small radius, Harold could see only mold-layered walls, dirt at his feet. It felt like miles, although he knew it couldn't be. He noticed other footprints, scattered heel indentations as if someone had hopped through the corridor. A troubling thought. Surely Domenick wouldn't come down here, not with his germ phobia. The airflow slowed, but a sound grew. Humming machinery.

Kyra stopped. "It's a door." Stating the obvious, something the girl excelled at. Harold held the phone high, examining the entryway. Rust coated the doorknob. Green mold — possibly black, but everything looked green beneath the phone's emerald ray — crept up the door like vines. Something else stained the door, small droplets spattered from the center blob. Harold didn't want to think about it.

"Whaddaya waiting for, little girl? Go on in."

The only possible way out. Suddenly the exit by the host's room appealed more.

The door opened at the girl's touch, surprisingly silent given its condition. Chains rankled. Harold jumped, expecting a leaping dog to rip out his throat. Kyra backed into him, one hand snatching his pant leg. At the end of the room, green light blurred. Together they shambled forward, a slow three-legged race.

A whisper nearly burst open Harold's heart.

"Who's *there*? *Please ... help* me."

With the phone shaking in his grasp, Harold inched toward the voice. The phone's beam fell on the mousy blonde he'd met that morning. Chained to the wall, looking like she'd seen better days. At first, Harold thought he'd stumbled upon the post swinger's party, an S&M jamboree. Something that didn't appeal to him at all. Why mix pain with pleasure?

"Get me *out* of here. Oh, thank God, praise him ..."

As they crept closer, Harold changed his mind. Definitely not a sex party. Shadows peeled back from the girl's face, revealing eyes like a cat's, jade colored and reflecting fear. And like a cat, her back hunched up as she hissed through clenched teeth. "Let me go *now*. The *key's* over there. You've *got* to ..."

Kyra, still afraid and clinging tightly to the back of Harold's shirt (something he oddly didn't mind; almost a little comforting), hesitantly approached the woman. With one hand on her knee, she bent over, staying well outside of the girl's range. "What're you doing down here?"

The woman jumped, her arms swinging toward Kyra. The chains jerked her back. She landed on her feet, stumbling like a drunk. "Shut *up*. They're in the next *room*." She rattled a chain toward the green light. "Just get me *out* of here."

Harold felt Kyra looking up at him, searching for answers. The only certainty Harold knew was he had to get the hell out of here. *Now*. Talk about out of the frying pan and into the fire. He didn't consider the implications, had no idea who'd chained the woman, didn't know who "they" in the green room were. Didn't care, either, thank you very much. Survival came first. And the Caribbean.

He hurried through the cellar, sweeping his phone along the walls. Beside the woman, he stumbled upon another door. If his generally unerring sense of direction hadn't failed him, it was the most likely way outside. The back of the inn, southern facing. The woman threw herself after him, the chains again choking her back. She just didn't learn. With his palms placed on the door, he felt wonderfully frigid temperatures.

"*No*! Don't *go*! *Please*! Don't *leave* me here! Don't ..." A wave of sobs rolled over her, obliterating her words into mush.

Harold debated with his conscience, something he hadn't done in years. "Sorry ..." He thought about saying more, perhaps telling her he'd call the police. Nope, no police involvement. His conscience, having atrophied after so many years of nonuse, lapsed back into a coma. Harold twisted the knob, icy in his hand.

"Mister, we can't leave her here! She might die!"

Why'd the damn brat have to say something? He'd almost made it out the door, his conscience clear. But the brat, the damned whiny, insufferable brat. Obviously, the woman's crying got to Kyra, something she knew a lot about. Sisterhood in tears. Yet, he hated to admit it; something about the little girl affected him. Downright embarrassing. *Dammit*. He didn't need an entourage. A loner all his life by choice (maybe a little by necessity, if he was absolutely honest), he didn't see things changing anytime soon. *Whatever, set the woman free, get the kid outside, then adios, it's been real.*

Harold's shoulders sagged, the briefcase weighing more than it should. "Fine, get the key, little girl. And free her. Make it *fast*. And be *quiet*."

The little girl scurried across the room. Harold attempted to provide her a pinch of light. On tiptoes, she stretched up against the wall, reaching for a ring of keys on a hook. Unable to snare them, she looked around. With an annoying "a-ha" face, she raced toward a workbench and picked up what looked like a stick. After several jumps, the stick loosened the keys. They hit the dirt with a jangle, much too loud for Harold's taste. He flicked a nervous look toward the green door.

Kyra's enthusiasm fizzled once she approached the captive blonde. She looked nervous, a wary child feeding an animal.

"*Please*! Just unlock me … please …"

Kyra knelt. Key after key slipped into the lock until a loud click jolted Kyra back onto her bottom. The blonde dropped one of the cuffs, then snagged the keys to free her other hand.

Despite his brief lapse into humanity, Harold had kept one hand on the door knob, ready to make a fast getaway. He'd done his good deed. From here on out, every man for himself.

He couldn't hear the clock upstairs ticking, not really, but in his mind, it ticked off every wasted second detaining him from his early retirement. Pounding and echoing like the gunfire he'd heard earlier.

But the footfalls of someone racing down the corridor sounded all too real.

❄ ❄ ❄

Brad lay in the middle of the street, unmoving, arms and legs out like a dead snow angel.

*I shot him.*

Splotches of his blood spoiled the snow's white blanket.

*I shot my husband. I killed him.*

Rebecca had pulled the trigger first. Terror had filled Brad's eyes, something she'd never seen from him before. As he fell back, his gun fired into the sky, a rocket declaring Rebecca's independence.

*Blew him away. He's dead. At my hand.*

Rebecca left the car. Her coat fell open. Stunned, the freezing conditions didn't bother her. In fact, she felt downright warm. It didn't bother her she took her husband's life. Quite the contrary; it felt good. He deserved it. Especially when he'd made it clear he meant to kill her and Kyra. Self-defense. The shock came in acknowledging her night-mare had ended. Finally, forever, once and for all. Truly Independence

Day.

While she stood over his body, she remembered everything he'd done to her. The memories scorched like burning lava. Tears dropped down her cheeks, freezing like her feelings. The tears weren't meant for Brad, but rather Kyra and herself.

But her other nightmare, the new one, awakened her.

*Kyra.*

She could look for the car keys, but it'd be a colossal waste of time in the snow. No telling where the bastard pitched them. And she had no desire to pat down Brad's pockets for his keys, the thought turning her stomach.

Down the street, the mansion loomed, its dark windows hiding whatever was going on inside.

With gun in hand — fitting quite comfortably, too — she hurried down the street toward the Dandy Drop Inn.

❉ ❉ ❉

Winston stumbled through the dark, feeling his way by hands and tenuous footsteps. Occasionally he fired up his lighter until the flame dipped and lapped at his finger. Hardly enough light to navigate, even an inch at a time. He passed a door that he presumed led into the house. Doubtful Kyra went through there. Particularly if she'd heard the gunfire. And he imagined he would've heard the commotion if something had happened. The walls appeared as thin as paper.

A stairwell nearly pitched him forward. His hand caught on the railing. Upstairs or down? Voices from below answered his question, so frantically strained they may as well've been yelling. And he thought he heard Kyra's high-pitched voice.

At the bottom of the stairs, he stopped, honing in on the hushed echoes of the conversation. A cavernous tunnel led to a door, the source of the voices. Never go through a closed door without listening first. Winston counted three voices. Chains shook and dropped.

After extinguishing the lighter, an afterimage of the flame flickered before it, too, snuffed out. He opened the door and stepped into a cool room. Wider than the corridor based on the airflow. He opened his mouth so as not to breathe in the terrible stench.

"Kyra?" His whisper sounded lonely, empty in the large, quiet room. Except for the voices mumbling behind a jade-struck door. Footsteps tramped toward him, light footed with a short stride. *Kyra.*

He flicked the lighter on. A white face darted toward him, contorted with fury. The blonde's savage eyes fixed on Winston, her teeth exposed like a dog's. Filthy hair snapped like whips as she jumped. Fingers clawed his face. Startled, he dropped the knife. Winston caught her hair and pulled. She stumbled outside the small circle of light. Her growl rose from the shadows. Something tugged at his arm. Winston turned fast, the lighter blowing out.

"*Stop*, Dave," Kyra whispered. "We need to *help* her." After several flicks, the lighter held. Kyra closed her eyes at the sudden light. Winston switched it back toward the woman. She had closed in, cowering, hands covering her face. Across the room, he saw an open door, meager light trickling in.

Winston tried to piece together the situation, but now wasn't the time. The voices behind the closed door rose, not in a friendly way. A pulsating sound, something he couldn't place, drowned out their words. "Kyra, we need to get you out of here. Now. Your mommy's looking for you." He gestured toward the open door. "That the way out?"

"The funny man went out that way. When he heard you."

No doubt who the funny man was. More reason to hurry. Perhaps Winston could still salvage his family's life if he collared Carsten and retrieved the cash. "What about her?" He jutted his chin toward the strange woman. "You know her?"

"Someone trapped her." Kyra's explanation made no sense, not that it mattered. But the woman bothered him, an itch he couldn't quite scratch. Only wild, cornered animals attacked like she had. When he turned the lighter back her way, she no longer appeared afraid. Her fists bunched, her shoulders up, ready for battle. Winston didn't need another enemy. "You follow us," said Winston. "Once outside, get into your car and leave. Don't stop until you're in the next town."

"I don't have my *keys*." Saliva flew from her lips.

"Fine. Go to a neighbor's house. But don't stay here." He hustled Kyra toward the door. As an afterthought, he added, "Count to thirty before you leave." Having someone trail you is always unsettling; having someone who's clearly insane behind you is plain suicidal.

Winston snatched Kyra up in one arm and peered through the door. A crack of light brightened the top of the stairs. Bitter coldness swept past him. Fresh snow dusted the upper steps. At the top, he pushed open a storm door. Snow swirled, a needed slap in the face after the cellar's stale air. The blizzard raged on.

He hefted up Kyra, who somersaulted into the snow. She scrambled to her feet, withdrawing into her heavy coat. Before he could climb off the top step, someone beat him to it. An arm wrapped around his neck, a hand snatching the back of his shirt. Kyra screamed while Winston flew toward a snow drift.

✱ ✱ ✱

Domenick was sleeping, a cold, uncomfortable slumber. Still, it was sleep, something he hesitated to give up. Dampness chilled his leg as if he'd wet himself. In his half-lucid state, the thought horrified him. Wearing his own waste, all sorts of germs onboard. He chipped away at the walls of consciousness, compelling body over mind. With startling clarity, the memory of the old man knocking him out rushed him into the here and now.

His eyes opened briefly, then the shades lowered again. Shudders coursed through him, his pants undeniably wet. He lay on something soft, his cheek pressed against something bristly. This time he forced his eyes open. He wished he hadn't.

Calvin lay beneath him, eyes open and milky. Dead, rotting with germs. Cheek to cheek with his nephew's body. And Calvin stank, the odor of death in his flesh. Revolted, Domenick imagined bacteria swarming off his nephew's body, infiltrating his organs. He threw himself back, his rear slamming down onto Calvin's legs. His feet scrabbled, slipped, then achieved a foothold. He backed into a wall. A cool, yielding wall that crumbled behind him. Dirt clumps fell upon him. He gagged, forced his mouth shut, afraid of throwing up on himself.

Several feet above, a rectangle of green light pulsated, high then low, strong then unhealthy. Something hummed, the earth singing around him. On his knees, he clawed the walls, his fingernails collecting dirt. Trying to climb. He split a worm in half, its body oozing and vile. Releasing toxins. More dirt slid down onto his head, his shoulders, into his mouth. He spat, did it again, stabbing his tongue out repeatedly hoping to cleanse his mouth. He was in a grave, something he never expected to see from this perspective.

The old man's head poked over the top. Emerald light cast shadows over his eyes, a geriatric grim reaper. His smile revealed a cob's worth of yellowed teeth. "Mother, he's awake."

"Get me ... the *hell* outta here!"

Like a gopher, an old lady's head popped into view. "Won't be awake for long, I reckon."

"What ... get me the *fuck* outta here! *Now*, goddammit!" Enraged, Domenick climbed to his feet and straddled his nephew. With raised arms, he jumped. The hole was deep, deeper than the traditional six feet he usually ordered. He couldn't reach the top, not like this. Calvin's body added a little more height. He jumped off his chest, thumped down, launched up again. More dirt dribbled into the hole. He paused, regaining his breath. "You don't know who you're fucking *dealing* with!"

"My, such language. It's been some time since we've heard so many eff-bombs." The woman reminded Domenick of his own mother: sugary, plump, flaky skin, a real walking pastry. Except his mother never tried to kill him. Not that he knew, at least.

"Reckon that's right, Mother. Listen up, Mister Domenick..." Immediately, Domenick patted down his pockets for his wallet, his lifeline. Old bastards stole it. "... we don't rightly give two hoots and a holler who you are. Makes no difference to us. But we don't much appreciate folks bringing guns into the Dandy Inn."

"Such nasty business, guns." The woman clicked her tongue, her gray head wagging.

Domenick's pulse banged away in his ears. His stomach threatened to expel his dinner, adding to his misery. The geezers weren't a threat; he could dispose of them in seconds. But he had to get out of the grave to do so. No matter the cost. Away from dirt, germs, bacteria, viruses. His filthy hands shook. He steadied them against his belly. Dirt smeared his shirt, the final indignation. His stomach knotted. Panic rose. Tremors began low, working their way up through his chest, his shoulders. Worst of all, his voice sounded warbly, a goddamn crybaby. "*Please*. Have *mercy* ... get me out of here. I'll give you *anything*. Anything you —"

"Look, mister, all we want to know is why you're here," said the old man.

Domenick clamped up, trying to snatch back the dignity the old bastards stole from him. They wanted information? His way out of the seven-foot grave. "Okay ... I'm, ah, I'm a Fed. Looking for Harold Carsten, wanted criminal. He —"

The old lady swatted a hand over the grave, all smiles, and disbelieving ones at that. "Pshaw. That Mister Carsten? A little peculiar, I'd wager, but he ain't no criminal."

"'Fraid I have to go along with my wife, Mister Domenick. I'd bet my bottom dollar you're lying. Didn't find no badge or F.B.I. identification on you. And that gun you was fixin' to use? I'm no expert, but it looked to me like it was fit with a silencer. Don't think that's jake with the ol' F.B.I."

Domenick realized his mistake. He should've begun with money, something that never failed. "Fine. Okay, whatever, you got me." Although it pained him, Domenick attempted a shamefaced grin. "I'm not a Fed. I'm a businessman. Carsten stole money from me. I just want it back. Now if —"

"Who knows you're here?"

Blood froze in Domenick's veins. Familiar with this line of interrogation, he'd seriously underestimated the old couple. But he knew the proper answer. "Practically everyone." He started ticking off fingers. "My wife, my associates, the police —"

"Pretty much 'spect you're lying again." The old man vanished while the woman shook her head, self-righteous pity on her wrinkled mug. Old or not, Domenick couldn't wait to blow off her face.

"*Wait!* I'm *not* lying! Call my —" A shower of dirt muffled his words. The shovel blade reappeared, flipped over, dumping another load. He sputtered, blowing the filth from his lips. "*Stop!* My *God*, what's *wrong* with you people? You *can't just* —"

"Oh, hush now, Mister Domenick. Ain't a thing wrong with us. Maybe you oughta think about your own issues, shootin' people and what not."

Just like his wife. Always about personal issues. "*Goddammit!* You *can't* bury me! I'll give you money, more money than you'll *ever* see in your *shitty* lives!"

*Tump, scratch* … Another shovelful unloaded.

"My, my, that's certainly no way to ask for mercy." A second shovel head appeared, smaller than the man's. His and Her shovels.

"Jesus Christ! How's one hundred grand sound? I'll give that to you as soon —"

*Flump, ritter, shoosh* …

"We don't want yer money." The old man laughed. "We don't need no money."

"Two hundred grand! How's that? You want more? Three …" Like an auctioneer, Domenick raised his offer. But the dirt kept falling. "Half a million bucks! More money than —"

"I think it's about time for you to shut your piehole, Mister Domenick. Money don't matter none to us."

"You said it, Poppa."

The shovel whisked above, sighing, dirt crying down on him. At the bottom, only Calvin's nose poked through the mounting dirt, a flesh-covered anthill.

Domenick snapped, his mind retreating. Tears unleashed, something he hadn't allowed — *swore* he'd never do again — since childhood. Civilized pleas swam into maudlin soup, bawled out in a voice that couldn't possibly be his. Forgetting his all-too-human phobia, he crouched like an animal, leaping at the walls, claws digging in. "*Don't do this, please, God, don't bury me, don't ...*"

"Poppa, shut him up already!"

"*Sweet Mary, don't bury me alive, please, let ...*"

*Thunk.*

Domenick didn't see the blade end coming this time. Swirling stars lowered him to the ground. He lay on top of his nephew, a bunk deathbed. The green rectangle above twisted, blurred, expanded, then closed in, smaller, smaller. Physically paralyzed, he remained mentally aware. Unable to speak. Impossible to move. But horribly alive. Watching the shower of dirt fall onto him, bit by bit.

"Here ya are, Mister Domenick." The old man pitched Domenick's pistol down. It thumped onto Domenick's chest and bounced next to his arm. "Why don't ya take that with you? We certainly don't have any need for guns."

"That's right, Poppa." *Swoosh, clatter, tsssss ...* "Nasty ol' things, I swan."

Black spots buried his vision. His eyes watered from irritation, turning the specks into running, disgusting mud. He swore he felt a worm slither over his forehead. Dirt fell into his mouth, filling it, packing it. And he watched his burial, unblinking.

"Like I said earlier, Mother, this is truly the best date night we've ever had."

He couldn't see much. Black polka dots connected, filling in the blanks. His open mouth filled, his throat blocked. Only his nostrils sustained him. Until they too were covered. Finally, the green light turned off.

Underground. Buried in dirt along with deadly microbes, invisible microorganisms of death. And still alive.

*Oh, my God, I'm still alive.*

From a distance, he heard the old couple laughing, exchanging hoots and hollers. And from very far away — could be he imagined it — he heard another scream, possibly a child.

Inside his mind, his screams raged the loudest, though.

# Chapter Eight

As soon as the man and the demonic girl left, Heather dropped to her knees. Fingers sifted through the dirt, searching. A prick to her finger released a drop of blood, God's precious life essence. The blade felt corroded and rusty. She'd have to work at it, but it'd do.

*Idiot.* The man had dropped his knife. Big mistake. Ironic, really. She'd use the blade on the man when she caught up, no looking back. Telling her to count to thirty, belittling her like a hide-and-seek playing child. God's work waits for no one. And the first man, the coward, he'd intended on leaving her for dead. Another soul she looked forward to ushering into Hell.

But the girl, she was the worst. Just being in her presence had proven a challenge. Definitely not one of God's children. The girl's whore of a mother had blatantly admitted as much. Said it arrogantly, too, as if she couldn't wait to lie down in Satan's welcoming arms.

If Heather had the knife when the demon spawn released her, she would've carved her soul loose right there. She deserved no better than to swim with the other sinners in the cellar, Hell on Earth. Heather didn't fall for her sweet act, not one bit. Now more than ever, she knew the devil donned sheep's clothing.

She had her work cut out for her. And there'd be a lot of cutting tonight in God's war. When she finished with everyone else, she'd come back for the gay abomination. Then the Dandys. Excitement kissed her like fluttering angel wings.

Heather flew up the stairs, unaffected by the cold. God's spirit kept her warm, His righteous blade her weapon. Then she heard the girl scream.

Perched on the top step, she peeked over the cellar door.

Out in the yard, the queer had his back to her, an easy target. Leaning over someone. Once again, God had delivered. Knife up, she ran ...

\* \* \*

"Run, Kyra!"

Christian jumped on Winston, crushing the air from his lungs. His arm wrapped around Winston's neck, tightening. He pulled Winston's head up by the hair. Winston gasped, his face cold from the snow, Christian's panting breath warm on his neck.

Kyra stood in three feet of snow, screaming. Winston tried to warn her again, but his voice erupted into a cough. He plunged his hands into the snow, digging deep for a rock, a stick, anything. A helluva time to remember he'd dropped the knife in the basement.

Winston jacked his head back, his skull striking Christian's chin. Christian grunted. His hold loosened. Even though Winston's head spiked with pain, he did it again. This host fell back, snow tossing up around him.

"Kyra, *run!*"

She didn't move, possibly didn't hear him. Winston scrabbled for solid ground, pulling himself up on all fours. His skull throbbed. Dizziness lightened his head, but he couldn't give in. He stood, his balance wavering. Bear arms locked around him. He jutted his elbow back, hoping for a lucky punch. But his luck had run out.

A human steamroller, Christian drove him back into the snow. The crook of his arm took Winston's neck, his hand firmly placed on Winston's temple. He intended to break Winston's neck and no doubt had the strength to do it. Winston pulled at his arm, tugged at his hand. His teeth sunk into Christian's hairy forearm. Delaying the inevitable, nothing more. Winston thought of Jules, his daughters. How he'd let them down.

A shrill sound overtook Kyra's screams. A banshee's wail, rising like whistling wind. A sudden impact forced Winston's face back into the snow, cold and suffocating. Christian's arm swept away, and he gasped. Winston raised his head, panting. Then Christian wheezed, a

134

gate swinging on rusty hinges. Warm wetness coated Winston's neck. Christian leaned back, his knees still pinning Winston in the snow. Hard bone pushed into Winston's legs. Winston lifted up on his elbows and craned his head around.

Christian's mouth opened and shut. His hands clamped around his neck. Blood spurted between his fingers, dribbling down onto his shirt. Behind him, a bony white hand raised in the air. Holding Winston's knife. The wild woman's head bobbed and vanished behind Christian's shoulder. Then she stood. Examined the knife. Then thunked it into Christian's back. She smiled, let out a chilling laugh. The words she yelled were incomprehensible. But the rage in them couldn't be denied.

Christian toppled. Snow clouded around his body. Kyra had stopped screaming, shaking in her solitary stance. The blond girl stood over her kill, enjoying the moment like a seasoned hunter.

Winston's throat burned. When he tried to speak, his voice cut like razor blades. He jumped to his feet, his body aching. But guarded and ready for another threat.

"*Kyra!*" Rebecca rounded the corner, running, defying the snow. Carrying his gun. Thank God, the gun. Maybe he still had a little luck left after all.

❄ ❄ ❄

Harold had made good time through the snow, much faster than he thought possible. Really just a matter of determination more than anything else, physical prowess need not apply. He had everything he needed in his briefcase.

In front of the inn, he spotted his car, or at least the huge, white lump where he had parked it. It looked like it had been partially cleared.

Now he just needed to hightail it through the front yard without being seen. No signs of Calvin or Domenick. He had no idea what had happened to them either. But the gunshots he'd heard earlier gave him hope. Yet he hesitated. Might they be hiding, waiting for him? Of course, he could take the long way around. Double back through the street, slip into his car, no one would ever see him. But the thought of trudging through all that snow just sounded like another unnecessary obstacle.

His car called to him. The cash in his hand urged him on. So close,

135

yet so far. One short jaunt through the snow, then *bam*, he was out of there. On his way to living a king's life. *King Harold.* Sounded proper, somewhat regal.

But something held him back. His getaway seemed too easy. The inn was quiet as a tomb, most of the lights off. With the gunfire, the host taking Calvin outside by the throat, a chained girl, and who knew what else, the place should've been abuzz with the fuzz. Or at least gangsters.

Briefly, his thoughts wandered to the girl, Kyra. Maybe he shouldn't've left her. Although he'd done his duty, showed her the way out. Gone way beyond duty, in fact. But when he heard the footsteps approaching, it was time to beat feet. No doubt Domenick ready to blast him away. Or someone else, it didn't matter. Definitely weird shit he didn't want to wade through. Much better to wade through snow.

With a deep breath that turned into several (a favorite procrastination tool), Harold hunkered down. His knees worked like scissors, cutting a path, a tiresome and slow method. The briefcase above his head weighed heavy after a while, more like gold than paper.

He chuckled at his earlier fears. Domenick wouldn't hide. Damn Neanderthal didn't know the meaning of the word.

He straightened and tossed his shoulders back. Decided to walk like a man, his head held high. With high steps, almost a march, he paraded through the yard.

From a distance, the little girl's screams broke the silence. He tore off, willing his cold legs to move faster. But like so many people in his life, his legs wouldn't cooperate. Slow, tedious, little progress. Side to side, he moved. Kicking proved to be another colossal waste of time. But the car drew nearer.

*Shit, shit, shit.*

The girl's screams didn't stop. Maybe he should go back. Nah, screw it. She had the creepy chick with her. And whoever the mystery person had been. What if it'd been Domenick? If so, there probably would've been a fireworks tent worth of explosions.

He pulled it together the best he could. No more guessing games, just couldn't think that way. Not with the car a few feet away.

His briefcase slammed onto the car roof. A safe haven for his cash while he cleared snow from the windows. Behind him, he heard something. Feet tramping through the snow, running down the street.

Then the sexy woman's shaky voice. "Kyra? *Kyra!*"

*What the hell's going on here tonight?*

He snatched the briefcase and dropped into a squat, not even sure why. The woman wouldn't hurt him. Other things she might do tempted him. But, after all the new developments, it was time to cut his losses and run.

When he looked again, the woman had fled the street, her shadow cutting through a neighbor's yard.

On aching legs, he duck walked to the driver's side, his ass cold and wet and trailing tracks behind him. Then he saw another path someone had made. Snow had been cleared from his tires. His two Goddamn flat tires.

He shot to his feet. Out of ideas, his immediate escape plan blown to hell. He thought about riding the damn wheel rims. In the snow, wouldn't it be pretty much like a sled? But it wouldn't get him far. The inn's other occupants had cars. Just needed to get the keys. His ordeal felt like some damn surrealistic film that was all the rage in the 60s — he just couldn't get out of this hellhole.

With a weary sigh, he trudged after the woman, staying out of sight. Following the girl's screams.

❋ ❋ ❋

When she heard Kyra, all thoughts of Brad vanished. Sheer adrenaline plowed the snow more than her legs. A knife of fear penetrated her heart. She pushed herself, faster, harder. And still Kyra screamed.

*Please, God, let her be all right, just let her be safe.*

After everything they'd been through with Brad, to have something happen to Kyra now seemed unspeakable. And that bastard, Dave. He swore he wouldn't let anything happen to her. *Swore* it. But Kyra was still alive, though, her screams the proof. Small comfort, just not enough. Rebecca'd never heard her daughter let loose a shriek like that. Not once. Not even when Brad had hit her.

*Hold on, baby, I'm coming. Just keep screaming. Let me know you're alive. I'll find you.*

Rebecca withheld tears. Her gut demanded action. She swallowed the lump in her throat, time for hysterics later. A blubbering mess can't fight. She tread on. Her coat flapped open. Hands jacked at her sides, propelling her faster. Kyra's screams rose, coming from the back of the inn. She considered making a vow to God, a desperate woman's last resort. Or a pact with the devil. But no time for contracts.

Her finger played over the gun's trigger, ready and armed. Five bullets left by her count. And she planned on making each bullet matter.

Falling snow blinded her as a wind gust ripped by. Her cheeks numbed. When she turned the corner of the inn, she dropped into a squat, gun raised and steady.

It took a minute for her mental synapses to process the scene before her. And she still didn't understand. But she saw her daughter. *Alive.*

"Kyra!"

Like a needle yanked off a record, Kyra abruptly hushed. "Mommy!" Slowly, she pushed through the snow with a wind-up toy's lumbering steps.

"Wait there, baby, I'll come to you." With the gun raised — safe enough to run with, close enough to use — she struggled toward her daughter. Dave stood behind Kyra, his shoulders heaving as if out of breath. Next to him she saw the blonde newlywed wearing nothing but a slip of a dress. A tea kettle's worth of steam billowed from her mouth. The knife in the woman's hand and dark-stained dress drove Rebecca harder.

She swooped Kyra into her free arm. Kyra curled up in a fetal position, warm and comforting against Rebecca's chest. She rested her chin on Kyra's head and wrapped her inside Dave's jacket, protecting her in a human cocoon. From a cursory glance, Kyra seemed unharmed — physically, at least. But Rebecca knew — the way all mother's know — the cold didn't cause her daughter's shudders.

She stopped six feet from Dave, well out of reach. Her gun arm locked rigid, showing Dave and the woman she was in charge. "What *happened?*" she hissed.

Dave came toward her, arms tossed up. "I'm not sure —"

"Stay *there*. I mean it." Another gun gesture, this time split between Dave and the woman. "What happened to Kyra?"

"She's all right." With a tired sigh, he lowered his hands. "I found Kyra in the basement. She was helping her ..." He nodded toward the woman. "... escape. We've got to go. I'll tell you —"

"Seems like you're damn good at postponing the truth. Give me *answers. What* was she escaping from? And *why* does she have a knife?"

"It was my knife. She ... took care of Christian."

It made no sense. None of it. Everything had been whispered, harsh and urgent, *rat-tat-tat*, too fast to put together the puzzle pieces. But now Rebecca understood the stains on the woman's dress. She swiveled, her gun leveled at the blonde. "God ... she *stabbed* him?"

"The sinner *deserved* it!" At the sound of the woman's voice, Kyra clung tighter to Rebecca.

With her gaze and gun locked on the woman, Rebecca said, "*Explain.*"

Dave patted the air. Given the circumstances, his calmness infuriated Rebecca. "Lower your voice. Christian tried to kill me." Clearly, he'd given up candy coating his words around Kyra. Not that it mattered. Rebecca suspected Kyra'd witnessed far worse tonight than unsettling words. But she demanded answers now.

"She saved me," Dave continued. "And ... Christian killed one of the gunmen."

He stuck his hand out, finger pointing toward a large mass. The snow had nearly buried Christian's body. Funny how, after seeing Brad's corpse, it didn't faze Rebecca.

"And the Dandys ... they killed Tommy ... chained me up," said the newlywed. "Left me to *die*. They're *crazy*."

*Much like you*, Rebecca thought. Frankly, it all sounded crazy. The Dandys as killers? But she'd sort everything out later. She sensed Dave's urgency, had seen more than enough to justify getting the hell out of there. Impossible to do without a car, though. Maybe she needed the religious zealot after all.

"Fine. Let's go. But we need a ride. And I'm keeping the gun. Anyone who tries anything gets a bullet."

"Rebecca, I —"

"Shut *up*, Dave. And you ..." Again she pointed the gun at the woman. "... if you're going with us, lose the knife. *Now*."

She smirked, a corner of her mouth twisted. At arm's length, she dropped the knife like a microphone.

"Better. Dave, we need a car. Your keys are gone. Which —"

"Jesus Christ." When he ran his hands through his hair, Rebecca noticed his glasses were missing. Made him look different, strangely more natural. "What happened?"

"Doesn't matter. *You* ... where's your car?"

"My name's *Heather*. Our car's in the carriage house's driveway. But Tommy has the keys. Wherever his mortal remains are." With folded hands, she looked skyward. Tears fell, her demeanor as heartfelt as a singing telegram. Definitely one to watch.

"We gotta go, even on foot. Away from here. Get out of the storm," said Dave.

Rebecca noticed calling the cops didn't seem high on Dave's itinerary. She couldn't trust any of them. "Let's go. Ladies and mystery men first." She waved them past her, using the gun like a traffic cop's baton. The blonde snarled, but strode through the snow. Dave hobbled by her, favoring one leg over the other. But in this weather, they'd all be hobbling. Three adults, two coats, one child, one gun. Rebecca liked the odds. She'd just enjoyed target practice with Brad after all.

"Um, do you mind if I join you?"

Rebecca whirled at the voice behind her. The odd man from breakfast wormed his way out of the shadows, his briefcase held in front of him.

Rebecca said, "Depends on if you have a car."

"Someone sliced my tires."

Kyra popped out from undercover. "He's my friend, Mommy. He helped me."

Rebecca hesitated. She didn't know this man. Even though Kyra vouched for him, a six year old's judgment couldn't be trusted. Not with everything going on. Still, safety in numbers. "Any weapons? Knives, guns? Seems everyone else is packing."

"What? *No.* Of *course* not." He appeared flustered, a little insulted, the way she imagined he always did. Too real to be a put on.

"Fine. In front with the rest. *Move.*"

Dave buried his hands in his pockets, his shoulders shaking from the cold. Rebecca considered giving him his coat back. Then thought not.

"All right, Dave, tell us where you had in mind."

"As far as we can get. Shopping district's two blocks away. Might provide cover. Maybe a workable phone."

Rebecca dreaded the trek through the storm. But she'd fought hard for her and Kyra's freedom. It wouldn't end at a bed and breakfast. "Fine. Lead the way."

Dave stopped at the porch, flattening against the railing. Carefully, he scanned the area, then waved them on with a military gesture. Much too polished for an insurance salesman. Even though she didn't trust him, Rebecca'd rather have him on her team.

Down the yard they trudged, staying low, Dave carving a path before them.

"The street's easier," said Rebecca.

Dave hesitated. "Okay. But you see any headlights, we take to the trees."

The house next door appeared dark. Dark enough to provide sanctuary. But Rebecca tossed out the notion. She remembered the Dandys saying how important they were in the town. A neighbor might not believe them about the Dandys. Frankly, she didn't know if she believed it. The nice old couple holding the blonde hostage. Killing people. Why, exactly? Still, with Kyra's life at stake, it left no room for gambling.

As if reading her mind, Dave said, "Not a neighbor's. Too close."

Behind them, a muffled voice cried out. Rebecca squinted, tenting her eyes with a hand. Frantically, Jim Dandy ran across his porch, slashing the air with a knife. Kyra folded, clutching Rebecca's sweatshirt.

A blood-curdling scream followed, colder than any blizzard. *Dolores.* Rebecca heard her anguish, mournful and soul shredding, the sound a mother who'd lost a child might make. She had no doubt Dolores had just discovered Christian's body.

"*Run!*"

❅ ❅ ❅

In the street, Brad sat up, shaking off snow. The pain in his side wouldn't stop, sharp and biting. His fingers found blood and swollen, raw skin surrounding the bullet wound. Painful as hell, like a rat gnawing his innards.

*Bitch shot me.*

His first thought, his most recent memory. Took him a minute to remember what led up to it. She'd tried to kill him. *Him!* He couldn't believe it. But he knew he'd live to see his wife and daughter die. Just needed a little TLC, that's all.

As painful as the wound felt, his headache unleashed a world of agony. The girl's incessant screaming intensified it. *Kyra.* Damn pissant wouldn't shut up. Sure, he wanted to make her pay along with his unfaithful wife, but if someone else got to her first, more power to him. Just leave him a piece. The game wasn't over, not by a long shot. Call it extra innings. He had another shot at bat.

First things first, though. Stop the bleeding. Worry about getting the bullet out when he called for an ambulance later. Only room for him onboard, of course.

He tried rolling over on his wounded side. Bad move. But he'd been through worse on the job, he'd muster through. Getting on his knees via his wound-free side proved a comparable snap. With a hand over the wound, he crawled toward the car his wife had been in. He clawed his way up, the car his mountain to scale. His fingers groped for the side mirror, a perfect handhold. Now the hard part. He bit down, bracing himself, then hopped upright. Lightning coursed through his body, striking nerve endings. It gave him a needed surge, slapping him into coherency.

He staggered toward his car. Once he slid in, he fell back, hyperventilating, shutting his eyes. Just for a moment. No, the worst thing he could do. He sat up straight and punched open the glove box. Everything he needed at his disposal. Couple of ballpoint pens, a knife, a lighter. Proof positive he was still in it to win it.

But he'd been wrong about one thing. He *still* had to face the worst part.

Every movement hurt. He couldn't think about what he had to do. Instead, his preparations took over, on autopilot. As natural as pissing. Hatred for Rebecca propelled him, his gold medal to strive for. What she'd done to him. Shot him. Leaving him to die in the snow. Bitch actually fucking shot him!

*She'll pay. By God, she'll pay.*

He rolled one of the pen's halves over the lighter's flame. Nice and sterilized. And red-hot. Like the fire he felt within.

*She actually shot me! Tried to kill me! Her plan all along!*

With the knife, he cut a strip of his shirt away, making sure it hadn't been tainted by blood or snow. He bit down on his leather wallet. His hands shook when he wrapped the rag around the heated tube.

*Shot me! I'll do far worse than that. Destroy her face first. Cut it. Make sure she feels every …*

Imagery of ripping Rebecca apart gave him something to live for. With a preemptive scream, he jammed the rag-covered pen into his wound.

*The pain. God, the pain!*

Legs stiffened, his feet slamming against the floorboard. His back arched. His breathing doubled, tripled. He couldn't get enough air, the torture nearly suffocating him. The wallet fell from his mouth.

With his last bit of strength, he yanked the tube out, the rag staying put. Slowing the bleeding. One last, agonizing step. He pulled out his lighter. Chomped down on his wallet again. Held the flame over his wound, cauterizing it. He screamed, focusing his pain, his torture of his wife.

*Goddamn bitch!*

The pain was her fault. All her fault. Every blistered, raw nerve end.

Somewhere along the way, Kyra'd quit screaming. No matter. He knew it, felt it in his throbbing wound, he'd have his vengeance.

His eyes closed. Before he passed out, he thought about the things he'd do to his wife and daughter. Maybe even jam pens into their bullet wounds, see how they liked it.

Probably the most restful sleep he'd had in a while.

✻ ✻ ✻

Winston shot a look over his shoulder. The old man jumped off the porch and ran around the house, hurrying toward his moaning wife. A diversion they desperately needed.

Running had no discernible effect, the snow hindering their speed. Yet for once, he was grateful for the storm. Sometime during his battle with Christian, he'd twisted his ankle. The snow acted as a cold compress, dulling the pain. The problem was everything else felt numb as well.

He thought he heard the old woman howl out Christian's name, a coyote baying at the moon. Then the old man joined her, shouting, blubbering. Indistinctive sounds, animalistic in nature. Absolutely chilling.

As they neared the end of the first block, his injured ankle felt heavier than a bag of sand, increasingly hard to move. With Kyra in her arms, Rebecca had taken the lead, apparently no longer worried about having them follow her. The accountant followed closely behind him. Far in the back, the blonde crept along, leaping through drifts like a timid jack rabbit. Although he'd rather keep her where he could see her, he doubted she'd catch up any time soon. She appeared to be taking her time, enjoying a leisurely stroll. Sure, she'd saved his life, but Winston suspected she hadn't done it out of any favor to him. Something about her made the hairs on his neck stand up.

To the left, a street led to the shopping district, all downhill. Hopefully easier to navigate, but no doubt slippery. Rebecca kept her daughter hidden in his coat, only a tuft of her hair visible. A joey in a kangaroo's pouch. Rebecca looked tired, her arms straining.

"Rebecca," he whispered, "how 'bout I carry Kyra for a while?"

"*No*." She turned her bundle away from him, spitting her answer through clenched teeth. "You're *not* touching her."

Can't say he blamed her, not really. He knew she wanted answers, a determined woman. But out of necessity, their journey had to be quiet. The time would come soon, though, for explanations. He wouldn't tell her the entire truth, at least not about himself, no reason for it. Bigger fish to fry, as they say.

And what the hell kind of fish was in the pan, anyway? The blonde, Heather, had been chained in the Dandys' cellar, purportedly by their hands. The host had killed Calvin, hid his body. And Christian'd meant to kill Winston. Clearly, they had more to worry about than Domenick, wherever he might be.

Behind him, Carsten struggled through the snow, adopting a haphazard half-run, half-walk down the hill. All the while sheltering the briefcase like a baby. The damn briefcase. He wished he'd never taken this job. Then again, Domenick wouldn't have accepted "no" as an answer. Hazards of the trade. But a murderous B&B was more than he'd signed on for.

Still, a pro inside and out, he intended on reclaiming the money and dealing with Carsten. Hopefully fix this mess. Make it good with Domenick and save his own family. Assuming he'd live long enough.

Unintentionally, the descent hastened their trek. Going down proved unsteady for Winston, especially on an unreliable foot. Every time his bad foot came down, it gave a little twist, splaying out to the side. More out of control than a car on an icy bridge. But if he stopped now, he'd tumble head first from the speed he'd accrued. Rebecca reached the bottom first, surefooted in her landing. Behind him, he heard a thump, followed by Carsten grunting. The accountant sat in the snow, briefcase held over his head.

"Get up," Winston whispered. He thought about ripping the case out of the accountant's hands. And, now that he's vulnerable, a simple bullet to the head would expedite matters. But he had witnesses. And he wouldn't pull the trigger in front of a young girl, just couldn't do it. Besides, Rebecca ruled the gun now, unwilling to relinquish it. He'd get it later. Win her trust somehow. Talk about an uphill battle.

Clearly humbled, Carsten groused while he crawled to his feet. Like a ghost, Heather drifted closer, her skin pale and blue from the reflecting snow.

Winston caught up to Rebecca. Her impatience obvious, she repeatedly tamped the snow down with her foot. "Where to now?"

Down the street, double-storied brick buildings sat on both sides, all of them dark except for a few stray window lights peeping out from behind curtained upper levels. A mountain of snow represented a solitary truck parked at a slant. Christmas decorations and banners drooped between streetlamps, ice tears dripping from them.

The stores promised warmth — blessed warmth! — and dryness. As a security man — and how he wished he'd never ventured beyond those origins — he knew how to spot alarms.

At the crest of the hill, thunder rumbled. No, not thunder. A deep, angry engine. Headlights poked up, then swept down as a pick-up truck plummeted down the street.

"Jesus. Go. *Go.*" Winston pointed toward an alley behind the stores and gave Rebecca a kick-starter shove. Once she took off, she never looked back. The damned accountant stood still, seemingly paralyzed, staring up the hill at the careening truck. Winston grabbed his collar, considered taking the case instead. But he might need him later. To prove his innocence to Domenick. Multiple scenarios raced through Winston's head, jockeying for lead, all within seconds. "Go, *Carsten, dammit!*"

As if awakening from a nap, Carsten snapped to, pushing his legs harder. Not fast enough. Even with Winston's bad ankle, he pulled ahead of the accountant. His ankle caught, turned, pain knifing up his leg. But he forced it to move. Even if he broke it, he couldn't tell, not in the cold.

The truck's engine growled. Headlights splashed over the area they'd fled, snow flittering like a swarm of gnats in the lamps. Rebecca had vanished down the alley.

"Christ, Carsten, move your ass!" Again, Winston grabbed him by the collar. Prodding turned into dragging. They reached the alley just as the truck bounced onto the level street. Tires slid like skis. Brakes squealed.

Still grasping Carsten by the neck, Winston hurried down the dark alley. The snow at his feet had turned to slush, melted by the buildings' barrier of warmth. No sign of Rebecca or Kyra. And he'd long lost sight of Heather. Deserving or not, she'd have to fend for herself. If the Dandys nabbed her, it might just save their lives, a sacrifice for their survival.

"In here." The whisper jolted Winston. *Rebecca.*

An afterimage of the truck's high beams burned his retinas. Next to impossible to see, he stopped, hands groping the brick walls. But he heard the truck on the other side of the stores clear as day. Idling, engine chugging. Light opened up overhead, spraying the sky, sweeping back and forth. A portable floodlight?

Winston's eyes adjusted. Rebecca stepped out of a garbage nook, Kyra still wrapped against her chest. "Now what?"

They had to get somewhere warm. Their only chance. One sneeze away from hypothermia. And getting captured. Winston released Carsten, frankly unaware he'd still been wrangling him by the collar. Like it or not, his lifeline.

He debated, took the chance, and flicked his lighter on. Using the torch, he found a store's back door, one in the middle of the block. Better odds. People searching for something will generally start at one end or the other, never in the middle. Assuming this also applied to psychopaths hunting for victims.

Three steps led up to the back door. He looked for tell-tale signs: tiny holes drilled into the framework, wires running down inside. No decals or other indications of security alarms. Hardly conclusive evidence, but he doubted the store was wired. Part intuition, part stereotype — a need for high security in a burg like this seemed doubtful, crime a rarity. Then again, after tonight's events, anything goes.

Better to take a chance. Out here, they were targets. If the Dandys didn't get them, then the storm surely would. He needed his coat for protection to pop out the door's bottom glass panel. But he also knew asking Rebecca for it might result in a bullet to the head. He'd prefer a glass cut over death any day. With his elbow pulled back, he let it fly. Glass tinkled inside, much louder than he'd like. The smallest of sounds could give them away.

On the other side of the building, he heard the truck door open. Footsteps crunched through snow, a long stride. Quite possibly Jim Dandy.

Winston reached through the hole. Glass shards caught his shirt sleeve. His fingers crawled up, found the chain lock. An easy slide, a twist of the knob. A heart-stopping lock click. The door opened.

\* \* \*

Harold powered past the woman, past his neighbor, Harton, into the store. Warmth caressed him, his body thankful, thawing.

He couldn't have lasted much longer outside. And why again was he on the run? At this point he no longer knew. Just following the crowd, the same old story. But from what he pieced together, Domenick was now only one of his problems. Maybe he should cut his losses, go it alone. The Dandys were after the others, not him. For once, being excluded sounded like a lovely option.

"Everyone be quiet. Stay low." With his back against the wall, Harton slid down to the floor, stretching his legs out. No one followed his lead. Harton — the alpha male, the one he hated upon first meeting — was trying to boss around the woman. Stupid thing to do when the woman's holding a gun.

"Now, *tell* me what the *hell's* going on here, *Dave*. And where's Heather?" Harold knew Rebecca was pissed at Harton, could hear it in her strained whisper. Which sort of pleased him.

"We lost her. Sit down. You need rest."

Scant light filtered in through the front windows. The air smelled musty and old, an odor Harold immediately associated with his past shopping tours with his ex-wife.

*Antiques. Why in the hell does it have to be antiques?*

Once his vision adjusted to the darkness, he saw the cutesy crap packing the store. Stand-up desks inexplicably given their own made-up titles: *secretaries*. *Doilies*. What kind of adult would even buy something called a doily? Ghastly furniture with flowered upholstery only a grandmother could love. Smiling, glass-faced dolls. Metal what's-its. Rusted lunch boxes, old records, moldy books. Statues of animals wearing clothing performing human activities. Fishing, a goddamn fishing frog. It didn't even make sense.

He'd entered hell. More reason to take his leave. Especially while the others were blathering on.

Harton said, "Rebecca, you should sit —"

"And *you* should quit telling *me* what to do!"

The little girl slid out of her mother's coat, her feet dropping to the hardwood floor with soft *thumps*. She rubbed her eyes, everything about her nearly too precious to stomach. Then she smiled at Harold.

Actually *smiled*. Christ, not exactly the time to play big brother to a snot-nosed brat.

"Tell me *what* you know. *Don't* leave anything out," continued Rebecca.

Harton sighed. "The woman, Heather, was chained up. She says the Dandys did it."

"You already *told* me this. I want to know *why*."

"I don't know, really, I don't. I'm not even sure if she's telling the truth. She —"

"Like someone *else* I know."

Harold had no idea why she'd said that to Harton. But it concerned him. As did something else, something that'd just happened. Like a half-grasped dream, though, he felt the memory flying away.

"Look, Rebecca, you want the truth? I'll *tell* you what I know. Just give me a chance."

"I'm listening." With a look that could freeze water, she grabbed her daughter and sat across from Harton. Harold, too, contemplated sitting. His legs hurt, the slow thaw jabbing needles into them. But he needed to be ready to rabbit at a moment's notice. For him, sitting didn't exactly provide a runner's starting block.

"Christian tried to kill me. He also killed one of the gunmen."

"Old news. You *still* haven't told me why this is *happening*."

"If I knew, Rebecca, I'd *tell* you. Something *sick's* going on. The people at the inn aren't right. They..."

*Blah, blah, blah*. Harold knew all this, already heard it. Nothing new. Antsy, he crept toward the front window. The truck sat outside, headlights on, the driver's door open. The truck's tires were tall, nearly as tall as Kyra. Snow swirled around the monster truck as if it'd kicked up a dust trail. But he couldn't see the driver. Domenick never left home without his precious Humvee. Had to be one of the Dandys searching for them, no doubt about it. Best not leave through the front door.

"For *God's* sake, Carsten, get *away* from the window."

Harold whirled, nearly tripping over a birdhouse. A fist clenched his heart and squeezed. Anxiety trickled down from his brain to his bladder. He recalled what had bothered him. Harold had never told Harton his last name.

He gripped the briefcase's handle, tight, tighter until his knuckles turned white. Ready to use it as a weapon, if necessary. Quickly, Harold sought sanctuary and lowered himself next to the woman. They had a common enemy now. And, of course, she had the gun. Time to turn the tables on his pursuer.

"I never ..." Harold's words faltered. After clearing his throat, he spoke louder. "I never *told* you my last name!"

The way Harton sputtered, Harold knew he'd tripped up on his lies. "I read ... I read your name on the inn's ledger. Everyone's a potential sales —"

"Bullshit." The little girl gasped, but Harold felt a rush of confidence. Manly, even, especially in front of Rebecca. "I know *what* you are, Harton. If that's your *real* name."

Rebecca raised an eyebrow and leaned forward. "Oh, *really*. I think Howard's —"

"Harold," he interjected, but the woman clearly didn't hear him.

"... right. I *know* you're not an insurance salesman. And you knew the gunmen. Tell me what you've dragged my daughter into!"

"Yeah, Harton, we're all ears." Too easy. Just too easy. Harold's big chance to play the hero, win the babe. After all, he'd already saved her daughter. He smiled, hugging his case and snuggling in against the wall, ready for story time. The little girl shot him another smile. Gave him the creeps. Nonetheless, he felt empowered. And, this time, he couldn't attribute money as the source of his power. "Please *do* tell what you've been up to." Sure it might be risky if Harton exposed what he'd done with Domenick's cash. But Rebecca already knew Harton to be a liar. Too damn easy.

Harton ran a hand through his hair. His *full* head of hair, one more reason to loathe him. Finally, he said, "Fine. Our friend, Harold here, stole money that didn't belong to him. Took it from a powerful, dangerous man —"

"Whoa, whoa, whoa!" Rebecca waved the gun with every "whoa." Harold flinched every time. A stray bullet he didn't need. "We're talking, what ... the *mob*?"

"Mommy, what's the —"

"Quiet, honey. Grown-ups are talking." She dropped an arm around the little girl's shoulders, her hand covering one of her ears. Keeping the world's dark secrets from her. Yeah, right. Better kids learn now so they don't get burned later. "And you're with the *mob*?"

"*No*. I just ... do some work for them on occasion. An independent contractor. I was sent to bring the money back."

Harton's eyes fell on Harold's briefcase. Harold slid it beneath him, sitting on it, guarding it with his body. Hearing the truth made him realize the seriousness of the game he put into play. Time to start back-pedaling. "I didn't *steal* the money. Domenick *owed* it to me. It's mine and —"

"Now who's talking bullshit? Why don't you just slide the brief-case over —"

"No! You're *not* taking it."

"*Dammit.*" Rebecca jumped up. Her daughter gasped, appearing ready to say something. Then she clammed up, a first time for every-thing. "You guys done? I don't give a *damn* about any money. I just want to know who's who and what's what in this ... this *nightmare!*"

"That's the truth, Rebecca. All I know."

"Except for his lies. The money's *always* been mine. I —" Harold shut up when Rebecca looked ready to smack him with the butt of the gun. He crawled a little more inside himself, the briefcase planting him into the earth.

"And this has *nothing* to do with the Dandys?" She directed her inquiry toward Harton, her interest in Harold obviously dwindling.

He shook his head. "As far as I know, no."

"As far as you *know*?"

"Okay, I *know* it doesn't."

Rebecca throttled her hands, apparently strangling stress. She paced the floor between the two men, her gun waving wildly about. Kyra took it all in matter-of-factly as if watching her beloved television. "So ... you're a hit man —"

"I'm *not* a hit man."

"Shut *up*. Howard's a criminal —"

"*Harold*. And I'm *not* —"

"I mean it, the next one who says a *damn* word gets shot! Mean-while, the Dandys are chaining people up, killing them ... Jesus. Where's Heather fit into this? And *how* did you lose her?"

"Rebecca, calm *down*. I don't know if Heather's involved. But I don't trust her. I don't know where she went. I couldn't save *everyone*."

"'Save?' This is *your* fault." Rebecca's pace picked up, growls fly-ing with every turn. "*Fine.* You want to be the big savior? Get us the hell —"

Something shuffled above them. Too heavy for rats. Rebecca froze. A clatter, footfalls bounding down a stairwell. Closer, louder.

Harton sprang to his feet, disappearing faster than Harold could rise. Next to Kyra, a door opened. A gun barrel pointed out. An old woman in pajamas followed.

"What the hell're you doin' in *my* shop?" Like a skeet shooter, she waved the barrel around, shifting back and forth between Harold and Rebecca. "Get *out*."

"Ma'am, we're *not* going to rob you." Although Rebecca hid the gun by her side, her hand trembled. *Not* a good sign. "We're in trouble. If you could call —"

With one eye shut, the old woman shifted the barrel about the store at a dizzying pace. "Don't give a rat's *ass* about your troubles, girl. I want you *outta* here 'fore I plug each and every one of you." She stepped forward, her gun gravitating toward Rebecca. Harold threw his hands around his head, waiting for the inevitable gun blast. Duck and cover as they taught him in school. Maybe not so much for gun fights.

"I *swear* we'll leave if you call the police. We don't mean any harm. Something's going on at the Dandy Drop Inn. We just —"

"You came from the Dandys'?" Her gun lowered, just for an instant. Close enough for Harold to grab the barrel. But he'd learned early on, heroes die noble deaths. Instead, he practiced what he knew best. Blend into the woodwork.

The woman raised her voice along with the gun. "I want *no* part of this. Get on *outta* here. *Now*, dammit. I mean it. And don't you tell *no one* you was here. *Go*."

Harold nearly shrieked when a shadow dropped over him. *Harton.* The hitman lunged forward, one hand clamping the woman's mouth shut, the other forcing the barrel up. The wall behind Harold rattled at the gun blast. Plaster floated down. Smoke twisted from the barrel. The woman struggled. With a clatter, the gun fell. Harton's arm went around her neck. Wrinkled hands tugged at Harton's hold until they dropped.

"Don't *kill* her," Rebecca shouted. Next to Harold, Kyra brought her fists up, cranking up a scream. Harold scooted over, pulling her to him, pushing her face into his chest. Smothering the scream.

The woman went limp in Harton's arms. Gently, he lowered her to the floor. "She's not dead. Just out," he said.

The front door knob rattled, fate tossing the dice. Harold knew his number was up — snake eyes. His heart pounded out a manic drum solo, impossibly fast and violent. *Painful.* Sensation left his arm, tingles zipping up to his shoulder. A face appeared at the window, hands cupped over eyes. *Jim Dandy.* Very much *not* to the rescue.

Dandy's flashlight spotlighted Harold. Dying in the corner and shuddering on the floor. Surrounded by antiques.

*Why'd it have to be antiques?*

# Chapter Nine

From behind the snow-covered hedgerow, Heather watched the truck slalom down the hill. Although she couldn't see the driver clearly, she had no doubt who commandeered the vehicle. The figure hunkered down behind the wheel, shoulders bunched up, too tall for the truck's roof. Her sinful tormentor, Jim Dandy.

After the others had left her behind, she hoped Dandy would capture them, chain them up like he'd done with her. At least the two men. She still wanted to shepherd the woman and daughter into Hell. Her God-given right. Maybe she'd still get her chance. But she needed relief from the cold, the storm. Clothing, food, enrichment of the spirit and body.

She didn't need the others. God protected her, this she knew. Invulnerability coursed through her, stoking her fire. Everything she'd been through tonight, she'd survived. God loves the righteous.

Long after Dandy braked, the truck kept sliding. Once it skidded to a stop, he left the truck, splashing a floodlight around the buildings. Her hatred for him spiked, everything he stood for. The way he and his loathsome wife had laughed at her beliefs, chaining her like an animal. More than ever, she had to get back to the inn and finish her work. Nothing, not even Satan himself, would stop her.

She studied the house behind her. A porch light burned dimly; all interior lights were off. One car sat in the driveway, buried in snow. A Christmas wreath with fake birds wired into it decorated the door, the kind her grandmother used to love. An elderly woman's house. *Perfect.*

The front door tempted her. But Heather knew the dangers of temptation. Dandy was too close, why take unnecessary risks? She pushed through the snow, her legs freezing. Her flats dragged like ice blocks glued to her feet. Suffering, just like Jesus had.

She stepped onto the back porch, pulled open the screen door and knocked. She kept knocking — quietly, but more determined than a woodpecker — until the skin broke over her knuckles. Splotches of blood froze on the wood. But she wouldn't give up, not now, not ever.

A light above the door blinked on, painting the snow the color of jaundice. The door pulled back, brought to a sudden halt by a chain. An eye, enlarged by bifocals, peered out.

Heather slipped on a mask of panic. "*Please*, let me in ... some men want to *hurt* me. They want to —"

"*Oh.*"

That was all it took. The woman's eye bugged before she closed the door. Inside, the chain scraped free. Once the door opened, Heather fell into frail arms.

"What happened to you, sweetie?" She stroked Heather's hair, the way Heather used to stroke dead animals. "Come in 'fore you catch your death of cold."

Heather looked around the living room. Folded throws lay over a sofa. Plastic sheeting unrolled a trail across the floor. Everything clean, immaculate. No children, no signs of a husband. God provides.

The woman took Heather's hand. On the way to the kitchen, she picked up a throw and wrapped it around Heather's shoulders, tightening it with a smile. She gestured toward the kitchen table, then fanned her face as if hot. "Now, sit. I'll start the tea while you tell me what happened."

"Does your phone work?"

"'Fraid not. The storm done knocked down the phone lines."

"Oh ... oh, no." *Good.*

"What *happened*, honey?" She ran water into a kettle, switched the stove on.

"Some men ... *attacked* me. Took me in their car. They tried ... they tried to *defile* me!" The crocodile tears came easy. Not hard to do when she thought of Tommy, of the indignation she'd been through tonight. But she thought it best to leave the Dandys out of her story.

More than anything, she wanted to return to the inn, wrap things up with a Heavenly bow. Police would just hinder her work.

"Oh, honey ... you okay? Shall I phone for an ambulance? Might take a while in this storm." She sat next to Heather, her hands on her knees.

"No ... I'm fine. Just ... shaken up."

"Land's sake. How horrible for you. You from around these parts?"

"No. My car broke down in the storm. I didn't know what else to do ..." She scaled her voice down, each note dropping dramatically. God blessed her with a beautiful singing voice.

"Shhh ... hush now, honey, everything's gonna be just fine. What's your name?"

"Heather," she sniffed.

"I'm Mabel. I ain't gonna let anything happen to you."

"I'm sorry ... if I woke you. Or your family."

She waved the notion away. "Pfft. Just been me in this ol' house for several years. Kids moved out long ago. And God took Kent a few years back."

Heather brightened. Possibly too much. But it couldn't be helped. Finding a Christian in this Godless city sounded celestial trumpets in her mind. "Kent ... was your husband?"

"Ayup." She leaned back, her eyes capturing a faraway memory. "God took him with the cancer. But he's in a better place now, honey, I just know it."

Jubilation coursed through Heather like rushing rapids. Mabel's soul shone brightly. Releasing her would be a joyous occasion.

The kettle whistled, jostling Mabel out of her reverie. "Some nice warm tea. Always good for the soul." With a slight hunch to her back, Mabel walked toward the stove.

Heather followed. "I know something that's even better for the soul."

Mabel turned. Her jaw bobbled, her top denture loose. "My, you startled me." A hand flew to her breast, patting her heart.

"Mabel, thank you for opening your Christian heart to me."

A beatific smile spread across the old woman's lips. Her eyes sparkled. Heather realized Mabel knew what came next and fully embraced it. "Why, honey, it's as you said. It's all a Christian can do."

Heather gripped the shorter woman's shoulders. "Would you like to be reunited with your husband?"

155

Mabel blinked, speedy bird-wing flutters. Confusion stripped her angelic outer shell. "Of course I do. But —"

"*Praise* him!" Heather reached for the knife block on the counter behind Mabel. Her fingers fell on the largest handle. Big and sharp and shiny; much better than the one she'd used on the queer. "Let me hasten your Heavenly arrival."

It surprised Heather, it truly did. Honestly, she couldn't help but feel a little disappointed. Mabel didn't join Heather in praying as she carried out her work.

✳ ✳ ✳

Jim Dandy banged on the store window with a knife, his face twisted with rage. Screaming. Rebecca couldn't hear his words, but his intent was clear.

*Dear God, he's found us!*

Kyra folded her knees to her chest, wide eyes peering over them. Next to her, Harold trembled, hyperventilating. Even in the wan light, he looked pale.

"Use the gun," yelled Dave. "Rebecca, if you won't shoot, give it to me!" He thrust a hand out, on the offense, a tiger waiting to pounce.

Rebecca froze, panic flushing away reason. Thoughts flurried through her head like the ongoing storm, relentless and terrible. The strange blond girl had said Jim killed Tommy, her husband. But she couldn't shoot the old man, not in cold blood, not without proof. She brought the gun up, holding it at arm's length. Alarm jangled her, indecision holding her back. Should she shoot Dandy? Dave? Use the gun as leverage to escape? But where could she and Kyra go in the storm?

Dave continued yelling, something Rebecca vaguely registered, no more effective than elevator music.

Everything had happened in the blink of an eye, so unreal and disjointed. The woman with the rifle. Dave choking her. The accountant falling to the floor. Now Dandy. No time to think, no time to plan, no clear course of action. Nowhere to run.

Harold's gasping slowed, tempered to an occasional wheeze. He tried climbing to his feet, fell back, his chest heaving great breaths.

Jim Dandy continued shrieking, raging against the blizzard. The knife tapped out a Morse code on the window.

"Mommy, do *something!*"

Kyra's panic slapped Rebecca into action. She pointed the gun toward the window, arm locked. Jim's features sharpened, carved out of furious creases.

Then the colors of the flag flashed outside. An all-American hallucination. Blue froze Dandy's scowl, red heated his frustration, the tints alternating. He stopped pounding and squinted down the street. The light show grew brighter. Dandy saddled up in his truck and rumbled out of sight. Fast, too fast for such a storm.

Seconds later, a cop cruiser stopped outside the store, red and blue cherries spinning.

Rebecca cradled the gun, something she intended on keeping, police or not.

Kyra pounced up, yanking on her mother's sleeve. "Mommy, it's the police."

Dave retreated into the darkness, something he had an unsettling knack for doing. The accountant's breathing regulated, the calm after his storm.

A silhouette peered through the front window. Rebecca recognized the outline of the hat, a trooper's hat. Not good enough. But when she heard his voice, she relaxed.

"Hello!" Deputy Gurley cupped his hands around his eyes, his nose pressed against the glass. "Everything all right in there?"

The gun nearly slipped from Rebecca's sweat-drenched palm. She inhaled deeply, let it out. Her heart settled. She drew Kyra toward her, unwilling to let go. "It's gonna be all right, now, baby. It's our friend, Deputy Gurley."

Kyra still felt tense, rigid as steel.

From the shadows, Dave said, "You'll be all right now, Rebecca. Go."

Rebecca couldn't see Dave. Not that it mattered. She still had no idea who he *really* was. Good enough reason for him not to make their plans. "We'll *all* go."

"I can't do that. Neither can Carsten."

"*What?* Don't pull this *martyr* crap on me, Dave. Help's here. And Harold needs medical attention."

A cough came from the floor. "No … he's right. No cops." The accountant sounded weak but unwavering in his decision. "Leave me here."

The tapping at the window stopped. A flashlight strobed through the store. When the light licked at Dave's shoes, he vanished further into the darkness.

"Rebecca, you and Kyra are safe now. Just *go*."

"Harold *needs* a damn *doctor.*"

When the beam licked at Rebecca, she shielded her eyes against the intense brightness.

"Rebecca?" called Gurley. "That you? You and Kyra all right?"

"I'll take care of Harold." Dave said it matter-of-factly, all business.

And it left Rebecca with no doubt what he meant. But she was sick of playing cloak-and-dagger games, her daughter's life in constant danger. Through no fault of her own. "Fine. Whatever. I quit. You boys go ahead and compare size, battle it out. Have fun. Shoot one another for all I care. But I'm done." She stormed toward the door. Gurley's face lit up, his smile welcoming.

"Rebecca." Dave raised his voice barely above a whisper.

"*What?*"

"The gun. Give me back my gun."

She looked at the weapon, considered it. Frankly, she'd be more than happy to relinquish it, having had her share of shooting. Didn't need it now anyway, not with Randy outside. But she knew, as soon as she left, what Dave would do with it. Although she felt hardened, toughened by the night, she wasn't heartless. Hastening Harold's death wouldn't be on her. "No can do." She gestured toward Harold. "Don't want your little game ending too soon, do we?" Her bitterness surprised her, something she usually didn't vocalize.

Dave sighed, obviously recognizing he'd lost the battle. "Fine. But don't tell the police about us. We were never here."

That much she supposed she could do. Even though Dave was skeevy, possibly a hitman, he'd tried to help. At least that's the way he'd presented himself. No matter, no skin off her back. Whatever. "Have it your way."

Gurley waited as Rebecca fumbled with the lock. Behind her, she heard Dave dragging Harold to the back of the store, possibly to his death. No longer her problem.

But before she opened the door, Kyra turned back. "Bye, Dave. Bye, Harold," she whispered to the living ghosts in her life.

❋ ❋ ❋

Winston slumped the accountant, a pile of human laundry, against the back door. Carsten had not once released the briefcase, dragging it across the floor like Jesus with his cross.

Pity, really, Carsten hadn't fallen to a heart attack. Certainly looked like a sure bet there for a while. Could've cleared up some things, particularly Winston's conscience. But against all odds, the accountant pulled through. Amazing. So relaxed now, he'd fallen asleep. His chest rose and fell like a tide, his even breath a sea breeze. He wasn't going anywhere. More damn lives than a cat.

Something ate at Winston, though. The whole thing with the cop. Rebecca knew him, vouched for him. Sure, he harbored a natural antagonism toward cops, purely instinctual like the never-ending animosity between cats and dogs. But there was more to it. Old man Dandy had taken his time leaving the scene of the crime. Not the way a killer would react. Winston had first-hand knowledge of a killer's mindset.

Outside, the cop's lights still rotated. Carefully sidestepping the artifacts scattered around the floor, Winston crept toward the window. On his knees, he looked out. The cop hung an arm around Rebecca's shoulders, more than just "Officer Friendly." With slow movements, he pinched at the gun in Rebecca's hand. She appeared hesitant, uncertain. Her shoulders twitched as she abruptly turned from the policeman. He came back strong. One hand clamped down on Rebecca's wrist, the other tugging the gun from her grasp. Rebecca stumbled back, Kyra her small shadow. He tucked the gun into the back of his pants. *Curious.* Even stranger? Once the cop escorted them to the back seat of the cruiser, he didn't consult his radio. Simply got in the car and drove away. These days cops don't sneeze without calling for backup, touching base, filling out paperwork. Then again, it's a small town.

But that small bit of reasoning felt like a lie to Winston. Lying to himself was a dead-end exercise, one he wanted to put behind him. An early New Year's resolution.

"Carsten ... Carsten, wake up." He shook the accountant, gently slapped his face. Actually, he would've enjoyed smacking him harder but restrained himself.

Carsten stirred, muttering like a nap-disturbed toddler, then nodded off again. Winston knew the accountant's caffeine. One quick yank and the briefcase released.

As expected, Carsten's eyelids snapped open. "Give that back, Harton! It's *mine*." His feeble attempt at grabbing for it ended with his hands falling to his lap.

"Ain't gonna happen."

"*Dammit*, give it —"

"Shut up, Carsten. You're *not* getting the money." He plopped down in front of the accountant, two buddies having a heart-to-heart. "You awake now?" Carsten nodded. "I'm gonna level with you. It's true Domenick sent me to get his cash back and take care of you."

"Kill me, you mean." Carsten abandoned his scrappiness, appearing resigned to his fate. But Winston had something else in mind.

"Semantics. I'm willing to make you a deal. You wanna deal?" A very weak nod from the accountant. His already non-existent chin dovetailed into his neck. "Thought as much. We're going back to the Dandy Drop —"

"*No*. Absolutely *not*. You're goddamned *crazy* if you think —"

"What about 'shut up' don't you understand? We're going back. I think something's off about the cop. I could be wrong. I'm usually not. But my gut's telling me the cop's taking them straight back into that hellhole. You help me and —"

"Why in the *hell* would I help you? It's *insane* going back there. You're —"

"*Christ*, Carsten, no *wonder* you're divorced. You talk to your ex that way?" A low blow, but at least he had the accountant's full attention.

"How ... how'd you know —"

Winston slapped a hand on Carsten's shoulder, a good-natured buddy shake followed with a smile. "Part of the job. Why would you help me? So I don't kill you." He let the thought simmer for a bit. It worked. Mental quicksand overtook Carsten, one agonizing granule at a time. He said nothing, just looked helpless. Winston almost felt sorry for him. "But I won't kill you if you help me save Rebecca and the girl."

"Jesus Christ ... Jesus ..." Carsten repeatedly stroked a strand of hair, the end result a clown's poof. "This is insane. Why even *save* them?"

Winston shrugged. "I like the little girl. And I suspect you have a soft spot for her as well." He waited a beat, then applied the final touch to his sales pitch. "You see how she smiled at you when she said goodbye? So for once ... why not be a hero?"

The color drained from Carsten's face. Fear swelled in his eyes like a balloon. Then Winston saw a spark in the accountant's eyes, a tiny one, but a start. Redemption, a powerful motivator. Winston would know. Truth be told, he sought a little redemption as well.

"Hero talk coming from a hit man." Carsten fought a grin, lost the battle. "We save the girl ... you'll let me go?"

"Man of my word." Winston prodded a finger toward him. The accountant's eyes crossed while he followed the tip. "But you have to disappear. Leave the country. Soon as this is over. Got it?"

"Can I have the money? How am I gonna travel without —"

"Jesus. No, you can't have the money."

"Just a little bit. Come on —"

"Don't press your luck, Carsten."

The accountant shut up after Winston thumped him in the chest. Winston needed quiet to think, possibly reconsider his foolish rescue mission. Really, he should take Carsten, steal a car, head home. Make friendly with Domenick, a good laugh had by all, break out the cigars. End of story. But if ever he felt compelled to do something, it was saving Kyra. He wouldn't be able to live with himself if he didn't at least try. And, truthfully, he knew Carsten wouldn't be much help. But a needed distraction? Carsten could fill that role with his eyes shut. Sometimes small sacrifices need to be made. Still, Winston had an awful feeling in the pit of his stomach, something nasty rotting inside. No gun. A bad ankle. A simpering accountant with a failing heart as his ally.

Time to go.

He knocked on the floor three times before he climbed to his feet.

❄ ❄ ❄

"Rebecca, you and Kyra okay?" Randy's eyes widened, his concern calming. Finally an island of safety in the ocean of insanity. Gently, he rubbed Rebecca's shoulders as he looked down into her eyes.

"We're fine. Just ... let's get in the car. The Dandys —"

"Hang on, hang on." His gaze switched to Kyra, then stayed on the gun. She hadn't thought to hide it, didn't think it necessary. "One of the shopkeepers called the station. Said he heard a shot fired." He squinted, looking into the store window. "Madge okay? She lives above her store."

"Haven't seen her. My gun fired outside. An accident. No damage. But *please* get us out of here. Something's going on at the Dandys.

They —"

"Whoa, slow down, little lady." Rebecca abhorred being called "little lady." So condescending, so belittling, designating her to a stature one step below helpless. Yet, somehow, Randy pulled it off. Charm counts. But now wasn't the time for deep brown eyes to sideswipe her from the bigger picture. "Y'all look a little rough. Let's get you in the car and hash it all out."

Rebecca doubted Randy would take the news about the Dandys lightly. Might not even believe her. Clearly, he's on good terms with them. But she had to report what she knew. Which wasn't much. Just hearsay. Still, if the Dandys are killing people, they needed to be stopped. "Randy, *listen* to me. The Dandys are taking people hostage. Maybe even —"

"Here, let me just take this before you shoot someone's foot off." As soon as he touched the gun's barrel, Rebecca flinched. Kyra clung onto her arm as they twisted away.

"I'd rather keep it." Rebecca held her ground. She gripped the butt, careful not to wrap her finger around the trigger.

Randy's hold tightened, two fingers turning into five. His permanent grin strained a bit. "Come on, now. Any gun fired in my town, I have to take. Just for a little while 'til we get everything straightened out. You'll get it back. Is it your gun?"

She wouldn't tell him about Dave, she didn't break promises. "It's, ah … it was my husband's. Think I told you he's a detective." At the mention of her father, Kyra's head lifted. Of course, Rebecca would have to tell the police she shot Brad. But not now, not like this, a hell of a way for Kyra to find out her father was dead. When the time was right, Rebecca would have a serious one-on-one with her daughter, no outsiders allowed. But that dreaded encounter needed to wait. Right now she just wanted to get somewhere safe; the next town over, the police station, anywhere but this damn snow-covered street with killers, mobsters, who knew what running amok. "Fine. Here's the gun. But I need it back."

"Sure you do." Randy grinned. But not the charming, flirtatious grin Rebecca had previously found so inviting. It looked more like a smirk, a withheld private joke. Suddenly she didn't feel so safe under the protection of Deputy Randy Gurley. After all she'd been through, surely she'd earned the right to be wary of everyone. "Come on, now. It's freezing out here."

Randy stuck the gun into the back of his pants, his fingerprints all over it. Not exactly the way Brad told her police confiscated weapons. Of course, Randy probably never had the need to confiscate a gun before.

When Randy snaked his arm around Rebecca, she jumped at his touch. Much too chummy under the circumstances.

*Is he really hitting on me now?*

He scuttled them toward the backseat, staying close. When he *thunked* the door shut, Rebecca realized it was a different cruiser than the one they'd been in previously. A fence separated them from the front seat. Her hand swept across the door, searching for a handle. The hardware had been removed, not exactly the most comforting thought.

Randy slid into the front seat, started the car. Rebecca's gut kicked like a bronco when he snapped off his police radio. "Nice and quiet so you can tell me what in the world's goin' on." Said with his typical devil-may-care nonchalance, heavy on the devil. "Now what were y'all doing out here in the storm? You said something about the Dandys?" He turned around, flashing a smile. A toothpick worked between his white teeth.

Anxiety nurtured Rebecca's growing dread. Randy seemed off; his movements appeared calculated, his actions not those of a seasoned policeman. But she needed to keep it together. Don't show fear, figure out if her suspicions were accurate. "Randy, you're going to need backup. Reinforcements." Rebecca knew police officers never tackled a call solo. Even in a small town.

Randy answered with a shrug, his go-to move for everything. "Only one on duty." He dropped the gear shift into reverse and pulled a U-turn in the street. "'Fraid you're stuck with me."

Rebecca wrapped a protective arm around Kyra. "Fine. Take us to the police station, please. I'll fill out a report there."

He charged up the snow-packed hill with a race-car driver's reckless confidence. "Say, I think I got a call earlier from your husband. Not a very friendly fella." Again, Kyra's eyes shot up. Rebecca couldn't meet her questioning gaze. Instead, she dragged Kyra closer, trying to love her daughter's future pain away. "Did he come around? That what this is all about?"

The lump in Rebecca's throat thickened. When she'd killed Brad, she hadn't had time to consider Kyra's torment. Everything seemed to be catching up to her, nothing adding up, all of it confusing. "No,

I haven't seen him." An extra squeeze to Kyra's shoulder.

*Dear God, please let Kyra forgive me.*

"'Spose that's good." As he manipulated the toothpick between his teeth, he glanced in the rearview mirror. "Now what's all this about the Dandys?"

Kyra blurted out, "They had a girl in the basement. And Christian killed some —"

"*Shoooot*, Kyra," he brayed, a red-neck squeal. "Now I *know* you're messin' with me. The Dandys wouldn't —"

"It's *true*! It *is*! I'm *not* lyin'!" Kyra's hands grappled at Rebecca's arm, clawing for conviction. "Mommy, I'm *tellin'* the truth! *Tell* him!"

Randy took off his hat, tossed it to the passenger side. He said nothing, but his burst of laughter shook Rebecca's bones.

"Shh, honey. Randy … I'm not comfortable with any of this. *Stop* the car. *Now*. Call for backup. Let us *out* until they get here."

"What? I ain't about to put two beautiful gals out in the storm." At the top of the hill, he turned left.

"*Dammit*, Randy. I *mean* it. Stop the *damn* car." Her fingers slid through the links, rattling the fence. "Let us out!"

"Sorry, ain't gonna happen. As an officer of the law, it's my duty to see things done right." The Dandy Drop Inn rose in front of them, an imposing glacier in the storm. "We'll just go straighten all this out with the Dandys."

"You *bastard*! Turn —"

"Mommy, I'm scared!" Kyra's shriek filled the car. Randy drove with one hand while ruffling through his hair with the other.

The cruiser crunched into the driveway.

"Goddamn it, we're *not* going back *in* there! They're *crazy*! Get us —"

"Come on now, gals, shush." He stopped at the head of the drive. "Just hush now." The horn beeped three times. "We're gonna straighten everything out."

"You son of a *bitch*! What're you *doing*? You can't —"

"Really shouldn't talk that way in front of your daughter, 'Becca." He ducked and dodged, looking at himself in the rearview mirror, finger combing his locks.

Rebecca's door wrenched open with a rusty cry.

Jim Dandy, axe perched on his shoulder, extended a welcome. "Glad y'all could drop back by."

Rebecca's scream overtook her daughter's. Falling on deaf ears.

More of Kyra's head-shattering screams, the same hellish lullaby Brad had passed out to, stirred him awake. But this time, Rebecca joined in the screeching. Christ, he wanted to kill them just to shut them up.

A cop cruiser sat in the drive. He watched the old man he'd seen earlier carry Kyra inside the inn. Behind him, a cop struggled with his faithless wife. Probably another lover. *Slut.* Time to worry about that later. Brad needed to pull it together. *Get 'er done* as they say at the station.

Sleep had refreshed his mind; his body not so much. Fire burned at his side. He swore he felt the flesh around his wound pulsing like a heartbeat. But "tough as leather tits" is how the rest of the precinct described him. Accurate, forget about flattering. A single bullet couldn't drop him. Not when he had a score to settle. Several scores, actually.

He checked his glock. Fourteen rounds left. More than enough to rid his life of leeches, plenty to take out witnesses. If the cop got in his way, so be it. His brotherhood didn't extend this far over the Kansas border. Besides, from where he was sitting, the yokel cop didn't act or look like good police anyway. Might even be the prick who tried to punk him earlier.

Excitement rejuvenated him. Hell yes, his wound raged. Even more so once he stumbled into the storm. But he wore it like a badge of honor, a painful symbol of how he'd been wronged.

No plan, no need for one. He intended to go in guns blazing, no pussyfooting around.

Show time. He couldn't wait for the curtain to rise, but more importantly, he couldn't wait for it to fall.

*Idiot. Foolish damn idiot.*

As they trudged up the hill, Harold couldn't believe the stupid task he'd agreed to. Especially after he'd suffered a mini-stroke, a taste of heart attacks to come. That's what it'd been, no doubt about it. Heart conditions ran through his family like rushing water. His mother certainly had regaled him with tales over the years of her body's failures. Another reason to thank his mother. Maybe drop her a bitchy postcard from the Caribbean.

He struggled up the steep, snow-packed sidewalk. Breathing like a broken vacuum pump. Following a mobster who had his money, ready to drop him with a bullet.

*Stupid.*

Yet, he felt revitalized. Not for the reasons Harton spouted back at the damned antique store, painfully evident in his manipulation attempts. Harold understood it, felt it, abhorred it. Shaming him into helping the little girl. Pathetic, really.

Harold felt no shame in his actions, never had, never would. Oddly enough, it was the things he hadn't done in his life that struck a chord in him. Strummed him like a banjo. The chance to play hero didn't come along often. Admittedly, he'd rather not see any harm done to the little girl, little what's-her-name. As far as kids go, she was tolerable enough, he supposed. And she seemed to actually care for Harold, something different, something he didn't experience in his world of solitary bookkeeping. Never thought he'd see the day. Harold Carsten, friend and protector of children. Of course, the grand prize for heroism lay in the kid's mother. Once he saved her kid, she'd slather him with kisses, caress his body with well-imagined favors.

Even with a clearly jacked-up foot, Harton still had a hundred feet or so on him. Dragging his peg leg through the snow. The briefcase banged against his leg like a loosened, wind-tossed house shutter. During their impossible journey, Harold's gaze never left the briefcase, his focal point. So close, so out of reach. Classic case of a carrot leading a horse. His carrot, his golden carrot.

Altruism's one thing. But always a realist, somewhat of a cynic, his eye never wavered from the ultimate prize. Crossing the finish line. Screw it. The briefcase outweighed even the hot woman. Rebecca was the champion horse, but the briefcase was the trophy.

Then again, it's not like Harold had been given a choice, not really. Harton made it clear he'd take Harold out if he didn't comply. Typical. Bullying never stops, no matter what they teach in high school. And it seemed damn clear Harton wanted Rebecca as well. The way big-muscled, hairy-assed cavemen always win women. With a big stick. But not if Harold beat him to the prize first. His life, his cash, his woman. Naturally, he didn't carry as big a stick as Harton. But Harold's I.Q. certainly soared above his opponent's. He suspected

Harton's intellectual growth stunted somewhere in his early stages, his gun a phallic extension of his manhood. In spite of the storm, his fears, his health, and his misery in general, Harold chuckled.

He had a plan. Find a weapon, an entire arsenal if necessary. Save the girl, win the woman, overpower Harton (shouldn't be that tough since he's basically operating on one leg), swoop up the money. Blow town. So simple.

This, of course, was all contingent upon his surviving the upcoming confrontation. Something he tried not to think about too hard. Simply couldn't. He had no idea what awaited him. Hell, he had no idea where reality stopped and started any longer. Murderers, hostages, goddamn antiques. Too much for his number-crunching world.

Harold's enthusiasm lost air, fizzling down to earth.

*Dear God, what have I got myself into?*

As if divinely answered, the briefcase's buckle glinted beneath the light of a dying streetlamp. A real hallelujah moment.

*Thank you, God.*

❄ ❄ ❄

*Dear God, what's happening to us?*

Rebecca's mind twisted, thoughts colliding. Nothing aligned, everything chaotic. The inn — the inn she'd earlier found so charming — jarred and jumped as Randy carried her toward it. Closer, closer. Jim Dandy had already rushed Kyra inside. Carrying her, stroking her back, whispering into her ear.

*Kyra. No ... no ...*

Randy's hand, secured over her mouth, smelled of cheap cologne. Handcuffs jangled at his waist. His arm wrapped around her stomach, pinning her arms to her sides. He pushed through the snow, easily hauling her with short, staccato steps. Rebecca's feet kicked above the ground. Something prodded into her thigh. *An erection?*

His hand muffled her scream. But the screams inside her head felt like a brain hemorrhage. Loud and terrible and unheard, threatening to break the thin ice of her sanity.

*Bastard. Dear God ... not another one!*

Two things tethered her to reality. Kyra. And killing Randy.

"Now, now, Rebecca. That ain't no way to be." His whisper heated her ear like toxic gas. "Ol' Randy Gurley will see you done up right and well. Show you what a real man's like. Bet you'd like that. Hmm?"

He loosened a finger from her mouth, stroked her cheek. Then brushed the side of her breast. Rebecca drew her legs up, impotently trying to kick back.

The door opened. Dolores greeted them with an axe, slapping the flat blade into a palm. Her features scrunched up, half the size of her usual friendly visage. She stood aside, directing them in. Quickly, Rebecca craned her head, searching for her daughter. No sign.

"Let the woman speak, Deputy. But hold her tight."

Randy straightened. Rebecca's feet hit the floor, numb and dead. The way her brain felt. He removed his hand from her mouth but kept a firm grip around her belly, just below her breasts. *Enjoying it.*

A sudden choke hold cut her new scream in half. Another vile whisper. "Rebecca, if I was you, I'd shut your yap." His tongue ran up her cheek. She uttered a gasp, her throat constricted.

"Gurley, none of that crap in our house! Don't want you doin' what you did with the last one!" Dolores stepped toward them, axe waving like a nun's finger. Shadows peeled away from her face, revealing a blotchy and patched complexion. The flesh around her eyes appeared swollen from crying.

"Sorry, Dolores. Your house, your rules." Randy sounded properly admonished, no doubt another act. His chin dropped onto Rebecca's shoulder, both arms wrapped around her stomach now. Randy swayed, dragging Rebecca with him, the way lovers marvel at the world.

"Best keep that in mind." Dolores's flats swished across the wooden floor until she reached Rebecca. Rebecca met her gaze, challenging her. She wouldn't flinch, give her any satisfaction. She'd had plenty past experience internalizing her fear.

*Don't scream. Look for a way out. All that matters, saving Kyra.*

"Why'd you kill *my son*?" Each word rose to a bitter crescendo.

"I ... if you're talking about ... Christian, I didn't. I wasn't even there." She forced the tremors out of her voice, keeping it steady and even.

Dolores rubbed her mouth. Between her fingers, she exposed receding gums. "Who did? And don't you *dare* lie to me!"

"I'm ... I think the newlywed girl did. That's what I was told." And the lucky murderer who got away. The ultimate irony.

The old woman's head bobbed, each time dipping lower. Her shoulders pinched up like a vulture's. Then the sobbing began.

Rebecca saw vulnerability, decided to massage it. "Dolores ...

I'm sorry. Really, I am. Sorry for your —"

"He was like a *son* to *me*," she wailed. Unexpectedly her hands gripped Rebecca's shoulders. Her head fell on Rebecca's chest. Rebecca stared down at the old woman's thinning hair, her white, dry scalp.

"I'm a parent, too, Dolores. I can't even imagine how horrible it'd be to lose a child. You have my sympathy. You really —" Rebecca yelped, stunned. Son-of-a-bitch Randy gave her ass an ugly pinch.

Dolores raised her head, tears dried, suspicion renewed.

Rebecca continued. "I'm sorry. But Kyra and I had nothing to do with it. *Nothing.* As one mother to another ... can't you just let us go? *Please?*"

Randy snorted. Then Dolores released a single laugh, the most mirth-free, unnerving laugh Rebecca'd ever heard. "Oh, Rebecca. I should've known you wouldn't have it in you to do something like that to my ... my Christian." For a second, she wavered, teetering on the edge of sadness again. But she snapped back like a rubber band. "No, girl. Your place ... Kyra's place ... is with us now."

"What ... *no*. Dolores, *please*! I just want to give Kyra a good life. She's already been through —"

"Why, young lady, that's exactly what we're going to give you and your precious daughter. A *good* life." All smiles and sunshine, her woes forgotten, Dolores patted Rebecca's shoulder with a parental touch.

"*No!* Kyra's my daughter! For *God*'s sake, Dolores, *please* —"

"Honey, I long ago learned ... God ain't got a thing to do with it. Now I'm gonna go see how Poppa's doin'. Deputy, take Rebecca to the basement."

"Don't do this, Dolores! Don't —"

"More than happy to, Dolores." With Randy's chin still imprinted on her shoulder, Rebecca felt his jaw tighten into a smile. "Just make sure I get my monthly cash stipend."

"You'll get your damn money, Gurley. You always do."

"Dolores, please, *please* let Kyra go. *Why* ... tell me why ..."

Dolores strolled away, a casual saunter. "Me and Poppa'll be down in a bit to talk to you, Rebecca. After we see how Kyra's adjusting." She hauled herself up the stairwell, clutching the railing, both feet shuffling on a step before moving on.

In a hushed tone, Randy said, "You're gonna *like* this."

❊ ❊ ❊

The old woman's release — *bless you, Mabel* — had been Heather's favorite yet. Truly a joy. Mabel's tears of elation had been contagious, moving Heather to join the old woman in celebration. While the release took much longer than she'd anticipated — knives were usually the most efficiently righteous tools — at the same time, it prolonged her ecstasy. Mabel hadn't struggled, completely surrendering to God, ready to join her husband beyond Heaven's gates.

Now, Mabel's spirit soared, dancing about the kitchen. Another light joined her. Her husband. The two green shapes merged, becoming one. Heather liked to think all the righteous became one in God's domain. As the souls departed, she wiped away the last of her tears, and whispered, "You're welcome."

Beautiful. The nice part of her work.

Invigorated by her holy high, she prepared for the task ahead. Banishing the bad souls of the others at the Dandy Drop Inn. The even nicer part of her job.

She modeled Mabel's winter coat in front of the full-length bedroom mirror. Sinfully decadent with a zoo's worth of fur, the coat's collar tickled her earlobes. The length draped the floor. So big, room enough for two or three Heathers. But not large enough to contain her holy spirit, bursting at her body's seams.

From the refrigerator, she downed a quart of milk and wolfed through a healthy chunk of cheddar cheese. Fortifying her body to do the spirit's work.

Mabel's car keys were a cinch to find. Like her mother, she kept them in a foyer nook. So obvious, yet oddly nostalgic.

Mabel also had a wonderful set of cutlery from which to select the tools she would need.

Outside, the coat provided ample protection from the bitter cold. She didn't bother clearing the car's back windshield or side windows. No need to. God was her co-pilot, guiding her through the most turbulent of storm-tossed times.

A police officer's car sat in the Dandy Drop Inn's driveway. As she ambled by, she rolled down the window. A very recent visitor based on the fresh tire tracks. Not a problem, just a little more work to accomplish.

She parked directly across the street from the inn. She stepped out, head in the clouds, invulnerable. Safe in God's hands.

Only once, ever so briefly, did she falter on her mission. She wished for boots as she trudged through the snow. Her flats provided no protection, her feet freezing. But it'd be sinful to pray for personal betterment, for material things. Instead, she remembered the glory of Mabel's delivery. It warmed her like a nice cup of hot chocolate, all the way down to her feet. After all, Jesus trudged bare foot on his way to His crucifixion.

She opened the cellar doors, knife ready, and entered Hell's gates.

# Chapter Ten

Old Mr. Dandy carried Kyra up the stairs, laughing and chatting like everything was fine. But ever since Kyra had gone into the basement, things had been scary in a way she didn't understand. Not scary like her daddy sometimes got. Scary like the movies he watched.

On the stairwell, she gave up screaming, just too tired. But the tears wouldn't stop.

"I want *Mommy*. Please, *please*, take me back."

"Don't you worry none, Kyra. We'll take care of your mommy. Just like we're gonna see to you, too. It'll be nice, you'll see. You're part of the Dandy's now." He smelled funny, old and rotten, like dirty clothes.

"I want my mommy ..."

Mr. Dandy kept on gabbing, saying things that didn't make sense. Ignoring Kyra, the way adults always do. "Everything's gonna be just fine. Mark my words. You're the granddaughter we never had, the one God done snatched away from us. And we got room for your momma as well." He rattled on, talking to her as if she were nothing but a doll, seen but not heard. "Things'll be a bit different now for you and your momma. Growing pains as they say. But dependin' on how fast you and your momma learn, you'll be happy here at the ol' Dandy Drop Inn. I just know it."

With each step up, Kyra bounced in his arms. He drew his fingers through her hair, stroking it, combing it. She shook his hand off, pushing her head back, keeping the stink away. "I don't *want* to live here. It's not my *home*."

Mr. Dandy's face cracked, a scary look, meaner looking than an owl. "None of that *talk* now, y'hear? You do as you're *told*, *when* you're told."

Kyra closed her eyes, too afraid to say anything else. Once they reached the top floor, Mr. Dandy let out a long sigh. Then he dug deep and found his nice voice again.

"I done heard you been to Jody's room already. How'd you like it?"

Kyra said nothing, just nodded, her voice lost.

"Well, now, that's just dandy. And *you* are, too." Quickly, he walked down the dark hallway. The blackness came alive, poking her with smoky, dark fingers and pressing in with shadowy fists. She heard Mommy downstairs talking to Mrs. Dandy. She sounded scared. Except for Daddy, nothing *ever* scared Mommy.

Mr. Dandy stopped, rattled a doorknob. When he opened the door, a familiar old smell blew over her like a breeze over a garbage dump. *Jody's room. The dolly room.*

Light on his feet, Mr. Dandy floated over to the bedside table and turned on the lamp. Nothing had changed in the room since her last visit. Except it felt different. Before the room had been filled with magic, packed with excitement, life dancing in the dolls' eyes. Now, the dolls looked unhappy, very angry. Their eyes glared, dead eyes, nothing but dim marbles. And like Kyra, they looked trapped. The hanging dolls no longer danced like ballerinas. Instead, the ribbons bound them into place. Yearning to escape and reunite with their missing mommies.

Gently, Mr. Dandy lowered Kyra to Jody's bed. "This is your bed now. Your room." He straightened like a giant, frightening and tall enough to reach the ceiling. His cap's bill draped curtains of shadows over his face. Except for the wide, green grin. "You're gonna be happy here."

Not knowing what to say, Kyra climbed under the bedspread, seeking shelter. With the blanket gripped to her nose, she carefully watched Mr. Dandy.

He chuckled. "Well, now, that's more like it. Makin' yourself at home already." When he messed her hair, his hand felt rough like sandpaper.

The door opened as did Kyra's hopes. But it wasn't Mommy. Mrs. Dandy's smile stretched like a jack-o'-lantern's, her eyes nearly closed. Her hands slapped her knees. She bent over and spoke to Kyra in the annoying way adults talk to their pets. "Who's a good little girl? *You*, that's who." She pinched Kyra's cheek, something old people liked to do. "*Yes*, you *are*. You *are*."

"Please, Missus Dandy ... can I see Mommy? I'm scared."

For whatever reason, they both laughed. "Child, ain't nothing to be scared about. Your momma's fine. We just need to ... talk to her. Teach her the way things will be. Soon as she cooperates, you can see her." When Mrs. Dandy sat on the bed, the mattress tilted, the springs squealing like pigs. "Now, I want you to get used to your new room. Isn't it *wonderful?*" As if praying, she folded her hands beneath her chin. Then she reached for the music box, the one that'd seemed so exciting before. The ballerina sprung up, twirling, dancing for her life. "There we go. Isn't that nice?"

They stared at her, waiting for an answer, one Kyra couldn't give them. It'd help if she understood things. The way they acted frightened her. On the outside, they seemed like nice old people, kind of like Grandma. But they kept her from seeing Mommy. Holding them both prisoner. But she'd learned adults wanted to hear things, things that made them happy. When you learned how to do that, life got easier. For now, she'd play along. Until she found Mommy. Mommy would know what to do, she always does.

"Yes, it's nice," she said, her voice smaller than the tiniest doll in the room. She cleared her throat and spoke louder. "I like it a lot." Her lips couldn't hold her smile. Tears stung behind her eyes, but she wouldn't loosen them. She wasn't a crybaby. She had to be strong. For herself and for Mommy.

"Why, that's just wonderful. *Wonderful.*" Mrs. Dandy clapped her hands and shrieked to the ceiling. "Ain't that wonderful, Poppa?"

"Darn tootin' it is." With a weird little growl, he tousled her hair again. "Think the lil gal's already fittin' right in."

Mrs. Dandy's cheeks wobbled as she nodded. "I think so, too." She looked funny, ready to laugh or cry, hard to tell. She leaned in, arms outstretched. Like Mr. Dandy, she smelled bad, but different. More like medicine, the strong kind that hurts your nose, the kind Mommy puts on cuts. She wrapped her arms around Kyra, squeezing her tight. Cheek to cheek, Mrs. Dandy's face scratched Kyra's, short hairs prickling her. Kyra clenched the bedspread, holding it like a security blanket. "You've had a long night, Kyra. Now give Grandma a kiss, and we'll let you sleep."

*Grandma?* She wasn't Kyra's grandma, nothing like her. But she thought she was. Or *wanted* to be her grandma.

Last night Mommy'd told Kyra Daddy was sick in the mind. She thought she understood it, maybe not completely. But she knew, absolutely *knew* the Dandy's had sick brains, too. Tremors swam over her, crashing through her like pounding waves.

*Help me, Mommy! I don't know what to do!*

She thought about how scary Mr. Dandy'd been. How he'd changed back and forth as easily as slipping on a Halloween mask. A bad face she didn't want to see again. She decided to pretend they were playing a game, the best way to get through this. Of course, she knew it wasn't a game. She wasn't a little kid. But even big girls can pretend sometimes.

"Good night, Grandma." She pecked Mrs. Dandy's cheek fast, then tried to pull away. But Mrs. Dandy hung on forever, wouldn't let go. When she hummed along with the music box, Kyra felt vibrations coming off Mrs. Dandy's chest, deep notes and not very pretty.

"Alright — 'Grandma'," said Mr. Dandy, "plenty time for that later. As you said, let's let the lil one get her beauty sleep. Not that she needs it. This one's prettier than the last one."

With a sad sigh, Mrs. Dandy finally released her. "Well, fine then. G'night, Kyra."

While Mrs. Dandy climbed off the bed, Mr. Dandy stood at the open door, a long and spooky shadow. Mrs. Dandy caught Kyra with camera eyes before turning off the light. Then she followed her husband out the door. A key rattled in the lock, followed by a couple of clicks.

*This one's prettier than the last one.*

Kyra couldn't be sure, but she had a pretty good idea what Mr. Dandy meant when he'd said that. She wasn't the first girl they captured.

Something snapped like a mousetrap.

Her first instinct was to burrow under the covers and not come out. But that's how a baby would act. She tapped the air until she found the lamp. Her fingers walked up the base, then snared the chain. Somehow the small circle of light made the rest of the room look even darker.

Again, another tick from the other side of the room. Where the dolls hung like tortured marionettes. Two clacks, a swish. The dolls awakening, dancing in the midnight hour.

She yanked the cover over her head, trying to block out the sounds, settling her imagination. But her imagination wouldn't rest. When she closed her eyes, she saw dolls unspooling from ribbons like yo-yos. Plastic knees stretched, wooden joints clacked. They spun, swinging their partners, dancing about the room to the song of the music box. Wearing their plastic frowns and staring with unblinking glass eyes. Glass, surely what their eyes were made of, nothing alive.

*No way.*

*Please don't let them be alive, God.*

*No, that's all just baby stuff. Scary stuff for little kids. Not real.*

The sounds continued. Soft clicks, dresses ruffling. Something skittered like a mouse. *Breathing?*

Kyra felt odd, out of place, out of time. Everything had happened like a bad dream. But she wouldn't let her imagination gobble her up. There were real things, scary things, happening at the Dandy Drop Inn. She didn't need any make-believe fears.

Behind the table, she found a long cord connecting the lamp to the wall. She wasn't chicken, not a fraidy-cat. She'd use the lamp to investigate. Her feet swung out from under the covers and lowered to the floor. The lamp upheld like a torch, she approached the hanging dolls.

It hadn't been her imagination. The lamp illuminated plastic legs in black shoes, swaying, gently jostling a neighbor doll. One doll twirled, glared at Kyra, then faced the wall and back again. She heard breathing, no doubt about it. Someone breathing heavily. Or *something* breathing. But dolls don't breathe, can't breathe. *Impossible.*

She raised the lamp. Two dolls clacked together like magnets.

She *felt* someone was there. Behind the dolls. She couldn't explain how, just absolutely knew it. She lowered into a squat, bringing the lamp with her. All she could see beneath the dolls were shadows. Moving shadows.

A frightened dog's whimper raised into a coyote's howl. But when the dolls parted, a bear with a human's head rushed out, knife in its paw.

❊ ❊ ❊

Randy whipped Rebecca's hands behind her back, bunching them together at the wrists. He shoved her toward the host's desk at the back of the inn.

"I bet we got us a little time to get fully acquainted, Rebecca."

She couldn't believe she'd found him appealing — sexy, even — last night. Now his foul nature sickened her. She seriously needed to reevaluate her taste in men once she and Kyra escaped. And they would escape, count on it.

"Be a real shame to not sample the goods." Menace changed his voice, now a sexual predator. Revulsion at the thought of his "sampling her goods" tore her stomach apart.

"Why're you *doing* this? Just *let* us —"

"Shh, shush now."

She wanted to bite the finger he pressed to her lips, but she controlled herself.

*Not now, not yet. Wait for an advantage. Keep him talking.*

With an arrogant swagger — the same he'd always had, just now intimidating — he pushed her past the desk, tilted his head to the door behind it. "Ladies first."

"I heard what Dolores said. You're doing this for *money?*"

"Go on. Through the door."

With an elbow, Rebecca nudged the door open. Hesitantly, she entered the room. An orange bulb, dangling from a wire, dripped carrot colors and ginger shades over the small room. A cot, unmade, was wedged into the corner. She recognized one of Christian's vests wadded up in a velvet ball. Undoubtedly his room, surprisingly filthy considering the fastidious nature of his duties as the Inn's host.

With a small shove, Randy followed her in and grinned at the cot. "Christian ain't gonna need that now. May as well put it to good use."

Rebecca turned. Randy stood close enough for her eyes to water at his cologne. Obviously, he'd splashed it on liberally for the occasion. "You owe me an explanation. This is just about money for you?"

How she'd grown to hate his shrugs. "Don't make much on a deputy's salary. Gotta supplement my habits somehow. Man's gotta live, right? When I found out what the Dandys were doin', I thought a little blackmail might be nice. But they recognized a good opportunity when they saw one. Put me on their payroll. I brought 'em stragglers I'd find. For an allowance, of course. Nothin' personal." He unbuttoned the top of his shirt, working his way down. His gaze never left Rebecca's chest. "Get undressed. Guarantee you're gonna like this. Ain't had no complaints yet."

Bile rose in Rebecca's throat. Especially at the thought of what she had to do next. But it was about survival, just acting. "You brought them … women so they could kill them?"

Randy clicked a side of his mouth, pinched his cheek up. "Not exactly. Bit more complicated than that. We're wastin' time. They'll be down soon. Take your damn clothes off."

"And you took money for them."

"That's about the size of it." He ran his hand over his crotch, leering.

It'd been a while since Rebecca had reason to act seductive. She hoped she hadn't lost her touch, forgotten how to bring the sexy. And it sickened her. But whatever it took. She bit her lip, grinding her fingernails into her palms. She wiped the fear — the disgust — from her face, easier than she thought. "I think that's *hot*." She came closer, an extra swing to her hips. Her arms fell on his shoulders, hands roaming his back.

His jaw dropped, an uncustomary look for him. Clearly, his victims had never given themselves willingly before. Her stomach kicked, a rebel in her body. Bitterness rocketed up into her throat, scathing and sour. She swallowed it, swallowing a bit of her soul with it. "What can I say? I like the bad boys." *Never again.*

"Well, all right, that's more like it. And I like me a woman who ain't afraid to go for what she wants."

She nuzzled his neck with the lightest of kisses. His cheap cologne filled her nose. To stop her gag reflex, she opened her mouth, drawing in air. Agitated breath whistled through his nose, a putrid smell riding it. Her lips found his earlobes. How easy it'd be to bite one off, so close, so tempting. But Rebecca had her eye on the bigger prize. She dropped a hand to his arm, moved it toward his back, massaging small circles, lowering. Her other hand found his crotch. His erection jumped at her touch, straining for freedom. He groaned, closed his eyes.

*Fool.*

Either he'd forgotten about the gun or was too ignorant to worry about it. She plucked the weapon — Harton's gun — out of his belt at the small of his back. Her knee jerked up into his crotch, aiming low and hammering hard.

"*Oof.*" His eyes squeezed tight, tears leaking from them, his pain palpable and earned. He doubled over, coughing, hands cradling his crotch. "You *bitch. Goddamn* you, I'm gonna —"

"You're not gonna do *shit*, asshole."

His eyes flew open at the click of the hammer. Rebecca relished his fear as he looked down the barrel of the gun. Something he'd probably never experienced, but certainly had no problem bringing to others.

"You ain't gonna shoot me, Rebecca." His confident voice derailed, squeaking, not so cocky with a gun in his face. "Don't have it in you. Now, what do you say you give me the —"

"Shut *up*." She grabbed the barrel, swung the gun. It landed with a satisfying smack to his temple. His legs shot out, dumping him to the floor like the trash he was.

He held a hand out, palm open and trembling. Pathetically begging. "No, don't —"

Bending over him, she pulled the gun back again. The second blow opened a small stream of blood, his yelp pathetic and tiny. She wanted nothing more than to blow him away. Like she'd done with Brad. But she couldn't risk the Dandys hearing the gunfire. Not when they had Kyra. She had to work quietly. And quickly.

She couldn't leave the groveling mess at her feet conscious, so this time she brought the gun down with the muscle of both arms. His nose cracked, blood seeping from his nostrils. And his whimpering continued.

"Shut *up*, you *pathetic* excuse for a human *being*." She struggled to keep her voice to a whisper. But a whisper just didn't work; it was completely inadequate to convey her rage. "Just *shut* the hell *up*." Her foot drew back. A kick to the crotch, followed by another. She wanted to permanently ruin him, keep him from ever raping another woman. He sobbed, one hand covering his face, the other protecting his crotch. Curled up in a fetal position. When Rebecca thought about how many women he'd probably reduced to such a position, she kicked harder.

One more blow to the head silenced him. Just to make sure — and because it felt damn good — she gave him one more for the road.

She stood, out of breath. With the gun cocked in the air, she peeked out the door, saw nothing. Once she reached the stairwell, voices rose from the kitchen. The Dandys, gleeful and pitched at giddiness. Dolores even sang, nothing but good times.

179

*Hold on, Kyra.*

Before Rebecca lowered her foot on the stairwell, the door snapped open at her back.

An all-too-familiar and hateful voice — a ghost — froze her. "*Die, bitch!*"

✳ ✳ ✳

As Brad staggered down the street, he thought he might pass out. The wound had worsened, the bullet eating away at his insides like a parasite. He saw all the colors of pain; biting red, stabbing yellow. His feet jabbed out sideways, forcing him in drunken half-circles before righting their course. But he wouldn't — couldn't — be denied. Not before he completed his job.

The trek took twice as long as it should've, but he'd made it. When he set foot on the porch, a second wind revitalized him. The worst behind him, the best yet to come. Blasting bullets into his whore of a wife would be cake compared to walking with a bullet in the gut.

At the front door, he peered through the window. The fates smiled upon him, or more than likely, his killer instinct. He always did have great timing, a true boon to being good police.

Rebecca stood at the foot of the stairwell, her back to him. No time like the present. But he wanted her to look at him when he killed her, his face the last one she'd ever see. For his pleasure, not her knowledge.

Gently, he turned the doorknob. Foot up, he kicked. The gun raised, steady in both hands. "*Die, bitch!*"

She turned, eyes wide. The way she always looked when he came at her, when she deserved it. A gun hung in her hand, but he had the drop on her. Confusion painted her face like whorish make-up.

He smiled. Payback's a bitch. The barrel honed in on her face. Slowly, he caressed the trigger, taking his time, making the moment last.

To his right, a door swung open. The old man raced out, then stopped. Holding something in his hand. A hatchet.

*What the hell?*

Brad lost his moment, his gut acknowledging it first. The old man barreled toward Brad, growling, hatchet above his head. Brad's forearm blocked the swinging hatchet. His finger bit into the trigger. A bullet cracked into the ceiling. Pain from Brad's side streamed up into his arm, his head, when he punched the old man's face. The hatchet clumped to the floor. His assailant tottered back, arms spiraling for balance, knees jerking high. The old man's back hit the swinging door. A clatter came from behind the door, exploding dishes and jangling silverware.

Brad swung the gun back on Rebecca. Still paralyzed, a stupid deer petrified by the great hunter. "You've had this *coming* for a *long* time, *whore*!"

"No guns in our *home*!" shouted the old man.

Brad shouldn't have looked. As soon as he did, he knew he'd made a mistake. Four bullets ripped into his stomach, his chest, verifying his fatal mistake.

No pain. Shock. A terrifying nothingness. His legs weakened, pliable as putty. He dropped to his knees, his gun slipping from his grasp. Blood soaked his shirt. Rushing out fast, too fast.

Rebecca stood in front of him, gun shaking in her hands. A smoking gun. She'd shot him. Again. He couldn't be sure — everything twisted and spun, images swirling together — but he thought he saw her smile. He fell forward, his chin smashing onto the floor, the last pain he'd ever feel.

And the last thing he ever heard was his adulterous wife, calmly saying, "No, you've had that coming for a long time."

✳ ✳ ✳

Winston couldn't believe how long it was taking the accountant. Hell, even with a bad ankle, he'd practically lapped Carsten. The guy made turtles seem speedy.

He stood before the Dandy Drop Inn's porch, weighing the situation. As he suspected, the cop cruiser sat in the driveway. Hadn't been there long, either, with only a light snow dusting the car's roof and hood. But Carsten needed to move his ass. Winston's gut — old reliable — told him Rebecca and Kyra didn't have much time.

Carsten finally caught up, huffing and puffing like a two-pack-a-day smoker. "Gotta rest."

"No time. We'll go in quietly. Check out the place, find the girls. Do whatever it takes to save them. You with me?"

Carsten bent over, hands on knees, acting like he'd just run a marathon. Plumes of icy breath rolled out of his mouth. "Yeah ... okay ... whatever."

"Kill anyone who gets in your way. Because they'll kill you in a heartbeat." The accountant didn't answer. Just stared at him behind fogged glasses. "Carsten, you understand?" His nod looked less than convincing. "You want the front or the back?"

"What? Why are we separating?"

"Gives us better odds. Front or back?"

"Back? You mean like ... the cellar back?" The accountant jabbed a thumb behind him, an uneasy hitchhiker.

"Yeah, Carsten, that's right." Winston had considered both of them entering through the cellar, taking advantage of the element of surprise. Making a grand entrance via the front door hardly seemed like a wise choice. Then again, better to cover both sides. And should Carsten fall to the Dandys, his sure-to-be-loud shrieks would let Winston know exactly where the old couple was at the moment.

Carsten rubbed his chin, gazing at the briefcase in Winston's hand. The briefcase troubled Winston. Cumbersome, surely not the best weapon to take into battle. But he had to keep it, no other option. The only thing keeping Carsten in line. Winston knew Carsten wouldn't make a run for it without the cash. And if Winston stashed the case, no doubt Carsten would double back to reclaim it. Or worse, someone else might stumble upon it. His ticket to his family's survival remained inside the case. Like it or not, it stayed with him.

"Guess I'll take the cellar," said Carsten. No surprise, really, the safer of the two options.

"Fine. Let's go." Carsten stared at him, still lethargic. Using the briefcase as a visual slap, Winston held it high and shook it. "If you're thinking of cutting out, Carsten, just remember the money stays with me." Of course, he had no intention of relinquishing it to the accountant. Not a dime. But Winston knew Carsten's mindset. Never say die when it comes to money. "*Go.*"

With his head down, the accountant trudged off, carefully deliberating each step, clearly delaying the inevitable. Finally, he vanished around the inn's corner.

Once Winston stepped onto the porch, he heard voices from within, loud and desperate. He lowered, trying not to scrape his bad foot across the ice-chiseled porch. The briefcase clumped to the floor, so loud Winston winced. A man's voice, an unfamiliar one, rose above the others.

A succession of gunshots cracked. Instinctively, he tossed the briefcase over his head. His bad ankle slipped, dumping him down. On his knees, he crawled to a window. Through the thin curtains, he saw Rebecca at the stairwell, gun locked in her hands. Jim Dandy stood by the kitchen door. A body lay on the floor, blood butter-flying beneath him.

If he entered now, Rebecca would most likely shoot him. Clearly fearless, nearly deranged looking, and most definitely ready to take down anyone in her path. And never enter a gunfight without a gun. He'd wait. See what happened next.

❋ ❋ ❋

*Shit.*

Harold had spent more time walking through snow tonight then he had in a lifetime in Kansas. A long, cold, miserable way to get to paradise. Before he rounded the west corner, he snuck a peek back at Harton. The hitman had stepped up onto the porch, the briefcase gripped tightly in his hand. It probably sounded a little callous, but Harold hoped Harton would get offed by the Dandys. The only way Harold would get his money back. Obviously, he couldn't overpower the hitman. But he had to get his fortune back somehow. The only real reason he continued with this farce.

Harold's bladder nudged him, full and aching for release. It'd been some time since he'd gone. Best to take care of business while he could. If his bladder blew out inside his slacks, it'd no doubt turn Rebecca off.

He braced himself, then unzipped. The cold gripped his genitalia like a fist of ice. Leaning against the side porch railing, he closed his eyes, focusing. Ocean waves licked at Caribbean sands. Splashing, rising, receding. Roaring water. He pushed harder, straining. When his bladder felt at full painful capacity, success kicked open the door. The stream trickled at first, then ferociously hissed like a rattlesnake. Steam rose, welcome warmth from his waste.

Then the sound of gunshots stopped him, a massive bladder block. Urine dribbled onto his shoes, down his pant leg.

*Dammit.*

Oddly enough, his soiled trousers bothered him more than the gunshots. Weird, really. Maybe the violence had desensitized him. But urine down his pants? Completely unacceptable.

*Goddammit.*

He grabbed a handful of snow and rubbed down the wet spots, achieving nothing but spreading it.

At the cellar door, he hesitated. Maybe he'd just wait it out. Tell Harton he'd gone inside, found nothing. Safest bet. But the temperature had dropped, and the damn snow wasn't gonna stop dropping anytime soon. He felt miserable, his pant leg freezing and chafing his skin. Crazy, but his best bet on surviving the night would be inside. Maybe he'd just hide on the cellar steps.

Harold entered the cellar, pulling the door closed behind him. He swiped at a top step and sat down. Folding his arms around him couldn't stop the shakes. His teeth chattered, *clack, clack, clacking* enamel away. Cold inhabited his bones, a very unwelcome traveler. And the dark threatened to drag him under.

Carefully, he moved down the steps on his bottom, the way children slide down stairs. *Children.* Something he'd never had, never wanted, probably never would. He thought of Kyra, how she'd treated him with kindness, no judgment.

He hoped she'd be okay and make it out alive. Well, after he survived and got his money, he hoped she'd be okay. Priorities.

❋ ❋ ❋

Intentionally or not, Jim Dandy had saved Rebecca's life. His sudden appearance had surprised Brad, the distraction she'd needed to blow his life away. For the second time. As she stared at her husband's lifeless body, a sliver of satisfaction dug into her. For better or worse, to death do us part.

*No way he's coming back from that.*

It'd been close, though, too close. For a few delirious seconds — when everything had happened fast as a wink — she actually thought Brad had returned as a vengeful ghost. Fear had gripped her, cementing the gun at her side. Jim's shouting had triggered her into action, though. Seemed so easy pulling the killing trigger, she barely remembered doing so.

She had a problem, though. A big one. After she sent the four bullets into Brad, she'd pulled the trigger again. Which ended with a despairing, empty click. No more bullets. In the confusion, she didn't think Jim'd noticed. She hoped not, at least. And she intended on keeping it that way. Call it leverage. Particularly since the Dandys have a strange aversion toward guns. Just not toward murder by hatchet.

Farewell smoke drifted from the gun barrel, Brad's undeserving funeral pyre.

Jim stepped over the body and gave a swift boot to Brad's gun. It scattered across the floor like a mechanical toy mouse, seeking refuge beneath a sofa. Far out of reach.

"No damn *guns!*" Jim bellowed. "Rebecca, you stop this foolishness right now, y'hear? Ain't no way to treat your folks!"

*Folks?*

She raised the empty gun, turning it on him. His lips twitched, a trace of fear. Good enough. "*Get* your hands *up*, Jim. *Now*, dammit!"

His hands raised, not much, barely to chest level. Behind him, Dolores appeared in the doorway. She carried an empty silver serving tray in front of her like a shield. "You okay, Poppa?" Her eyes flit between Rebecca and her husband, barely alighting on the corpse. Apparently not a big deal in their world. "Now, Rebecca, put down that gun. We don't cotton to them things. Not one bit."

"I don't know what in the *hell's* going on. But I'm getting my daughter, and we're *leaving*. First one of you tries to stop me gets a bullet between the eyes." She nodded her chin toward her late husband. "Proof's on the floor."

"Land's sake, child, just —"

"Shut *up*, Dolores! You're both *sick*. Where the *hell's* my *daughter?*"

They shared a look, an uncomfortable one, one loaded with hidden meaning. Dolores said, "Top floor. But, child, listen to —"

"I'm *done* listening!" She nudged the gun toward them. Jim's shoulders bunched up, his hands covering his ears. "Get in the *kitchen*. *Stay* there. First one comes out is *dead*."

"Don't do nothin' you'll regret," said Dolores, as they backed through the kitchen door.

A shriek ripped out. Far away, yet long and terrifying. Unmistakably Kyra. Ice ran down Rebecca's back. She twisted, her toe catching on the bottom step. Her knees, then her chin, banged onto the steps. Kyra screamed again, driving Rebecca into a crawling sprint. Her hands clawed the stairs, pushing her to her feet as she climbed.

Halfway up the stairs, a hand snagged her ankle. *Dolores.*

"Stop *now!*" Jim Dandy's croak echoed up the stairwell. Rebecca dropped. She kicked back, her foot contacting Dolores' face. Dolores tumbled, rolling down the stairs, a deep drumbeat.

"*No!* Not *again*, it *can't* happen again!" Torment twisted Jim's voice.

Dolores lay at the bottom of the steps, her dress flipped up over her chest. Moaning, still alive. Beside her, Jim dropped into a squat.

"*Mother!* You all right? *Tell* me you're all right. Dolores, *talk* —"

"I'm fine." She coughed, sounding less than fine.

Rebecca didn't stick around to find out. The next shriek propelled her up, around the landing, vaulting two steps at a time to the third floor.

❄ ❄ ❄

Darkness encased Heather, a tight humid tomb. But the brighter God's will burned in her, so did her determination, enabling her to sense her way through the dark. Another power bestowed upon her by the Lord. She had swept through the horrible cellar where the evil couple had chained her. She'd raced down a long corridor until she literally tripped onto a staircase.

Up she went, her flats whispering over the wooden steps. From somewhere within the inn, she heard voices shouting. Mostly the little devil spawn wailing like a demon. Her shrieks sounded just on the other side of the wall. Reaching upward. The only place anyone should aspire to go. Too late for the little girl, though.

On the third floor, Heather fled down another narrow passage. The hall ended with a door to the right, small and barely visible. Upon pressing the paneling, it bounced open with a minuscule click.

She stepped over the threshold and into a trap. Objects dangled from the ceiling, swinging, bouncing into her. Something — ribbons, strings? — entangled her like webs. She felt hair, harsh and coarse; miniature plastic faces. Dolls.

Another door in the room opened. She grabbed the moving dolls, stilling them.

And she waited. Waited for what seemed like hours while the old couple cooed and made a fuss over the mewling little demon. Lapping at the cloven feet of Satan. Talking about new beginnings. How right they were; they just didn't know yet the nature of their new beginnings. But she couldn't deliver the three at once into Hell. Even with the knife, they outnumbered her. Besides, she wouldn't be able to enjoy her work if it happened in a hurry. Sometimes good things come to those who wait.

The lamp winked out, and the Dandys left. Soon, like a moth drawn to Heather's inner flame, the sinful spawn came toward her.

Inch by inch ...

Heather parted the dolls and dove out. The lamp dropped from the girl's hands. She screamed. Heather screamed, too, hers an exhilarating battle cry. Her foot tripped on the bottom of Mabel's fur coat, sprawling her to the floor. She looked up. Behind a bed, the hellish girl cowered. She hurled a doll at Heather, falling far short of her target. Then another and another, dropping to the floor like fallen souls.

Heather climbed to her feet, shedding the coat like a serpent's skin. She twisted her knife, admiring how her eyes reflected on the blade.

"*Mommy!*"

The Devil answered the girl's summons. The Whore of the Midwest burst through the door.

✳ ✳ ✳

Rebecca rattled the doorknob before she saw the key hanging in the lock. She twisted it and flung open the door.

She took one look, didn't stop to think. The blonde bitch, Heather, carried a knife, stalking Kyra across the room. Steeped in adrenaline, fear, and anger, Rebecca roared. She ran toward the woman, gun out at arm's length. The sight didn't faze Heather. Ignoring Rebecca, Heather turned back toward her prey. Rebecca drove her arms into the blond woman, carrying them both into a bookshelf. Objects rained down, an avalanche of dolls and toys. Rebecca gripped Heather's knife-wielding hand and banged it into the bookshelf. Heather's eyes, the wild orbs of a rabid dog, glowered. She bared yellow teeth, snapping them. And she possessed a likewise animalistic strength. The knife wavered, the point gravitating toward Rebecca's face. The blade lowered, deadly metal inching closer to Rebecca's right eye. One chance. Rebecca dropped the gun, grasped Heather's throat. Squeezed. And still the knife drew closer. But Rebecca knew she had the weight advantage, hoped gravity wouldn't let her down.

A split second. Risky as hell.

Rebecca jerked Heather forward, dodging left. She tossed her body weight back, Heather tumbling with her. And twisted. The knife cut across Rebecca's shoulder as Heather retracted her arm. Rebecca bounced off the bed to the floor. Heather fell into a bedside table, teetering for balance. She dropped, the table overturning on her. Her arms crawled up the wall, bloated, pale slugs.

From somewhere, a soft lullaby began playing.

Rebecca picked up the table, raised it over her head. A tablecloth slid off, falling to the floor. Heather ripped at the air with empty claws, the knife lost in the clutter. One of her eyes crossed, rolled up, a white eggshell. Rebecca cracked the eggshell with the table. Heather's arms flopped down. So did Rebecca's adrenaline spike. Her muscles ached beneath the table's weight, her shoulder burning from the knife wound. She lifted the table again. Six inches above Heather, the last of her strength spent, the table crunched down.

But Heather hadn't given up yet. She coughed, licked her lips. Spewing gibberish, threats spoken in tongue. Her one good eye fixed on Rebecca, sharper than a knife. Everything Rebecca needed to know.

Rebecca collapsed, her knees pinning the girl. The air left Heather with a rush. And still she struggled. Rebecca swung her fist into Heather's face. Her knuckles slashed Heather's cheek. A tooth popped out; a trickle of blood traced Heather's cheekbone to her neck. Rebecca hit her again.

"*Kill you and your little bitch! I'll* —"

"*Why* don't you *just* ... *die!*" Rebecca didn't know how many times she hit her. Her arm throbbed, her hand felt like it'd fallen asleep, needles prickling nerve endings. Skin tore back on her knuckles, leaving them raw and bloodied. Heather looked worse, her face a mass of blood, teeth, and muscle.

Repulsed, Rebecca stood. She wobbled, steadying herself against the wall. Kyra stopped screaming and ran to her.

Down the hall, footsteps pounded the stairs.

*Get it together, Rebecca.*

"Kyra ... we gotta go."

Kyra nodded, yanking on Rebecca's arm. "This way, Mommy."

Half-dizzy, Rebecca let Kyra lead her by the hand. To where, she had no idea. Her brain hadn't yet caught up to her body. But Kyra seemed confident. The best defense either one had at the moment.

The footfalls banged down the hallway.

"*Come on, Mommy.*" Kyra pulled a mass of hanging dolls back like drapes, shoving Rebecca into the inanimate mob. Her daughter's foot raised and kicked the wall. A door, invisible at first glance, snapped open.

Rebecca shook her head, took a breath, chased away her stupor. And followed her daughter into the dim corridor. As soon as they closed the door behind them, they heard Jim Dandy tear into the room, cursing like a land-locked sailor.

# Chapter Eleven

Kyra hurried down the black corridor, fleet-footed and assured. Like she knew the rat maze by heart. Rebecca thought she probably did, too. A minor blessing brought about by bratty behavior. She led Rebecca by the hand, no clear vision, no verbal communication. Kyra, like Rebecca, must've understood any sound could give them away. And she hated that her daughter had to fear for her life; she was too young to have such fears.

*Bastards.*

Beating two people senseless (maybe to death, in Heather's case) had taken its toll on Rebecca. Frankly, she never knew she had it in her. It surprised her, made her wonder what would've happened had she stood up for herself instead of being Brad's punching bag. Still, inside, she felt tense, a coil waiting to spring; outside, she ached as if she'd been on the receiving end of the beatings. Her hand had swollen, possibly a broken bone or two. Raw knuckles bled, the hallway's dampness intensifying the pain. Every muscle screamed for relief, a time-out. Something she couldn't risk.

Suddenly, Kyra stopped at the end of the narrow passage.

"We gotta go down," she whispered. Kyra descended slowly, carefully attending to her mother. Which hurt. Rebecca should be the one leading her daughter to safety, not the other way around. Since the nightmare began, Rebecca hadn't had a moment to gather her thoughts, think things through. Pin some semblance of reality on the night. And it wouldn't happen anytime soon, either.

Behind them, Jim Dandy howled through the hidden bedroom door. "We ain't gonna hurt ya! No damn way to treat your kin!" Then he entered the third-floor corridor above them. His footsteps crashed, rumbling like thunder, his pace fast with long strides. Wouldn't take long for him to catch up.

"*Go*, Kyra." Her daughter kept their hand bond sealed as they ran down the stairs. Rebecca's toe hooked on a step, almost landing her atop Kyra. She forced a shoulder against the rotted wood, grabbed the railing, and straightened.

"You're just makin' this harder on yourself! You're not goin' nowhere!" From above, Jim Dandy's voice boomed like a giant's. And Rebecca felt as helpless as Jack at the bottom of a bean stalk. But even Jack persevered.

Kyra stopped on the second flight of steps. A strip of light trickled out from beneath a door. "Mommy, that goes to Christian's room."

Rebecca took a step toward it, stopped. Their way out. And she could grab Brad's gun from beneath the couch. But Brad's body lay in there, bloody, contorted on the floor. After everything else Kyra'd seen, Rebecca wouldn't have her daughter discovering her father's corpse. "What's downstairs?"

"The cellar. And a way outside."

"*Go*."

They coasted down the stairs, swiveled to the final flight. A dark figure stood at the bottom, backlit by wan light. Short, squat, unwavering. One foot perched on a step, a hand raised.

"Now you gals just stop right there," said Dolores. "The very *idea*. No way to start your new lives."

The step groaned as Dolores lifted herself up. At their backs, Jim approached, slowing, closer. So close, Rebecca heard him hyperventilating. She felt his body warmth at her back, smelled rank sweat rolling off him.

Rebecca cradled Kyra's chin, drew her in. "*Please*. For *God's* sake, Dolores. Just let us *go*."

Dolores smacked her gums, working up saliva to lubricate her words. "You just don't understand, honey. We're *givin'* you and Kyra a new life. Sooner you understand that, the better off you'll be."

"That's right, Mother." Jim's baritone bounced off the walls. Something *thwacked*, a chopping sound. Then a mouse-squeak of metal.

While Dolores used false words of kindness, Jim intimidated with a knife, an axe, a hatchet, whatever. *Didn't matter.* The Dandys wouldn't touch a hair on Kyra's head. The plan Rebecca had used on Randy worked earlier; play along, wait for the right opportunity. Then strike like a venomous cobra.

Kyra, shaking like a tambourine, grabbed the tail of Rebecca's sweatshirt and draped it over her face.

The Dandys were beyond reason, clearly insane. Several times they'd referred to Rebecca as "family." But if she could get them talking, establish some sort of rapport, maybe she could use it to her advantage. "Just *tell* me what this is all about, Dolores. Tell me what you *want!*"

"Why, before all the fuss and whatnot, we was fixin' you a food tray," said Dolores. "And we were gonna tell you about your new life, Jody."

*Jody. They think I'm their daughter, Jody.*

Rebecca said nothing, while thoughts corralled her mind. If only she could see in the darkness, find something to fight with.

"Where's that fool Gurley anyway?" Dolores's friendly tone slipped away.

"He ... he tried to attack me. I got away."

Behind them, Jim roared. "Damn that man! Knew he was no good!"

"Poppa, language! Not in front of our little one."

Kyra bonded closer, small fingers gluing onto Rebecca's arm. Rebecca, likewise, wrapped her arm around Kyra, stroking her hair. Reassuring her, the only thing a mother could do.

"Sorry, Mother. But I knew Gurley was trouble. We jes' may have to get rid of that boy."

While Rebecca couldn't agree more, she had to keep Dolores on track. Work her melancholy like a pump. Remain calm, feign interest. Save Kyra's life. "You said something about our new lives."

Although Dolores's face remained in shadows, her shoulders noticeably sagged, followed by a sigh of contentment. No longer on guard. "Well, now ... maybe it's best we just show you."

Jim sputtered. Spittle landed on the back of Rebecca's neck. "Mother ... you sure the wee one's ready?"

"No! Kyra stays with us. *All* of us. Like ... *family*." No matter what new horrors awaited them, Rebecca wouldn't let Kyra out of her sight. Not again.

"Rightly said, Jody. After all, we're kin now" Dolores clapped her hands, a circus ringleader presenting the next macabre act. "Girl has to see it some time."

"Reckon you're right, Mother. Let's get on with it then."

Cautiously, Dolores left the stairs, utilizing a four-point turn. Rebecca noticed a shoulder striking down when she favored her left foot. The fall down the stairs must've done some damage. *Good.*

Behind them, Rebecca heard something slapping into flesh, a rhythmic beat. Jim brandishing his weapon into his palm. Nowhere near as trusting as his wife.

Like guarded prisoners, the Dandys escorted Rebecca and Kyra down a wider, cavern-like corridor. Rebecca shuffled heavy feet across the dirt floor, navigating through the darkness. A small glow outlined a door, hardly the light at the end of the tunnel.

Dolores led them into the cellar. At the opposite end of the room, green light slipped out around a door, pulsating as if alive. Rebecca looked around for an opportunity, a weapon, an escape route. Chains attached to a wall added to the dungeon-like atmosphere. Rebecca had no doubt they were intended for her. A shiver coursed through her, one she couldn't hide. It possessed her body, shaking her sanity. Then Kyra grabbed her hand. Her anchor, her lifeline. She took a deep breath, the only thing on her mind: *survival.*

"Now who left this open?" Dolores waddled toward a side door, opened just a crack. A cold draft blew in, a light tide of snow piggy-backing on it. She wrinkled her face and sniffed. "Why do I smell urine?" A strange thing to ask, particularly since Rebecca couldn't smell anything over the permeating stench of rot. "No matter, I reckon." She shut the door, smiled at Rebecca. "Come on now, gals. It's time to visit our special room."

Jim Dandy stuck right on their heels. Dead leaves crunched beneath his feet as he prodded them toward the green-lit door. Dolores stopped, pushed the door open with a hip and an elbow. Emerald flashes blinded Rebecca, then dimmed. Bright, muted, dead, the cycle continued. The ground beneath her feet shook as an engine dropped to a low growl, an electronic dirge.

"Go on, then." Jim prodded a finger over Rebecca's shoulder. "Go on." Rebecca noted pride in his tone, the sort someone might display over a job well done. The green aura lit up his beaming face, his teeth the color of spinach.

Rebecca grabbed her daughter's hand, squeezed it tight as if their lives depended on it. Together they crossed the threshold ...

❄ ❄ ❄

Outside the window, Winston watched the old woman topple down the stairs. The tall, elderly man — the same one who'd hunted them at the antique store, no doubt Jim Dandy — rushed to her aid. Near tears, he nestled the woman's head in his arms, not at all the man who'd stalked them. Although thin and lanky, his flannel shirt drew taut across his back, muscles straining at the shoulders, his neck. A farmer's body. Not someone to underestimate.

Using a surprisingly gentle touch, Dandy helped his wife to her feet. She strode to the back of the inn, tenacity in her gait, a hobble in her step. Her husband pounded up the stairs, two at a time. Even from outside, Winston felt tremors on the porch.

Safe to enter if he moved fast. Winston stepped over the body inside the front door. Blood stains decorated the corpse's chest and stomach, his arm cocked behind him at an unnatural angle. Militaristic buzz-cut, cheap off-the-rack suit, scuffed dress shoes, broken blood vessels crossing his nose and striking out into his cheeks, in shape except for the start of a beer belly. Doubtless a cop. But not the uniformed policeman Winston saw earlier.

Having procured a weapon earlier, he knew where to look. He listened at the kitchen door. Unsettling silence. In the kitchen, most of the knives looked ready for the melting pot; dull, tarnished, showing the onset of rust. Clearly, the Dandys kept their best cutlery elsewhere, but he grabbed the best blade available. Even a stick could be a deadly weapon given the right amount of force; it was just a matter of physics.

At the stairwell, he stopped. Frantic voices from above, a scuffle, furniture banging over. Rebecca's voice receded while Jim Dandy's rose. Rebecca had the gun, and Winston knew she could protect herself. But Kyra's voice wasn't among the ruckus. His gut told him to go to the cellar, the same damned gut that brought him back to the Dandy Inn in the first place. The Dandys had held Heather there. Why not Kyra?

And where the hell was Carsten, anyway? No matter; it fell on Winston to save the young girl.

Him and a little luck, of course. At the host's desk, he rapped the wood three times. Gave it one last hard knock, hoping it might up the good fortune ante. There's no such thing as too much luck. When he thought his axiom might likewise apply to bad luck, he faltered. Chasing it from his mind, he ran down the hall to Rebecca's room and down into the cellar.

❋ ❋ ❋

For a moment, Deputy Randy Gurley thought he was back in his parents' house, his mom pounding on the door, bitching at him to get out of bed. A true nightmare. After hearing the last knock, he jolted, a true sure-as-shitting how-do-you-do from the waking world.

But now he longed for the comfort of sleep again. Blood matted his hair. He couldn't breathe, not easily. When he inhaled, it felt like he was snorting razor blades. Skin flattened over his nose, the tissue tender to the touch, clearly broken cartilage.

*Goddamn. She broke my nose. A real wild one.*

In spite of his injuries, he smiled. Which hurt in an entirely different way. But he liked a challenge, especially from women. And it made him want Rebecca even more. Call it revenge sex, call it what you like, but she'd be his. Even if he did have a bit of residual nausea after she kicked him in the junk.

When he stood, he nearly toppled. Dizziness swept up, tilting the floor. He fell onto Christian's cot, holding his head until the world stopped swimming. At first, he thought he might have a concussion. But, hell, he'd recovered from worse hangovers than this.

Pretty dumb of him to let Rebecca get the gun. In his defense, though, he'd always had an eye for the hot ones, a soft touch for the softer sex.

At least he still had his gun, his police-issued model. Of course, the creepy Dandys had some weird hang up about gun use in their home. Ever since the incident years ago. Whatever. If he needed it, he'd sure as hell use it and damn the Dandys. What're they gonna do? Fire him? Hardly. Not after everything he knew.

The room quit rocking. He stood, unstrapped his gun. Nice and smooth and hard. Couldn't wait to fire the bad boy.

As he left the room, he felt woozy again, sick to his stomach. Mind over matter, he demanded his body to suck it up. Damn if it didn't listen to him.

He heard a door click at the end of the hallway. Rebecca's room.

Using police-trained stealth, he sidled down the hall, gun up. Just off to the side of the door, he gently inched it open. The room appeared empty. But the hidden door to the servant's hallway stood open. Once he moved into the darkness, he allowed his eyes time to adjust. Instead, he saw stars and comet trails of orange and yellow blazing across his mind's landscape. Nothing wrong with his ears, though. Footsteps dashed down the stairwell at the end of the servant's corridor, heading for the cellar. Quieter than church, he followed. When he reached the cellar, he saw a figure at the end of the hall, limping toward the door.

Down the cavern he sidestepped — not too different from the country two-step he was famous for — gun cocked, raised, and primed for sweet release.

❋ ❋ ❋

Of course, Winston knew someone was behind him. Heard him coming down the stairwell. The bigger his stalker's attempts at covertness, the louder he sounded. A step on a leaf, the giveaway creak of leather. And the smallest of jangles. Handcuffs. The cop. A dirty cop. And all cops, good or dirty, carry firearms. He couldn't take him out at a distance. Especially not in the dark. It'd have to be a close fight, one where he could see his opponent.

By the time he reached the door, his plan took shape. Not much of one, but improvisation had worked out so far. His damn ankle didn't make things easy, though; rather, it put him at a decided disadvantage.

He estimated his pursuer at twenty-five feet behind him. The cop's feet brushed through leaves, awkward leaps defining his location. The doorknob gave in Winston's hand and, mercifully, the door opened. Had it been locked, he may as well've been lined up in front of a firing squad.

As soon as he closed the door, Winston flattened against the wall. He switched the briefcase to his left hand, the knife to his right. Sucking in a breath, he held it. Not so he wouldn't be heard, rather he needed to hear.

Slowly, the knob turned, clicking like a cricket. The door cracked open. Winston heard the cop's breathing intensify. The door swung inward. No one entered. A metallic tick, one Winston knew well.

Before the cop's foot landed on the dirt, Winston swung the briefcase. The thud felt solid, flesh folding beneath the case. The cop grunted, fell back a step. Winston brought the case back again, his other hand raising the knife. Then he realized his screw up. Too late. *Amateur.* He left his torso unprotected. For one precious second.

The cop rebounded fast. He hurled into Winston, a go-for-broke leap. Winston crashed back, the cop on top of him. The briefcase dropped, but Winston held onto the knife. Dirt softened the blow to his head, still a startling internal crunch. The cop struggled, working his hand between their pressed-together stomachs. Winston felt the gun's hard contours, its barrel dragging across his skin. With a downward plunge, Winston's knife sliced into the cop's back. His assailant's body stiffened at the knife's penetration.

But this time physics didn't quite work the way Winston had hoped.

Reflexively, the cop's finger squeezed the trigger. Winston didn't hear the big bang he expected. Just a muffled *phunt*, stifled by their bodies, very anticlimactic. Especially considering Winston knew it was his last call.

He knew it as sure as he knew when he first fell in love with his wife. Or the intense feeling of unconditional love when his first daughter was born, a genetic desire to protect and provide so strong he thought it'd tear him up at times. Road marks in a man's life, never again crossed. And now his impending death provided the final road stop. Something inevitable, something instinctually understood. He envied the man who's suddenly pulverized by a car, never seeing his death coming.

His stomach burned, outside and in. He felt the lodged bullet spreading damage like a fast-acting tumor. And shock held him in its anesthetizing clutch. Just a matter of minutes, seconds, for the shock to dissipate. Until the real pain came for him, hand in hand with death.

He rolled the cop off him, twisting the knife out of his back. Winston wasn't alone in shock. The cop's feet kicked, his hands scratching the air. Gasping and gulping for life. Tears ran down his cheeks, a soundless mourning. Better than he deserved.

The simple act of propping up on an elbow felt like Winston's skin ripped open, cascading his guts to the ground. The knife slipped into the cop's throat, though, nice and easy. Before he died, the cop locked eyes with Winston, giving him a dumbfounded look, a sort of *what-did-I-do-to-deserve-this* look.

At least Winston accomplished something. The cop would never terrorize anyone again.

He lay back down. Above him, dimly lit webs tangled, flapping in a sudden breeze. Wind caressed his face, cooling his forehead's sweat.

He thought of Jules and the kids, how he'd never see them again. What they'd think of him. Would they find out the truth? He didn't know, everything rational just mere blips on his weakening radar. The trust fund he'd set up for them should be untouchable no matter the outcome. A small comfort. But he'd let them down. An ugly truth he couldn't whitewash no matter how much paint he applied.

The gentle wind stopped. He thought he heard footsteps, soft as cotton, treading the dirt. Death coming for him at a leisurely stroll, getting paid by the hour it seemed.

Then he thought about the reason he took on his desperate rescue mission, his go-for-glory last hurrah: Rebecca and Kyra. The blood erupting from his mouth tasted like death; salty, sharp, and bitter. He let out a single chuckle, didn't have the strength do it again. But he found the situation ridiculously ironic. Only now did he realize why he wanted to save Rebecca and her daughter. Surrogates for his family, plain and simple. And like his family, he let them down as well.

The footsteps shuffled closer. Maybe an angel preparing to whisk him to Heaven. But he knew he'd burned that bridge long ago.

Still, an angel appeared above him. An upside down head, a drifting balloon with cartoon features. Not what he expected. Thick bifocals magnified his eyes. God had stiffed this particular angel on a chin. His hair appeared greasy, thinning. An angel wearing the body of an accountant.

"Carsten."

Carsten nervously flit his gaze about. "Keep your voice down, Harton. They're in the other room." His whisper came out loud. Too loud, as if Winston's auditory skills had been amplified tenfold, better than a bat's. "You're dying."

The accountant had a knack for stating the obvious. And the unhelpful. "Yeah. Listen, Carsten, find the cop's gun. Get Rebecca … and her daughter. Take the … goddamn money. I don't … care." Dryness in his throat quieted his words. When he inhaled, an elephant sat on his chest. "Just … save them. Do … it for Kyra. You're … the only …" Winston's words simply stopped. No energy, his body's equipment repossessed by the reaper.

Above him, Carsten blurred, features swirling in a whirlpool. When he came back into focus, only for a second, Winston saw the accountant nodding, a silly head-wagging, eyes-closed, painful-looking nod. "Fine, Harton. I'll do it. Or at least try."

*Who'd 'a thought the damn accountant would be my angel?*

Winston shut his eyes and departed with a smile.

❄ ❄ ❄

*Hell, no, I'm not going into that room!*

Harold had tossed Harton a bone, nothing more, fulfilling a dying man's last wish. If only by lip service. Harton had died. What he didn't know wouldn't kill him. Harold chuckled, then clamped a hand over his mouth. He shot a look toward the door. Half-way expecting to see the Dandys rushing out of it. But he saw nothing. Just heard and felt the *throb, throb, throbbing* coming from beyond the door.

He couldn't believe how everything had fallen into his lap. Especially after the night he'd endured. Waiting on the steps, freezing his ass off. Every time he'd heard a shout, a scream, people running above him, his heart nearly iced over. Then when old lady Dandy stopped at the door he hid behind, he thought, *Game over.* How in the hell she'd smelled his sodden pants was one of life's unexplained mysteries. One he could live without knowing the answer to.

But the Dandys had moved on. Into the green-lit room. The hot woman and her daughter in tow. He'd almost left, too. Didn't quite know why he stayed. Actually, he did. The money, of course. But, in reality, he thought the chance of reclaiming it was a long shot at best. Then he heard the scuffle. Opened the door a hair to watch it play out. Harton and the cop fighting. To the death as luck would have it. Once the proverbial smoke cleared, he risked it all, snuck over. The money trail led to and ended at Harton.

Now Harold's heart *rat-tat-tatted* as he searched for the briefcase. Too damned dark. But he couldn't give up now. On his knees, he went spelunking, combing the dirt with his fingers. Finally, he found the mother lode.

*Happy days are here again.*

It felt like a reunion with a long-lost friend. Not that he'd experienced many of those. But this had to be sweeter, much sweeter.

He stepped on the cop's wrist. The gun lay at his outstretched fingertips. While the briefcase tasted like dessert, the gun would provide the cherry on top. Protection. Out of this antique and death-ridden hellhole.

At first, the gun felt like a snake in his grip; deadly, revolting to the touch. It didn't take long for its charms to win him over, though. *Harold Carsten, snake charmer.*

No fond farewells, he sure as hell wouldn't miss the place. If anything, he'd miss his unfulfilled fantasies involving Rebecca. Pity. Just not in the cards, though.

And Kyra. Poor girl didn't deserve whatever the Dandys had in store for her. Sure, she was a snot-nosed brat. But the only brat he'd ever known, even tolerate. She'd be fine, though, he told himself. The cops were gonna bust down the doors any second.

Loaded down with treasure, he hurried toward the door, his escape hatch. One, two, three, *poof*, gone like a magician's assistant.

Yet, he hesitated.

The cops were already here, dead on the ground. Harton saw to that. This shithole burg probably didn't have more than one cop on duty at a time.

Not his problem.

*Kyra.* So innocent, a full life ahead of her. One she probably wouldn't squander. Not like he had.

*Jesus, get it together. Remember the Caribbean.*

For some reason, though, his mantra sounded more like, *Remember the Alamo.* A morbid notion, to be sure, but one that stuck to him like flypaper, the kind he could never detach from his fingers.

A scream rose from the green room. High pitched, chilling. *Kyra.*
*Jesus Christ ...*

Either blasphemy or the start of a prayer. Harold couldn't distinguish the difference. Not anymore.

Before his balls detached — as his ex used to joke about at cocktail parties — Harold walked toward the green-washed door. The closer he came, the tighter his throat constricted. His heart raced, asking, *Knock-knock, who's there?*

*A foolish-assed idiot, that's who.*

He didn't give himself time to think, rethink, ponder, change his mind. Most of his life had been spent inside his head, playing these contrary games. To no discernible end.

With the gun raised, the briefcase tucked beneath his arm, he turned the knob.

\* \* \*

The pulsing green light bathed the entire cavernous room in an unhealthy display of scrub blues and pine greens. A holding cell for terminal patients, but far, far worse: a graveyard.

Kyra screamed. Almost an act of violence, Rebecca slapped her palm over Kyra's eyes, keeping her from seeing the worst.

*Dear God, please don't let Kyra have seen it.*

Rebecca hoisted her daughter up, burying her face into her chest. A protective arm swathed her, shielding her from the ungodly sights. Kyra gave in willingly, shaking beneath Rebecca's shelter.

Just beyond the door lay a rectangle of dirt, darker than the surrounding ground. Freshly overturned dirt. Next to it was another with two entwined planks of wood at the head. A grave marker. In a childish red scrawl, *Jody Two* bled across the horizontal timber. The line continued down the cavern, an underground cemetery. A succession of buried Jodies. *Jody Three, Jody Four...*

Rebecca's stomach contracted, her chest muscles tightening. Nausea flushed through her, a fierce tidal wave. She pitched forward, coughing, dry heaving over Kyra's head. Keeping beat with the throbbing that shook the entire room. When the empty sickness passed, she straightened. And, God, she wished she hadn't.

Because the graves weren't the worst sight. Not by a mile.

At the far end of the cave, past the graves, Dolores sat in a folding chair. Shifting shades of green illuminated her relaxed features. With folded hands in her lap, she looked extremely reverent. Several other chairs sat in a row, all facing the centerpiece. The blasphemous centerpiece.

A six-foot-long glass tank sat on a stand. Bubbles spewed out of a wooden box at the bottom before popping out of existence. Thick tubes of various colors draped out of the tank like dead octopus tentacles. They connected to a black, chugging machine, the source of the thumping sound. The engine — a sump pump of sorts — shook on its wooden platform, an evil, living entity. Smoke spouted from its gaskets, its manufactured snout. Behind the tank, a series of bright floodlights dimmed and brightened to the tune of the engine's rhythm, scorching the entire room green.

Rebecca gripped Kyra tighter when she saw what rested in the tank.

A desiccated corpse. Remnants of flesh floated in the green water. A tattered dress waved like seaweed. The top of the skull was missing, only the nose and jaw left in a death grin. A wig had been attached. Black and long, drifting coal-dark shadows in the green water. Skeletal fingers waggled, a greeting from the grave. And nestled within the corpse's other arm, cradled to its sunken chest and connected with chicken wire, rested a baby's skeleton. Small, unformed, curled like a fetus.

Rebecca thought her stomach had nothing left to give. Her body rebelled against the idea. Dry heaves folded her over. Kyra curled up at her belly like a mirror image of the horrific tableau in the tank.

"Dear ... *God* ... my *God* ..."

The throbbing ground down. Green light birthed, died, and began the cycle again. The color of death.

Jim stood by Rebecca, thumbs tucked under his armpits, a proud farmer surveying the fruits of his labor. His pride slipped into disappointment once he saw Rebecca's reaction. "What's the matter? Cat gotcher tongue?"

He draped an arm across Rebecca's shoulder. She flinched at his touch.

*Dear God, help me to keep it together. Please, God, don't let Kyra see this ...*

Jim's brow pulled down. "Come on over and sit for a spell. Let Mother tell you our story."

The tenuous line between sanity and insanity pulled taut, ready to snap like a tightly tuned guitar string. As if Kyra felt it, she pinched Rebecca's shoulder. An awakening, a warning not to let the tide of insanity engulf her.

Rebecca sought inner control, forcing steel into her voice. All she could manage, without breaking into screams, were tinny, one-word sentences. "Fine."

As Jim led Rebecca to his wife, she couldn't look at the fish tank. Her eyes flit everywhere but there. Each step closer, the green brightened. She longed for total darkness again.

"Okay, baby?" she whispered into Kyra's ear.

Kyra said nothing. Her hair rose and fell in a nod, sweeping against Rebecca's palm.

Dolores patted a hand on the chair next to her. The chugging machine ate whatever she attempted to say to Rebecca. One glance to her husband and she twisted the air. Jim obliged, adjusting the power on the pump. The roar diminished to a steady hum. Out of the corner of her eye, Rebecca saw dwindling bubbles, escapees climbing to oxygen.

"Now, honey, this is ... I guess, you might call it our special memory room for Jody."

"Ain't this room a peach?" added Jim. "Back in the day, the slaves dug out the cave. Reckon they was caught before they finished their escape route properly."

Rebecca focused on Dolores. The lesser evil in the room; maybe not. Beneath the green light, she noticed Dolores's eye for the first time since her plunge down the stairs. A hideous blood moon, the white obscured behind red clouds. Rebecca hoped she'd get the chance to finish the job for good this time. Make it a double Dandy drop.

"If it's ... okay, Dolores, I'd ... I'd rather Kyra not see this." Usually, Kyra would rise to the challenge, a dare to peek. Not tonight.

Dolores narrowed her one good eye, the blood-filled one inert. "Well, I don't rightly know what the bother —"

"I mean for *now*, at least," Rebecca blurted. "She needs ... time."

"Ah, let Kyra rest, Mother." Jim dropped into the next chair, his knees cracking. "She'll come along given time. Her momma's right." Jim Dandy to the rescue. *Bastard.*

"I suppose. Anyhoo, this is our daughter." Dolores gave a half-hearted gesture toward the corpse. Her chest swelled with a deep sigh. "Now we know our daughter — and our granddaughter — ain't alive. We're not off our rockers."

"Absolutely right." When Jim dropped a hand on Rebecca's knee, she jerked.

"Of course not." Rebecca's words rang false. She just hoped the Dandys wouldn't see through her subterfuge. Every word, every movement counted for survival.

"But, after the incident ...," continued Dolores, "... that awful day, we wanted to remember Jody. Remember her as she was."

*As a corpse?* The back of Rebecca's throat bucked, threatening another round of dry heaves. She said nothing, couldn't if she wanted to.

"It happened so long ago ... but seems like yesterday, really." Dolores stared into the tank, green light catching the tears dripping from her good eye. The red one remained dry. "Jody'd ran away. Just seventeen at the time. Eight months later she showed up out of the blue. Like nothing had happened. 'Cept for the telling belly bump." Jim sniffed, cleared his throat. "A baby out of wedlock. Can you imagine?" Dolores stared at Rebecca, clearly in her mind, the idea of a bastard baby more horrific than anything in the cellar. "She said she was leavin' with the baby daddy. Then she'd ... she'd ..."

As if psychically linked, like all long-time couples, Jim took up the narrative. "Give the baby up for adoption. She *knew* we was against such a thing. We told her we'd raise the child as our own, wouldn't have it no other way. And she stood right in front of me with a big ol' grin and said she wouldn't let us lay a hand on the child. She came back just to *taunt* us, enjoying every minute of it. Well ... we wouldn't have none of that, no sir. I ran for my shotgun. Course I never meant to use it. Just put the fear of her parents, of God, back into our child. But, stubborn as a mule our Jody, she went right on down the stairs. I went after her. She turned on me, clawing and screamin'. And ... oh, Lord ... the gun went off. An accident ... a stupid accident ..." Jim sunk his head, sobbing into his hands. Kyra snuck a quick peak before retreating to her shelter.

"It's all right, Poppa. It was a terrible accident, not your fault at all." Dolores reached behind Rebecca, stroking Jim's shoulder. His chair quaked, his shoulders tossing. "But, the worst part? The worst part, Rebecca? You know what that was?"

Rebecca didn't know, nor did she want to. But as a captive audience, she didn't have much choice. She shook her head, playing at empathy, hiding her terror. She squeezed Kyra tight, so tight they were one.

"I *felt* the baby kick in our dead daughter's belly. I *swear* to you I felt her kick." Dolores looked lost and swept away, oblivious to her surroundings.

After a moment's silence, a proper grieving period, Jim continued. "Growin' up on a farm and all, I'd done delivered my fair share of foals. So ... I performed an operation, spur of the moment, mind you. Tryin' to save one life after the loss of another. But somethin' went wrong. Terribly wrong." He reached the hollow place people do after a good cry: emotionless and passive. His lifelessness jarred Rebecca more than his fits of rage; a matter-of-fact detailing of a macabre event that would give sane people nightmares forever. "Baby rolled out, deader than a doornail. I tried smackin' her little behind again and again. Tryin' to whup the life into her." Kyra's tremors shook Rebecca. The chair's leg hopped, digging a circle into the dirt. "But it was no use ... no use. That day, God — a dead-to-me God — took both our babies from us."

"And with me bein' barren and all ..." Dolores spread her hands, clearly seeking understanding, sympathy. "We just couldn't accept the loss. So we been tryin' to find a daughter again since. And a grand-daughter." She leaned over, all smiles and grandmotherly warmth, attempting to ignite a spark from Kyra. "The other gals — the other Jodies — just didn't understand. Not one iota. But ... now we've found someone special in you, Jody. You and Kyra."

As Jim's tears drained dry, so did Rebecca's nausea. While the story revolted her, a numbness of mind triumphed over her physical upheaval. A coping device.

Plain as day, the Dandys had been kidnapping women, little girls. Holding them captive. And if they didn't comply? They were buried beneath the Dandy Drop Inn where no one could ever mourn them.

The last thing Rebecca meant to do was stir the pot, tip over the Dandys' stew of insanity. But their casual demeanor, their blithe acceptance of kidnapping and murder infuriated Rebecca. She demanded justice. For her, for Kyra, for the past, forgotten victims.

She jerked a thumb behind her, spitting bile in her voice. "And if these other ...'*Jodies*' didn't go along with you? You ... *killed* them?"

The Dandys shared a look, not one of guilt. Contented smiles spread, a post-coital comfort.

Dolores said, "That's not how we prefer to look at it, Jody. We was lucky enough to find Christian early. The only man we ever considered takin' into our family. Soon enough we found out he was different. Like us." A momentary flicker of sadness drew her jowls down. "Became a son to us. And, as we opened up our hearts to him, he taught us to enjoy certain ... *things.*"

"Put a spark in our love life," said Jim.

"Jim Dandy! Not in front of the little one." Dolores placed wrinkled fingers over her lips, pretending, not succeeding, to murder a laugh. "We got to where we considered it 'date night'. Somethin' we looked forward to. Then Deputy Gurley kept bringin' in more and more. Folks who didn't have no family to speak of. Gals who rightly shoulda loved to join our family."

Sudden fury blew away any empathy Rebecca had for the Dandys.

She knew they were insane, absolutely so. Driven that way by their daughter's death. A small defense, but something to hang a sliver of humanity on. But with a great deal of pleasure, they'd just admitted to killing people. And enjoying it. *Date night.*

Rebecca forced herself to look at the tank. This time she saw a means to destroy the Dandys, even if just emotionally so. Her last recourse. Kick the tank over, smash the glass, destroy their shrine and what might be left of their shriveled hearts. But why stop there? She'd grab a sliver, poke their eyes out, cut their throats. Perhaps next to impossible while holding her daughter, but she had to try. And she wouldn't let go, either; not of Kyra, her sanity, or their chance for survival.

She jumped up, the chair crashing back. Her scream swelled, flying through the cavern like a howling wind. The scream fortified her, building her inner strength.

Behind them, the door opened. And a small voice, nearly lost in the depths of the room, said, "*Stop.*"

❊ ❊ ❊

Immediately, Harold regretted his decision. He tried to bind reason to the scene before him. Just the way his brain operated. But his brain fizzled, refusing to lock these grotesque puzzle pieces together.

"*Stop,*" he repeated, but much less forcefully.

Rebecca held Kyra, screaming. The Dandys flanked them. Sitting in front of a skeleton in a tank. Totally irrational.

"What the *hell? Rebecca, Kyra,* let's *go. I'll* save you." His confidence blew him away. Such power, such controlled domination over the room's inhabitants. A real Alpha male waving his gun around. Or maybe the money in his other hand empowered him. Either way, he liked what he heard. Not so much what he saw.

Mr. Dandy bolted out of his chair, all six-foot-scary-plus of him. The intermittent, flashing green light tracked him as he galloped toward Harold. But like a distrustful strobe light — missing frames from a film print — half of Dandy's approach slipped into darkness. Time jumped as Dandy ran. He loomed close, closer. One blink away.

Harold locked his arm and pulled the trigger. The recoil jerked his arm back, knocked his teeth together. His glasses dropped, his vision crippled.

A red-and-blue blur of flannel swam up on Harold. A hazy comet trail followed Dandy. Harold planted his feet, fired again. The moving target dodged. With a roar — an extremely macho one, he thought — Harold swept bullets throughout the cave, merciless in his approach, mercenary in his haphazard aim.

A bullet thunked into wood. Glass tinkled. A scream — the old woman? — flared, a gaggle of shrieking old ladies echoing off the walls. Harold fired another arc, his arm sawing back and forth.

When Harold lowered the gun, Jim Dandy rose in front of him. Now in focus. A very undesirable focus.

Dandy's arm flashed. Something thumped into Harold's chest. It didn't hurt. Not really. Until he looked down and saw a hatchet handle dangling from his chest. A power tie that *really* killed.

The gun dropped. Harold's hand flew to his chest. Warm life's blood dripped from his fingers. With a hand bracing Harold's shoulder, Dandy tugged the hatchet out of Harold's chest. Pulled his arm back. Harold raised the briefcase. The hatchet attacked his cash, chopping into the leather. The briefcase opened. A kaleidoscope of green paper butterflies fluttered through the air, turning and twisting. Wafting gently to the ground. Beautiful. Absolutely *beautiful*.

As Harold fell, he snatched one in midair. On his knees, he clutched the bill to his chest. And fell down on top of it. Contrary to the saying, he had every intention of taking it with him.

More screams rose. Agonized howls. Enraged cries. Strangely muted sounds from far-away shores. Perhaps even Caribbean shores. Somewhere along the coastline, he thought he even heard Kyra crying out his name.

*"Harold."*

*Harold Carsten, hero.*

When the accountant came in, gun blazing, Rebecca wasted no time. Jim Dandy hurtled through the cave toward Harold, one less immediate obstacle. Clearly shocked, Dolores tried to haul herself up, scooting along the chair's edge. More than happy to help, Rebecca grabbed the back of the chair and pitched the old woman forward. Even one handed, it only took a nudge. Green dust rose beneath Dolores's body as she writhed in the dirt.

A bullet zipped by Rebecca. So close, a small breeze brushed her cheek. The glass at her back shattered. She whirled. Green water sloshed out of the broken tank. Jagged glass teeth caught the corpse as it tried to escape. The body rose and fell with the moving water, its arms dangling down.

Rebecca held Kyra, tucking her inside Harton's coat. Keeping her innocent mind, her eyes, from witnessing the chaos.

More bullets cracked, a succession of explosions.

On all fours, Dolores crawled toward the tank. Her arm stretched out, wavering hand reaching for her daughter's remains.

Rebecca's opportunity, the one she'd been waiting for. She latched onto Dolores's arm, dragging her to her feet. Rebecca turned Kyra aside. Then plunged Dolores's head down. Glass ate into the old woman's neck. Dark liquid iced the shards. Dolores's bun of hair provided the perfect handle. Rebecca grabbed it and steered Dolores's neck across the glass.

At the far end of the room, Jim bayed, a terrible sound. He stared at Rebecca, square jaw unhinged, then again at his dying wife.

Dolores's feet stopped jerking. Her shoulders sagged against the tank's frame. Her last gasp of breath sounded like a cat spitting up a hairball. Yet she'd managed to wrap her arms around the skeleton. Both of them. Bobbing next to her daughter's remains. Three generations of Dandys reunited in death.

With jacking fists and giant leaps, Dandy ran back toward Rebecca. With Kyra in tow, she tore down the opposite side of the cavern, the graves separating them by six feet. But Rebecca knew he only had eyes for his wife. For now. An edge of time, one she wouldn't squander.

Rebecca hopped over Harold's body. The only time Kyra braved a look. She murmured his name into her mother's arm, "*Harold ... Harold.*" Then hid again beneath the coat's folds.

In the next room, Rebecca nearly tripped. She toed the object, felt rigid skin and muscle bounce, then snap back into place. A body. Two of them. Harton and Gurley. Harton must've taken Gurley out, reason enough for her gratitude. Not that he needed it now.

"Kyra, I'm gonna put you down. Just for a minute. Shut your eyes, baby, 'kay?"

Kyra slid down Rebecca's body, her feet tapping the ground. Rebecca dropped onto Gurley, her knees on his chest.

From the green room, Dandy wailed, moaning his wife's name. "*Dolores ... no, oh, God ... Mother ...*"

Shivers settled into Rebecca's spine.

*Don't listen to him, time's running out, hurry.*

With shaking hands, she patted down the dead bastard. Something he no doubt would've enjoyed had he been alive. Her stomach pitched as she entered his pocket, grazing his groin through the thin material.

A clink. *Success.* She yanked the keys out, jangled them to hear their reassuring solidity. She'd hoped to find his gun, too. But maybe that was the one Harold had used. No time to go back, too dark to search the floor. She snatched up Kyra again.

Dandy's crying slowed. But his muttering built, steeping into anger. Seconds before he exploded.

"Outside?" Rebecca pointed toward the door Dolores had closed earlier.

Kyra peeked and nodded. Rebecca launched up the narrow steps. Near the top of the steps, her foot slipped. Terrified, she thrust an arm above her, catching herself against the cellar door. Pain wrenched her back, but she needed to stay ahead of the pain. Keep going. She threw the door open and lifted Kyra into the snow.

Below, Dandy's screams escalated. Footsteps thrummed across the floor. Louder, faster, deadlier.

*"Hurry, Mommy!"* Kyra squatted in the snow, her arms outstretched.

Rebecca climbed out, shook off the cold. As soon as she kicked the cellar door shut, she slid her fingers down the splintered exterior until they found a latch. Her fingers froze, numb, practically useless. Harder than threading a needle, she hooked the latch.

*The lock on the outside.* Unlucky for past victims, good luck for her and Kyra.

The door cracked, banging up an inch, then snapping back.

Dandy's fingers slid through the opening. White snakes slithering over the hook. *"Goddamn you, woman!* I'll *see* you *die* a *long* and —"

"Don't listen, baby." With Kyra in her arms, Rebecca pushed through the snow. One last haul. She had to beat Dandy. Beat him to Gurley's cruiser. As long as Dandy kept banging at the cellar door, she stood a chance. Small, but possible. If he doubled back through the inn, though, he'd gain on them.

The snow didn't give, not without a fight. Her legs strained, scooping snow up on her ankles like shovels. Lifting fifty-pound weights with her feet. Kyra grew heavier. Her arms shook, weakening. And still the snow fell.

"Hurry, Mommy. *Faster.*" Kyra's voice grew distant, a tired whisper as if she'd given up hope.

Rebecca said nothing, reserving her strength. Willing it into her legs.

*One step at a time, keep going, don't stop …*

Her foot stumbled into a small trench. A recently plowed path. She moved faster, almost at a sprint.

Dandy's stream of threats stopped once they reached the corner of the inn. Terror filled her. Her bladder tightened. *Don't hesitate.* The cruiser sat in the drive, a stallion to whisk them into the sunset. If they lived to see another sunset.

Behind the inn's curtains, Rebecca glimpsed a shadow swim past one window, vanish, fly over a second. Stretching beyond human size and running toward the front door.

One final surge. She quit battling the snow and, instead, adapted to it. Her legs lifted high, rising above the drifts, chopping down like jackhammers.

*Faster. One chance. Keep going. The final leg.*

Six feet to the car, six long feet. Six feet under, the alternative.

She held the keys in her hand before she reached the car. A ring of keys. Not enough light available to read an automobile make on any of them. She started with the biggest one. It fit in the door, didn't turn.

The Dandy Drop Inn's front door banged open. A rectangle of light lengthened across the snow.

The key ring jangled an awful tune as Rebecca fumbled for another key. The lock flipped up. So did hope.

"Gonna make you *suffer, woman. Suffer* like —"

*Dear God, help us, just a few more seconds.*

Snow didn't slow Dandy. His legs cut through it like butter, knees pitching high.

The car door opened. Rebecca hoisted Kyra inside like a pillow. As she slipped behind the wheel, the key scratched at the ignition, found its mate. The engine fired up as the locks went down.

*Bam.*

Kyra screamed. Dandy flattened his hands against the passenger window, howling. A red fist banged the pane. Then the hatchet appeared. His damned hatchet. The blade screeched across the glass, leaving a slug's trail of scratches. The next blow cracked the window. Kyra turned away, shielding her face in her hands.

Rebecca dropped into reverse. She floored the pedal, the tires sizzling. The back end wobbled, going nowhere. Something caught, the magic spot. Like a rocket, the cruiser shot back. Dandy drew sparks across the hood with the hatchet's edge until he fell face first into the snow.

Rebecca craned her head, looking back, steering the car in a straight line. She risked one quick glimpse up front for Dandy. *Gone.*

At the foot of the driveway, a thump stopped them. Rebecca's heart stuttered. The tires spun, the back end bouncing.

*Runch.*

Dandy sprawled out on the hood, clawing his way toward the windshield.

"Don't look, baby." Rebecca's back hooked with pain again as she nudged Kyra down. "Hug the floor and hold on."

Kyra slid down to the floorboard, tucking beneath the glove box.

Rebecca dropped the gear into first. Then stepped on the pedal. The engine's roar grew. With a lurch, the car jumped forward.

Dandy's eyes widened. He slashed the hatchet down onto the hood. The weapon opened the metal like a can opener. His hand slid into the gash, and he held on.

"Hold on tight. Cover your head. Brace yourself."

*Just let Kyra be safe.*

Rebecca's foot met the floor. The car barreled forward. The front end plowed through a snow-covered hedge, slowing the car. But the inn's wall stopped them.

Rebecca launched up. Her teeth gnashed as her head banged the roof. The steering wheel caught her chest as she dropped. Her ribs felt like they split upon impact. The car bounced back a foot, stopped, the seat reclaiming her.

She shook dizziness away the best she could. A hand clawed up in front of the hood, poking through a snowy grave. Then another hand. Finally, Dandy's leering, bloody face.

With a strange calm, Rebecca applied a remarkable accuracy of pressure to the pedal. The car reversed over the flattened hedge, delivering safe passage into the driveway. With one arm over the seat, Rebecca backed up to the driveway's foot.

The headlights caught Dandy on a stage of snow, the inn his backdrop. Drunkenly staggering to his feet. One arm crooked up as if for protection.

*Good luck with that.*

"One more time will do it, baby. We're almost safe. Hang on a-gain."

*No pain, no gain.*

Now at an advantage, Rebecca strapped on her seatbelt. She stomped the gas. Like a beast, the car roared, bounding toward Dandy. His wide-eyed panic made Rebecca smile. This time the impact had a buffer, a human buffer to soften the blow.

The front end crunched. Just like her car from the other night, a wisp of smoke curled up from beneath the hood. But unlike her car, the cruiser was built to last.

She backed up. Beneath the car's fallen bumper lay Dandy's corpse. One hand stuck up, fingers dangling, a farewell wave of how-do-you-die hospitality. Blood smeared the front wall. Jim Dandy'd left his final mark on the Dandy Drop Inn.

Rebecca checked Kyra, saw she was fine. Even had her answer some questions about her name, the date, silly medical questions. She double-checked her seatbelt with a tug and a lengthy hug.

It took a little effort to get out of the driveway.

The snow had stopped. At last, the storm had ended. Black ribbons of clear sky marbled the cloud coverage. Stars winked, blinked, and promised blue skies ahead. Rebecca turned on the heater, let it blast until they toasted. The first warmth Rebecca'd felt in some time.

She intended to keep driving until they reached the next town. After Gurley, the Dandys, everyone, she didn't trust Hilston, Missouri, its inhabitants, anything about the town. But once she crossed the border, she'd light up the cop cruiser's cherries, blast the siren, throw an attention-grabbing parade. Until the local cops pulled her over. Or a battalion of truck drivers escorted them to safety.

Rebecca smiled at Kyra. Asleep. Enjoying good dreams, she hoped. She'd earned them, certainly would need them. Especially once she finds out about her father, a topic Rebecca'd rather not face. Or have Kyra face. But after tonight, she knew her daughter could live through anything.

Hell, for that matter, so could she.

❄ ❄ ❄

Heather sat on the cellar's dirt floor, legs crossed. Cradling in her lap the baby's empty shell she'd found, stroking its tiny bones. God's little lost soul.

Even though Heather couldn't see much of anything — the witch had seen to that by pulverizing her eyes into swollen ham hocks — she still felt the baby's soul lingering in the cellar. Finally, she watched its spirit soar, taking wing to Heaven.

Another one delivered.

She struggled to stand. Her entire body hurt, one big, walking wound.

A real shame she hadn't been able to do her proper work, particularly on the woman and her little devil spawn. Maybe another time.

Her feet shuffled across the dirt, tapping into bodies wherever she ventured. Most of them weren't worth ushering into Heaven, of course. Quite obvious from the night's events and all the sinning she'd witnessed.

But near the green room's door, she found something interesting. The accountant's body. And more money than she could imagine.

Carefully, she gathered it, stacked it back into the briefcase. Money to continue her work. Across the country. Maybe even the world. She might even buy some fancy new white teeth since the vile bitch knocked out most of hers.

Once again, God had seen to her needs.

The Lord gives.

Across the street, she unlocked Mabel's car. From far away, sirens cried. No doubt clean-up crews for the mortal remains. But her work here was finished.

She began her trek across Heaven's Highway, singing joyous hymns as the sun rose.

# ABOUT THE AUTHOR

Stuart R. West is a lifelong resident of Kansas, which he considers both a curse and a blessing. It's a curse because...well, it's Kansas. But it's great because...well, it's Kansas. Lots of cool, strange and creepy things happen in the Midwest, and Stuart takes advantage of them in his work. Call it "Kansas Noir". Stuart writes thrillers tinged with horror and horror tinged with thriller, both for adult and young adult audiences. He writes at the crossroads of horror and sneaky humor. *Dread & Breakfast* is Stuart's fourteenth published novel and Stuart feels funny talking about himself this way. Stuart spent twenty-five years in the corporate sector and now writes full time. He's married to a professor of pharmacy (who greatly appreciates the fact he cooks dinner for her every night) and has a twenty-two year old daughter who's still deciding what to do with her life. But that's okay. It took him twenty-five years to figure that out.

Stuart's blog can be found at http://stuartrwest.blogspot.com/. Drop in on him at Facebook at: https://www.facebook.com/stuartrwestwrite

Press
Presents

Deep beneath the streets of Detroit, someone — or something — is picking off the miners working the Detroit Salt Combine's salt mine. The company refuses to do anything, so the miners turn to the Attican Detective Agency's Jasper O'Malley to get to the bottom of things. Teamed with Sadie Dupree, a geologist, and Amelia Rio, a get-away driver for the local mob boss, Jasper delves into the secrets of the mine. Will they be able to unearth the truth, or will they suffer the same unfortunate fate of the Detroit Salt Combine's workers?

REUNION

DAN FOLEY

Something lurks beneath the surface of Cooper Lake. Something
hungry. Something intelligent. Something that preys on those who venture
too close to its domain. The native Indians had a name for it. ONIARE In
1939, its victim was a young drifter. Dave Longo fought and killed it then,
but it won't stay dead. It returned in 1956 to claim the lives of two young
men. For Dave, its return was a reunion in Hell. It's now 2014 and the
creature has returned again, but Dave Longo is not around to face it a third
time. The task becomes the responsibility of Ryan Lowell, a child the oniare
had terrorized back in '56, but can he overcome his childhood fears to
vanquish the oniare once and for all.

There's something in Troughton's Moss that speaks to the people of
Ellsford; it whispers in their ears, burrows into their minds, like a
Brainworm, and tells them what to do.

THE MADONNA
Twenty years ago it spoke to Paul Cunningham and set the wheels in
motion.
He brutally murdered, then raped a young woman.
A short while later, within the narrow confines of her grave, she gave birth
to ...

THE CHILD
Grown to young adulthood, it moves undetected among the people of
Ellsford with only one purpose.

THE END TIMES
The time has come. The Moss is beginning to give up its dead,
sacrifices made in its name throughout the ages.

THE CHOSEN ONE
Dobson Heather, a child of the Moss himself, has been marked. But is
he Ellsford's salvation, or their damnation?

The Caribbean Sea, 1708 AD. In Port Royal many have heard the legend of the Black Brig, a ship of the damned bringing a fate worse than death to the isolated colonies of the Caribbean Sea. But few know the true story behind the tavern tales. As the war between the Northern Alliance and the League of the Antilles looms on the horizon, an old captain is ready to embark on a venture to cease the blight of the Black Brig once for all and have his revenge. Set in an alternate historical setting, where a supernatural plague caused the fall of the European powers and where what was left of humanity struggles to survive in the New World, *Dead Men Tell No Tales* narrates the ghastly voyage pirate captain Daniel Drake Davies underwent in 1676, and the events that will force him to confront those same horrors thirty years later. For the dead do not rest peacefully in the Devil's Sea. Pirates, voodoo, and seagoing undead await you in this fantastic journey in a land that never was.

www.ingramcontent.com/pod-product-compliance
Lightning Source LLC
Chambersburg PA
CBHW070105260626
47160CB00004B/1328